# The Sincerest Flattery

A TWIST UPON A REGENCY TALE
BOOK 6

## BY JUDE KNIGHT

## ARE YOU SIGNED UP FOR DRAGONBLADE'S BLOG?

You'll get the latest news and information on exclusive giveaways, exclusive excerpts, coming releases, sales, free books, cover reveals and more.

Check out our complete list of authors, too!

No spam, no junk. That's a promise!

### Sign Up Here

www.dragonbladepublishing.com

*Dearest Reader;*

*Thank you for your support of a small press. At Dragonblade Publishing, we strive to bring you the highest quality Historical Romance from some of the best authors in the business. Without your support, there is no 'us', so we sincerely hope you adore these stories and find some new favorite authors along the way.*

*Happy Reading!*

*CEO, Dragonblade Publishing*

# About the Book

When Percival Lord Thornstead heads to the far north of England to meet the bride his father has arranged for him to marry, bad weather, the ague, and a crooked valet disrupt his travel plans. Turned away at the door of the manor, he takes a job minding sheep to stay close.

Lady Aurelia Byrne sneaks away from the house dressed as a kitchen maid. She is angry at being told she must marry someone she has never met. She'd rather marry the shepherd she meets in the fields than the London fop her father has chosen for her.

Percy guesses who Lia is and is charmed. Lia discovers who Percy is and falls in love. If not for Lia's overbearing mother all would be perfect.

Then Percy's father intervenes to carry Lia off to London to make her debut with Percy's sister. She is having the time of her life when her mother makes public accusations that call her reputation into question. A hasty marriage restores her to favor. Deep in the throes of love, the young couple are blissfully happy, and have fashionable London at their feet.

Until a former mistress of Percy's comes seeking a boon that takes him away from Lia's side, and old rumors about Lia's mother are revived, causing Lia to be shunned by the highest sticklers. Their marriage will be tested to breaking point.

⚬⚬⚬

# Chapter One



*February 1792*

"RIDE ON AHEAD, Lance," Percy begged. "Let them know I have been delayed." At least, that is what he intended to say, though his stuffed-up nose and raw throat garbled the words.

His brother apparently grasped his meaning, for he shook his head. "I shouldn't leave you, Percy. I won't leave you, at least not until after I've spoken with the physician."

"Can't keep a lady waiting," Percy insisted, but he might have saved himself the trouble. Lance might be nearly five years his junior, and mostly content to go along with his older brother's plans and schemes, but when he dug his toes in, there was no moving him.

A knock on the door. Perhaps it was the physician? It was the innkeeper's wife, with a tray. "Some chicken soup for the young lord," she offered.

Percy didn't want food, but Lance and the innkeeper's wife insisted he would recover more quickly if he kept up his strength. He succumbed to having his pillows plumped so he could sit up, at least enough to have the tray put on the bed.

But his head hurt too much to lift it, and the spoon felt as if it was ten times the size it looked and made of granite. In the end,

Lance fed him, a spoonful at a time, until he covered his mouth after the sixth spoonful. "Enough. Let me lie down, Lance. There's a good chap."

The innkeeper's wife, who was hovering, asked, "Did you understand him, my lord?"

"He has had enough, and wants to lie back down," Lance explained. "I daresay your head hurts, old chap." He had picked up the tray and handed it the woman, and was supporting Percy with one arm, while rearranging the pillows with the other. "You should let me stay and nurse you, Percy."

Percy shook his head, a slow and tiny movement from side to side, so as not to burst his pounding head right open.

Another knock on the door, and this time it was the physician. Lance hustled the innkeeper's wife away and fetched Martin while the doctor did his examination. That was a relief. If he had brought Martin to listen to instructions for Percy's care, then Lance intended to follow his brother's instructions.

The brothers were on their way to meet the girl to whom Percy was betrothed. It would be rude to keep Lady Aurelia waiting. Percy could already tell—and was unsurprised to hear the physician telling his brother—that he would be a week or more in bed with this wretched cold.

This *ague*, rather, which is what the doctor called it. Was an ague different to a cold? Worse? Percy couldn't see that it mattered. Nothing did, except for the wretched head, the throat, the blocked nose, the cough that seemed to twist his ribs inside his chest and tear his muscles.

The doctor droned on, and Percy heard bits and pieces in between bouts of coughing and musings about Lady Aurelia. Her miniature was pretty. His father had seen her when he was last in Berwick, near where her parents lived. His father and hers were sometime associates in the House of Lords and rivals in the breeding of sheep to produce the perfect wool clip.

His Grace, Percy's father, said Lady Aurelia was a comely chit. She had never had a Season, but then she was only seventeen, just a few months younger than Percy's sister Guinevere.

Their parents had signed the marriage agreements. The wedding was to be in six months. No one seemed to think it necessary for the two principals to the marriage to actually meet before the parents agreed the betrothal, although it would not be announced until after Lady Aurelia arrived in town with her parents for the Season.

Once the betrothal was announced, of course, the wedding must follow, or there would be scandal.

When Percy came up with the scheme to ride north and introduce himself to the lady and her family, the duke did not object. All he said was, "Comport yourself like a Versey, Thornstead. And take young Lance with you."

Of course, that didn't prevent his father from organizing their travel, complete with carriages full of servants and branded with the crest of the Duke of Dellborough. Percy and Lance abandoned them on the first day out from home, riding ahead and changing horses every couple of hours. Which brought them here, traveling on horseback with just Martin to attend them, a couple of days behind the letter announcing their visit and perhaps as much as a fortnight ahead of the carriages with the rest of their servants and luggage.

The doctor had apparently finished, and was turning back to Percy. "Rest, Lord Thornstead. That's the best—the only possibly medicine. I have left instructions for various ways to soothe your symptoms, but sleep is what you need more than anything."

He left, taking the innkeeper's wife with him. Lance picked up Percy's hand and looked into his eyes, worried. "I do not want to leave you," he said.

Percy squeezed Lance's hand. "Lady Aurelia," he said, though it sounded more like, "Laay Aweia."

Lance sighed. "Yes, I know."

"I will look after Lord Thornstead," Martin assured Lance.

Still Lance stayed, supervising the administration of the potion the doctor had ordered, which contained something in it that soothed the throat and sent Percy into the prescribed sleep. Next time he surfaced, Lance wasn't there, which was a good thing, but Percy could not remember why. It was a woman who spooned stuff down his throat—chicken soup and some more of the doctor's medicine. He thought she washed his face, too, but he was sinking back into sleep, his last thought as he succumbed, "The innkeeper's wife!" Yes. That was who she was.

RAIN WAS LOOMING and the head gardener insisted that a storm was on the way. Lady Aurelia Byrne dashed out of the house as soon as her mother released her from the latest session with the dressmaker. Lia's betrothed was expected in the next few days, and Mama was determined that Lia would be dressed as finely as any lady in London. Any young lady, that was, who favored pastel colors and over-embellished garments. Lia's mother had never seen a frill she didn't like. On some of the gowns, even the frills had frills.

Lia had looked forward to leaving behind the plain skirts of childhood, hemmed mid-calf. She had not realized how hard it would be to run, or even to move quickly, in hems that swept the floor. But Mama had said she was grown, and could not emerge from her bed chamber without the gowns that signified her transition from girl to woman, stays or a corset to confine and shape her breasts, and with her hair dressed high on her head with a forest of pins.

Her mirror told her that she looked short, fat, and sallow. Her mother bemoaned the same three failings.

New dress or not, frills or not, she had to escape. Staying inside had become impossible. She was too full of all the resentments Mama and Father would not allow her to express. New dresses! *Is that all they can think of? Do they think a few gowns I do not even like make up for landing me with a betrothed? Someone* she had not even met, let alone had a chance to know?

She had been presented to the Duke of Dellborough, her betrothed's father, several months ago, during a rare visit to Berwick on Tweed. She retained the impression of an extremely tall gentleman, austere, and coldly polite. No one had told her at the time that she was being inspected to see if she would be a suitable wife for the man's son.

Beyond a doubt, anyone her mother thought perfect for her was going to be impossible! Her mother's ideas and her own were so far divergent on every issue that she could not imagine liking, let alone being married to, anyone her mother admired. Though, to be sure, her mother's conversation on the matter circled around the duke. Even Mama had not yet met Lord Thornstead, the duke's son.

Lia managed to walk sedately while she could be seen from the house, but it was a close-run thing. Once she passed into the Yew Walk, she was going to run.

Then she stopped. A rider was coming up the drive, hunched over his horse's neck. It was a beautiful piece of bloodstock. That was her first impression, her eyes drawn to the horse ahead of the gentleman.

He was a gentleman, as witnessed by the greatcoat he wore against the cold. It had five capes, and his head retained a top hat despite his collapsed position. Was he hurt? Forgetting any possible watchers, she ran across the lawn while the horse followed the curve of the drive, and reached the arch to the stable yard just before the rider.

He had managed to draw himself erect. He was more boy than man—younger than her, Lia would guess. His face was hectic with fever and his eyes looked through her without seeing her.

"Sir," she said loudly, and for a moment his eyes focused on hers.

"Lady Aurelia." His voice was hoarse, but the words were clear. "Profound apologies..." And then his eyes rolled back, and he slumped again, this time so fully that the top hat finally fell.

Lia caught the horse by its bridle before it could move suddenly and dislodge its owner. She led it into the stable yard, waving to the head groom, who was just crossing from the kitchen.

"Lady Aurelia! What have ye there?"

"A gentleman," Lia said, "I think he is sick. Or injured, perhaps. I do not know who he is, but he called me by name."

The head groom's whistle brought several more grooms, and within a couple of breaths, she was relieved of her place at the horse's head, and two of the men were lowering the rider into their arms.

"Would ye let Mr. Buxstead know what has happened, my lady?" the head groom asked, and Lia nodded and hurried in through the side door to find the butler. He sent a footman for her father and a maid for the housekeeper. Lia didn't wait for them, but rushed back to watch the men carrying the traveler inside.

Several people arrived together as the two grooms stood in the kitchen, one holding the man's legs and the other his shoulders. The housekeeper touched the gentleman's forehead, and said, "Oh, dear." Another groom came in with the man's saddle bags. Lia's father appeared, saying, "What have we here?"

Lia did her best to shrink into a corner, for this was the most interesting thing that had happened all week, and she did not want to be sent away like a child.

Several people spoke at once, but Father pointed to the head groom. "He rode in," the head groom said. "Dressed like a gentleman, and on an expensive horse. Mentioned Lady Aurelia, my lord."

Father's eyebrows shot up. "Did he, indeed?" He nodded toward the housekeeper.

"He's burning up, my lord. An ague." The gentleman coughed without waking, though it was a long hard cough that shook his body.

"Then we had better get him into bed and send for a physician. Are those his belongings?" He held out a hand to the groom with the saddle bags.

The housekeeper was giving orders to a little group of maids, who disappeared in different directions, two to make up the blue room, one to speak to the cook about a soothing drink, and one to fetch the housekeeper's favorite simples from the still room. "Come along," she said to the grooms, and led them away.

Lia made to follow, but her father, without looking up from the contents of the saddle bag, which he was spreading across the kitchen table, said, "Not you, Aurelia. Aha!" He took a signet ring from a handkerchief he had just unwrapped, and held it up so he could read the motif, then nodded. "So." He looked up and met her eyes. "It seems your betrothed has arrived, child. Leave the servants to do their work. When he is better, your mother and I will allow you to meet him. Now off you go. I am sure your mother would be most displeased to find you in the kitchen."

Sent away, just as Lia had expected. She was on her way from the room, and already wondering whether she could sneak into Lord Thornstead's bedchamber, when her father spoke again. "And Aurelia? I shall be very unhappy if you try to enter the young man's bedchamber. Not only would it be most improper, but I will not have you catching whatever makes Lord Thornstead sick. Now run along."

She did not sigh until she was on the other side of the door, but then she could not resist. When would her parents stop treating her like a child?

LORD THORNSTEAD HAD the ague, Miss Walton told Lia. Miss Walton was Lia's governess, but there would be no lessons today, for Miss Walton was going to sit with the young gentleman until other arrangements had been made. Her mother had decreed that

Lia would not be permitted to meet him until he was out of danger. "You are not to worry, my dear," Miss Walton said. "The physician believes he has every chance to recover fully. I will not lie to you, Aurelia, for you are not a baby who needs to be protected from the truth, and the boy is, after all, your betrothed. He is seriously ill and will need careful nursing. However, he shall have that, and he is young and fit. I do not despair of an excellent outcome."

"I can help with the nursing," Lia offered, though without much hope.

"I'm sorry, Lady Aurelia. Your Mama has left her instructions. You will not go near the sickroom. Indeed, you should not even enter the West Wing."

Lia knew there was no point in arguing. "You will keep me informed, Wally, will you not?"

"Of course, dear. I know you must be concerned."

And with that, Lia had to be content.

At dinner, Mama had said that the young lord was much the same, but that he was being nursed. As usual, Mama proved to be less informative than Pansy Kirsop, the chambermaid whose responsibilities included Lia's room.

Pansy, who came to turn down Lia's sheets and place a warming pan between them, said the earl had brought Miss Hatfield, the vicar's sister, from the village to oversee Lord Thornstead's care. That was a relief. Miss Hatfield had a reputation for her care of the sick. Besides, Lia was concerned about Miss Walton, who was not a young lady and should not be staying up all night with a patient.

Since a single lady could not be alone with—or, indeed, put her hands on—a single gentleman, two of the footmen had been assigned to actually nurse the young lord, taking turns so someone was always at his bedside.

In her private thoughts, Lia thought propriety should take a back seat to saving a life, but she did not express that opinion. Pansy was loyal, but she also talked. A lot. If she happened to mention Lia's thoughts on the matter to someone else, then word might get back to Mama or even, Heavens forbid, Father.

The patient was still ill. Worse, in fact, than when he rode into the courtyard. His fever was very high. The footman on duty spent a lot of his time washing him with cool clothes to bring down his fever, and he was also being given willow-bark tea, for the same purpose.

He slept much of the time, but restlessly. "He keeps calling for you, my lady," Pansy told Lia. "Isn't that romantic?"

In Lia's opinion, it was peculiar. After all, they had not met until that afternoon. "What does he say?" she asked.

"Just your name, my lady. Lady Aurelia. And then something about a purse. Purse is coming. Wait for purse." Pansy shrugged. "Charlie—he's one of the footmen looking after his lordship—says maybe he wants to buy you a present?"

Lia had no idea. She hoped he would get better, for he was only a young man and she had nothing against him except that he had agreed to marry her without even meeting her and without her having a Season.

But if he died, Mama and Father would have to find someone else, and meanwhile, she could go to London. She indulged herself in a little fantasy in which she wore a black ribbon, and everyone asked her about it, and the most handsome gentlemen competed with one another to bring her flowers and take her for carriage rides, to comfort her for her loss.

Then she felt guilty and said a prayer for Lord Thornstead. After all, she did not wish the poor boy dead. She just wished he had refused the betrothal. That said, he was not much older than her and looked even younger, so she supposed this betrothal was no more his choice than it was hers.

The following day, the news was no better and neither was the weather. The physician returned. Lia heard the knock on the front door and abandoned her needlework to look down from the gallery into the entry hall. She saw him enter the house under an umbrella held by one of the footmen. The butler led him upstairs and Lia hurried back to the little parlor before her mother caught her watching.

Nonetheless, she took the risk of walking around the gallery in the direction of the West Wing to try to meet the doctor when he left his patient. She had circled the gallery five and a half times before she saw him approach, shaking his head and looking grim. Then he saw her, bowed, and said, "Good day, Lady Aurelia. No need to worry your head about your guest. Strong young gentleman."

She smiled and gave a small curtsey. "Thank you, sir," she said, politely, wondering what he was not saying.

The butler escorted him down the stairs and then turned away from the front door in the direction of Father's study. Lia picked up a candle and lit it from the fire in the parlor. She opened one of the hidden doors that let onto the maze of servants' passages. The stairs she chose were steep, but she hurried down them with practiced ease. She had been using the hidden servants' ways for years.

She knew servants seldom came this way at this time of day, and sure enough, she met no one on her way to her goal—the passage that ran alongside Father's study. Sure enough, if she put her ear to the door that opened into the study, she could hear the physician.

"I would send for his family, my lord. I am still hopeful of his recovery, but I'll not deny there is cause for concern. Better to call them here unnecessarily than to leave it until too late."

"Very well." That was Father's voice. "If a messenger can get through. In this weather, I would not be surprised to hear that the road is blocked—though it must have been open when that foolish young man came through. What possessed him to ride in that condition? And in the rain? If he had just waited another two months, we would have been in London. He could have met… Well, never mind. We must do our best for him, Doctor."

Lia heard the light patter of footsteps, and had straightened by the time one of the parlor maids turned the corner. She nodded and smiled. The maid looked at her askance, but asked no questions. Lia squeezed past the maid, and walked off the way the maid had come, thinking about what she had overheard. Poor Lord Thornstead.

# Chapter Two

P ERCY WAS VAGUELY aware that the innkeeper's wife had taken over his care. Where was Martin? It was two days before he felt interested enough to ask. All he got was lips pressed tightly together, a shake of the head, and the instruction to swallow his medicine and not to bother his head.

On the third day, he woke feeling much better. He sat up, cautiously. His head spun a little, but then settled. When he looked around the room, though, he wondered if he was still unconscious. He had been moved into a room smaller than any he had ever occupied—one right up in the garrets, by the sloping roof and tiny dormer window, and only a little larger than the bed. That was another thing. The bed, too, was undersized— barely long enough for him to sleep in with his legs tucked up, and narrow, too.

Furthermore, none of his things were around him. What was going on? He swung his legs over the side of the bed and waited again for the room to settle. This time, the dizziness came with a side serving of nausea. Perhaps standing up was a bad idea.

He was still sitting, hoping he'd feel better in a minute, when the innkeeper's wife opened the door. She had a heavy tray, and Percy instinctively rose to carry it for her, but subsided back on the bed with a moan. Standing up was definitely a bad idea.

The innkeeper's wife thought so, too. She put the tray down on the table beside the bed, and came to tip him back onto his pillows, scolding all the time. "Tried to get up too quickly, didn't you, young man? The idea of it, when you have been out of your mind with fever these three days. But I have to say, you are looking better. A few good meals and you'll be back on your feet again." She frowned. "But who is to pay for it? That is what I would like to know."

Percy could not understand the question. "My valet, Martin. He has my purse." He looked around the little room. "And my bag, I assume?"

"Hah!" said the innkeeper from the doorway. "That's the question, ain't it? And your horse, too. If it was your horse, and if he was your valet, which I doubt. All part of a plan, wasn't it? To cheat us out of board and lodging when you was took sick."

The words were all in English, but Percy could not make sense of them. "I beg your pardon?"

"Now, dear," said the innkeeper's wife, "don't be bothering the young gentleman. You can see he is still sick."

The innkeeper glared, but kept his mouth shut.

"No," Percy said. "Tell me. What do you mean? What has happened to my horse?"

As far as he could work out, Martin had stayed one night after Lance left then had ridden off with both the remaining horses and all Percy's luggage. And his purse. The innkeeper made his opinion very clear. The three of them were in collusion, with Lance departing first, then Martin, and Percy left behind since he could not be moved.

"And who will pay the bill?" the innkeeper demanded. "Unless you have some money hidden somewhere?"

"I will write to my father," Percy offered. "My father is the Duke of Dellborough. He will pay you all you are owed and reward you for your nursing."

The innkeeper laughed. "Pull the other one, you young rogue. I should throw you into the street. That's what I should do."

His wife tugged him from the room, to argue with her husband in the passage outside the door. What they said, he couldn't hear, but the rise and fall of voices suggested that the wife was winning.

Percy let himself fall back on the bed. Whatever happened, he had to sleep.

A WEEK AFTER Lord Thornstead had arrived, Lia had still not met him. He had been very sick for the first four days—so sick, the doctor had moved into the mansion, and Mama and Father had tiptoed through the house with grim faces. Lia knew they had not been able to send for his father the duke, for she had asked in the stables and been told that the messenger had been turned back by slips on the road out of their valley. How awful for his family if he should die.

After that, he began to recover, or so Lia was told. Apparently, he still slept most of the time, and Lia was still not permitted to see him. As soon as the road out of the valley was open, Father and Mama had sent letters to Lord Thornstead's father. It was as well the road had been blocked, Mama reasoned, for she was able to reassure the duke that his son was on the mend.

One benefit of Mama's preoccupation with the young lord and his illness was that she had failed for several days in a row to set Lia's tasks for the day, and today was no exception. As soon as it was light, Lia dressed in the old clothes she kept at the bottom of her clothes chest. Mama would not be up yet, and if Lia asked nicely in the kitchen, she should be able to take a basket of food with her.

Some to eat and some to share, for if she offered to carry the basket to the shepherd's hut, Bessie the kitchen maid would be delighted to be spared the task. Bessie had not spoken to Horace, the shepherd who usually took the night watch, since the last night of shearing, when he had disappeared from the celebration fire with one of the upstairs maids.

Lia was certain she could make it out of doors and out of sight before her mother missed her. If she was very lucky, her absence would not be noticed at all, and she would be home, tidied, and doing her music practice before Mama came looking. Her music practice, both because she enjoyed it and because Mama would hear her playing and know her daughter was dutifully occupied. Which meant she was less likely, on a busy day, to come looking.

Lia risked a beating. It was unlikely to be a bad one with Lord Thornstead presumably expecting to be presented to his betrothed once he recovered just a little more. It would be worth it. She could not bear to remain immured inside.

Fifteen minutes later, Lia came over the hill into the sheep fields, keen to count the early lambs. Wool was the wealth of the Earls of Harrowby, and the breeding ewes were always moved close to the manor and the home farm as lambing approached.

She stopped on the top of the hill to assess the sky. Another spring storm was coming. Mrs. Murford, the cook, had declared it yesterday, based on the ache in her bones. Now Lia could see the clouds for herself. Rain was worse than snow for the newborn lambs, which was why they were in this field with its roofed pens, the gates left open so the mothers could take cover if things got bad.

There was a hut on wheels by the shelters—a shepherd's hut that was rolled to wherever it was needed. During lambing, a shepherd would stay in the hut at night, checking on the ewes and lambs during the night in case one of them needed help, and making sure that no foolish woolly mother stayed out in the rain with her young one. Lia would knock on the door and tell Horace to help himself from the basket.

And there he was, stepping out of the door and stretching.

Did he sleep the night away? She'd have something to say

about it if he did. She strode down the hill swinging her basket. As she approached, though, she realized that the man on the steps of the hut was not Horace.

Whoever it was greeted her with a charming grin and a short bow. "The maid with the basket! Would you excuse me a minute? I'm just off to check one of the ewes. She gave birth to twins in the night, and I moved them into the shelter, because it was drizzling. You are most welcome to come and see, if you wish."

Not waiting for an answer, he headed for the nearest shelter. He had been up in the night, then. But who was he? She was sure that she'd not seen him before, and she would have noticed him, she was certain. He was tall—taller than her father—with fair hair and warm blue eyes. It should be a contradiction, for she thought of blue as a cold color, but certainly the new shepherd's eyes were warm.

She had no business thinking he was handsome, or so Mama would say. "We do not notice whether servants are handsome or not," she would scold. "We notice whether they perform their tasks, and we thank them for good service. Their physical appearance is not important, and is none of our business."

By the time Lia put down the basket and followed the shepherd, he was already opening the gate to the shelter to let the ewe and her lambs out into the field. "They will probably need to be shut in again tonight or if it comes on to rain too hard," he said, cheerfully. "But meanwhile, being out in the fresh air will be good for them."

The ewe had delivered two sturdy lambs, both of whom followed their mother, bleating for her to slow down. As soon as she did, they latched on, one each side, their tails going like propellers as they drank as if they had been starved up until this minute. The shepherd admired them, leaning back against the gate with his elbows on the top rail.

Lia stared at the lambs as well. Better than staring at their keeper, who was even more attractive in his current pose than he had been stepping, yawning, from the hut.

After a moment, he straightened. "I am Percy," he introduced himself. "And I do hope I am correct, and that my breakfast is in that basket."

*My goodness.* Bessie the kitchen maid would be kicking herself for shirking this task!

WHEN PERCY HAD arrived yesterday at the manor house known as Byrnewick, the butler who opened the door to his knock threatened to set the dogs on to him. True, his clothing was hardly suitable to his rank. It was all they would give him at the inn, and that reluctantly and only because the innkeeper's good wife insisted they could not turn him out wearing nothing but one of the two shirts that were the only clothing Martin had left with him. And then only because he had been wearing one in his bed and the other was in the laundry.

The shirts were, of course, of the finest quality, but not the rest of the clothing. He had on a pair of trousers left behind by a somewhat fatter guest, pinned so they would not fall down, some old workman's boots, going through at the sole, and a rough coat.

They were all grimy, too, for the lifts he'd managed to cadge on his way here from the inn had been on the backs of wagons, and shared with crops or animals.

It was a shock to be told that Lord Thornstead had arrived days earlier and was asleep upstairs, and even more of a shock to be threatened with bodily violence when he tried to argue.

He had retreated, and walked around to the stable block, hoping to find his father's coachmen or one of the grooms, though it was unlikely they'd arrived yet.

Harrowby's grooms might have run him off, too, except that one of the horses was being exercised in the stable yard and took exception to a kitten who bounced out from a hidden corner. The horse had reared, pulled its lead rope from the groom's hands, and took off for the arch that led out to the carriage way.

Percy had thrown himself on the lead rope, leapt to grasp the halter, and talked soothingly but firmly the whole time. He was carried along a few feet, but managed to bring the beast to stop. He'd been patting it and praising it when the groom came to take over again.

As a result, his conversation with the stable master began on a friendly note, but threatened to deteriorate when he asked if the stable had any visiting horses and grooms.

"What's it to you?" The stable master frowned at him with narrowed eyes.

Percy tried to think of a reason. "If you were busy," he said, "you might have work for me."

The stable master, though, said he had no need of extra grooms, Tthough you have a good hand with a horse, I'll give you that. But we have just the one horse visiting, and that belongs to the poor sick lord who is betrothed to our lady. He came on his own, and if he has a carriage and men, they've not arrived. Could have been caught up in the storms further south."

Lance was sick ? It had to be Lance, for who else would be pretending to be him? Not Martin, who had no reason to visit Byrnewick, and every reason not to. Percy could imagine him stealing Percy's identity somewhere else, but not at Byrnewick. On the other hand, the only other person it was likely to be was Lance, and Percy could not imagine why Lance would do so.

"Are you any good with sheep?" said one of the other men present. "Only, our Horace broke 'is arm this day and the lambin' has started. We need some-un to take Horace's place."

The Dellborough wealth had been founded six centuries ago on Cotswold wool, and in his boyhood, Percy had served his time out in the fields during lambing and shearing. Indeed, rams were part of the dowry of his intended bride, for the Earl of Harrowby was a notable breeder of Border Leicesters, and His Grace,

Percy's father, intended to use the Leicester rams over his Cotswold ewes to produce lambs that were good for both meat and wool.

Without conscious thought, Percy had found himself assessing the flocks as he trudged his way up through the estate. "I know sheep," he admitted to the shepherd. "I daresay your Leicesters birth their lambs much the same way as the Cotswolds we have back where I come from."

The shepherd shot a few questions at Percy, all of which he was able to answer, and the next thing he knew he was on the payroll. Which at least gave him a place to sleep and regular food while he found out what game his brother was playing. Or Martin, if it was Martin. Either way, his entourage would soon arrive. They could identify him.

After that brief interview, he'd been sent to help move a flock of ewes from the far reaches of the estate to a field nearer the house, then welcomed to the head shepherd's cottage for dinner and a sleep before taking his turn in the shepherd's hut.

The accommodation in the shepherd's hut was comfortable enough. Warm, too. Percy was out of the habit of keeping a night watch, and was worried enough about sleeping right through a difficult birth and losing one of his charges that he barely slept a wink, instead doing the rounds of the field every half hour through the night.

As it were, the one ewe who gave birth popped her twins out one after the other with little trouble, though she had chosen the wettest and windiest place in the whole field. As soon as the lambs were both up on their feet and had taken their first meal, Percy had lifted them up and led the anxious mother to the pens, where he reunited the family and shut them up to keep safe through the night.

He had made one more round of the field, then put his head down in the hut, and the next thing he knew the sun had risen and was just above the horizon, lighting up the clouds. He got up to check on the sheep once again, but when he stepped out of the hut, one of the loveliest girls he had ever seen was walking towards him with him with a basket.

They had told him a maid would bring him breakfast, but they didn't tell him she would be so beautiful! Her dark brown hair glinted golden in the sun as she looked at him from large gray eyes. Her lips were the color of a rose—he would bet they were as soft as a rose petal, too. She was short, the top of her head not even as high as his shoulder, but at no risk of being taken for a boy, with a shape that made his mouth water.

A quick glance around the field confirmed all was well with the sheep, but he had better let the new mother out of the pen. She'd need to eat her fill now, for there'd be rain later, and she and her babes would need to be shut up again to keep the little ones from the worst of the weather.

He excused himself to the maid, who followed him to watch as he let his charges from the pen. She stood beside him for a minute, watching the twins feed.

Percy would have happily watched the maid, but he supposed his current thoughts were inappropriate for a gentleman who was betrothed, however unwillingly. Better to think about satisfying another appetite instead. "I am Percy," he introduced himself to the girl. "And I do hope I am correct, and that my breakfast is in that basket."

THE SHEPHERD WAS very forward, but then she supposed if he were new, he might not know who she was. What fun! She could pretend to be a maid, if she remembered to speak Northumbrian, and not the educated speech she'd been schooled in as an earl's daughter.

"Aye," she said. "I'll put it in t'hut for ye."

"May I be permitted to know your name?" Percy asked.

"That's for me to know and you to find out," Lia replied.

Percy's face lit with amusement. "Then you will have to stay and give me a fair chance to coax it from you," he declared. "Why don't you sit on the steps and share a bite with me? I'll just wash my hands."

*A peasant who worried about clean hands.* Bemused, Lia sat on the steps as asked while Percy walked over to the little waterfall that fed into the stream running through the field, pulled up his sleeves, and bent over to wash his hands in the water.

Lia opened up the basket and pulled out several cloth-wrapped bundles. One proved to be fresh crusty bread still hot from the oven. One contained a pat of butter and a small jar of jam. The third held a generous wedge of cheese. The basket also contained a bottle of small ale, a knife, and a couple of apples.

No plates or cups. She was frowning at the array, wondering how they would manage a joint meal given the lack, when Percy returned from the stream. He cast an eye over the meal and said, "I think there are cups and plates in the hut. I don't know how clean they are, though. I'll check, shall I?"

He mounted the steps, skipping the one she was using, and disappeared into the hut. A moment later he emerged again, waving a mug and a bowl. "These seem clean. You use them, Miss No-Name, and I shall drink from the bottle and eat off the napkin."

He took a giant stride over the step again, and sat on the next step down. He handed her the mug and the bowl. When his hand brushed hers, she felt a tingle right up her arm from the point of contact. The shepherd did not seem to notice. "Ladies first. Serve yourself, Miss No-Name."

"Lia," she told him. "My name is Lia."

He bowed, gracious in victory. "Miss Lia. I am pleased to meet you."

Bother. Calling her No-Name had been a trick, and she had fallen for it. She broke the loaf in half and cut a slice off the cheese while trying to think how she could regain the upper hand.

"What happened to Horace?" she asked.

"He broke his arm—slipped and fell while bringing in the sheep yesterday afternoon."

Lia regarded Percy with narrowed eyes. "I've never seen you around here before."

"I'm new to the estate," Percy replied. His own eyes were startlingly direct. He regarded her with interest, and not a hint of subservience, and something about his gaze set those tingles off again, rioting through her breasts and down to her core. It was most uncomfortable.

He was still talking. She made herself ignore the strange feelings and listen. "I arrived yesterday. Horace's bad luck was good for me. I asked for work at the stable, and the head shepherd overheard."

She buttered her bread then picked up the jam jar and examined it. Where was the jam spoon?

"Wipe your knife clean on the edge of your bread and use that," Percy suggested.

He was irritatingly observant. She supposed that was useful in a peasant. She followed his advice, and then remembered her obligations as his hostess, in some sort, and poured herself an ale so he could have his own meal.

"The rest is for you," she told him. "Boys eat more than girls." Or so her governess always said when nurse complained that Lia's brothers never stopped eating.

"That's what my Aunt Enid says," Percy laughed. "Though my sisters think it is just that men get the best of everything."

"How many sisters do you have?" Lia asked. "I've always wanted a sister."

"Four sisters and three brothers. Are you an only child, then, Miss Lia?"

Lia shook her head. "Two brothers. They are younger than me." She almost said they were away at school, but caught herself in time. Maids didn't have brothers who went away to school.

"I'm the oldest," Percy said. A shadow passed over his face. "Lia, may I ask you something? I've heard about the sick lord—

the one who arrived just before the storm. How is he? Have you seen him?"

That was an odd thing to ask. "Why do you want to know?" Lia demanded.

Percy seemed to be choosing his words carefully. "I had the ague myself. My, ah, family had to leave me behind, and then I got robbed, which is why I was so pleased to have a job for a few days just during the lambing. Especially one where I get to sleep during the day, and be fed so well. I'm still recovering, you see. I guess I just feel for the poor fellow. That's all."

"I saw him arrive. He was already sick, and he nearly fell off his horse." Lia supposed that was safe enough. After all, any maid might have seen him arrive. "The servants looking after him say he is getting better. He is able to sit up to eat, and his fever is gone, except in the evenings."

If LANCE HAD been sick enough to nearly fall off his horse, that would explain why the household might have guessed he was Percy. Poor Lance hadn't been able to tell them his name. Although now he was recovering, he could correct the error. It was a mystery that he hadn't.

Perhaps it was Martin, but Percy was nearly certain it must be Lance. Once he was off work, he would check the horse in the stables, and that would settle it either way.

If it were Lance, Percy could think of one reason for him to prevaricate? Except Lia spoke as if she had no personal knowledge of Lance's condition. "He is betrothed to the earl's daughter they tell me," he commented, watching Lia closely. "I suppose she has been able to comfort him in his illness?"

Her nostrils flared and she pressed her lips together. "Unlikely," she snapped. "She has never met him. Her father made the betrothal without asking her, and will not allow her into the sickroom. When he is no longer sick, I suppose they shall be introduced."

She had completely forgotten her rather lame attempt to mimic the accent he'd heard from the stable hands and shepherds, and was speaking like the lady she was. He had guessed when he saw her hands, which were certainly not those of a kitchen maid. He had been nearly certain when she told him her name. A maid called Lia in the household where the daughter of the lord was Lady Aurelia? Possible, but suspicious.

The accent she kept slipping back into confirmed it. Why his future wife was carrying a basket of food to a shepherd, he did not know. She had set his mind at rest over the possibility that Lance had taken one look at her and decided to go on being Percy for as long as possible. He was embarrassed he even thought it. Lance was still only a boy, and besides, Lance would never betray him.

On the other hand, Lady Aurelia might. She was clearly not happy about the betrothal, and one of her first questions was about Horace the shepherd. Was she in the habit of sneaking away from the house to meet the scoundrel? Percy had not yet met Horace, but he imagined him, a village Lothario with black curls and broad shoulders.

A pity Horace was injured, for Percy wanted to hit him. If he found out that Horace had taken advantage of Percy's betrothed, he wouldn't allow such gentlemanly considerations to stay his hand. He would break the man's other arm.

Lady Aurelia was packing the paraphernalia from the breakfast back into the basket. "Do you bring breakfast every day, Miss Lia?" Percy asked. "Will I see you tomorrow?"

She shook her head. "Bessie usually brings the basket. I offered today, as I wanted a walk before the rain traps us indoors once more. I doubt I will be able to get away again."

"That's a pity," said Percy. "I've enjoyed our chat."

"You can chat with Bessie," Lady Aurelia told him. "She will enjoy it, I am certain."

"I doubt Bessie is as pretty as you," Percy grumbled. He was flirting, but he also meant it. His bride was one of the loveliest young ladies he had ever seen, but her conversation and something about the way she ate her breakfast hinted there was more to her than her looks. How did he get so lucky? If, that is, she did not have assignations with shepherds.

A pair of raised eyebrows conveyed her skepticism. Did she not know how pretty she was? "I do not expect we will have the opportunity to meet again," she told him. "However, I have enjoyed our breakfast together, Percy. Thank you for showing me the lambs."

He stood as she did. "I will see you to the top of the field," he said.

After he had held her hand to assist her over the stile, he did the rounds of the field, checking on the ewes. Those who were already mothers seemed to be devoted to their lambs, all of which were thriving. He noted that three who had yet to lamb had wandered away from the flock—an indication they might be about to give birth.

As could any of the rest, of course. Seeking isolation from the flock was a sure sign, but the reverse didn't apply. Perhaps, as with people, some sheep were more sociable than others.

He yawned. The exhaustion of the ague had not completely left him, and the last few days had been trying.

His relief would arrive in a couple of hours. After that, he would go to the stables to look at the guest's horse, and then to the bed the head shepherd had offered him. Making another attempt to see Lance could wait until after that.

# Chapter Three

L IA RETURNED THE basket to the kitchen and took the servants'
stairs to her room. The most dangerous stretch was between
the stair door and her bedchamber. It had been easier when her
room was on the schoolroom floor. Her governess was growing
old. She slept deeply and woke slowly in the mornings. Her
brothers were away most of the time, as were her mother and her
father. And she was friends with the servants who saw to the
schoolroom floor. She trusted them not to betray her.

However, the marriage negotiations had prompted her
mother to have her moved down to the same floor as her parents.
"If you are old enough to be married, Lia, you are old enough to
have an adult bedchamber of your own, with your own sitting
room instead of one shared with your brothers."

The benefits might outweigh the disadvantages if her brothers were home. They would not return to Byrnewick until the
summer holidays, however, and her parents planned for her to be
married by then. The move had therefore increased the risk of
being caught by her mother, without giving her any advantage in
return.

Still, this time, she reached her room without being seen,
except by Pansy who was building up her fire. Pansy already had
a ewer of hot water waiting for Lia's wash, and clothes laid out on

the bed.

Lia stood by the fire and allowed Pansy to undo her coat and her gown. "Pansy, there is a new night shepherd. A temporary one, I suppose. He is filling in for Horace, who has broken his arm."

Pansy raised her eyebrows. "Did you take him a basket, my lady?"

At Lia's nod, Pansy added, "I hope he is not handsome. Bessie will be in an awful sulk if he is handsome, and she did not get to see him first."

"He is one of the most handsome men I have ever seen," Lia admitted. "Very bold, though." Her hand had still not recovered from holding his as she stepped over the style. She felt the absurd urge not to wash it. A shepherd! How awful!

A knock on the door was followed directly by her mother's entrance. "Kirsop." Mama nodded to Pansy. "You may wait in the next room."

Pansy curtseyed and left the room.

"Aurelia, your father must go to Berwick, and I have decided to accompany him. We will be back tomorrow."

The only response her mother wanted was a curtsey and a nod. Lia gave them to her, though she did wonder why her mother had come if that was all she had to say. She could not begin to guess the number of times her parents had left for a journey of far more than two days with no more notice than a note to her nurse or later, to her governess, delivered after the earl and his countess had left. Perhaps Mama recognized that she was now an adult?

That hopeful view was soon dashed. "You are not to visit Lord Thornstead, Aurelia. Your father and I will arrange an introduction once he is well enough to come downstairs. I will not have you spoiling this excellent match your father has been good enough to arrange for you."

Lia curtseyed again, nodded, and said, "Mama," for good measure. Mama could take that as agreement if she liked, but Lia had made no promises. Mama's remarks made her even less inclined to comply than usual.

"Very well. I have assured your father that we can trust to your good sense and the propriety you have been taught."

That was something of a facer, as her brothers would say. Lia could not remember her mother ever saying anything that hinted of approval before. Good sense? How awkward! Now how was Lia to go directly against her mother's orders without feeling guilty?

She was still determined to do so, for she had to meet her betrothed. Now, more than ever, for the man her parents had chosen for her felt like safety after the disturbing feelings Percy the shepherd had aroused. How awful, to be attracted to a shepherd! It had never happened before, but then she had never met such a handsome young man before, either.

Her misguided attraction was probably just she had never met a young man of her own class. Now one was here, almost within arm's reach. She could not possibly give up the opportunity to see if he aroused the same uncomfortable feelings, even if he did seem far too young to be her husband.

After weeks of wishing Lord Thornstead on the other side of the world, she was now delighted to have him under her own roof. She just hoped he would one day grow to be as physically appealing to her as the shepherd.

With that in mind, she chose one of the gowns Mama had had made in the village for her to wear in London, and let Pansy style her hair in a more adult fashion than her usual crown of plaits or loose roll.

She put her plan into action as soon as her parents' carriage was out of sight. The first step was to talk to Charlie, the footman. Geordie, the other footman assigned to the young lord's care, had also succumbed to the ague, but Lord Thornstead no longer needed a constant attendant. Miss Hatfield might have been a wiser choice as unwitting coconspirator, but she had been sent back to the vicarage yesterday. Which was good, in its way, for it meant Lord Thornstead must be much better.

Lia spoke to her governess, first. Miss Walton was sympathetic to her wish to discover her fiancé's state of health. "I do think, my dear, that Lord and Lady Harrowby would have no objection to you speaking to the footman who has been nursing him," she agreed.

*Phew.* Mama tended to ignore Miss Walton, except when issuing edicts regarding another subject to be added to the long list of skills and charms that Lia would need to practice before her debut in two months. But there had always been the chance that she might have thought to instruct poor Miss Walton to keep Lia from showing an interest in her betrothed. As if Miss Walton had ever been able to stop Lia from doing as she pleased.

They had Charlie meet them in the pink drawing room, which had been given over to Lia's lessons now she had graduated from the schoolroom. He was happy to talk about Lord Thornstead. "He is much better today, my lady. He had a good night's sleep, and his cough is nearly gone. He ate a good breakfast, too. He sent me down to the library for some books, so I guess his headache is gone." He chuckled. "Wanted to know if I could play chess, my lady. Where would I have learned to play chess? We played a few hands of cards, but I was no match for him. He showed me where I was going wrong, though. That's the sort of young gentleman he is, my lady. Polite to the likes of me. Says 'thank you.' He's kind, my lady. That's what he is."

Kind was probably a good quality in a husband, but what she really wanted to know was whether he would make her tingle. Since she could not quite think to ask whether Lord Thornstead was good looking, Lia decided the information Charlie had given her was enough. But Miss Walton had an idea. "You play chess, Lady Aurelia. There can be no objection to you playing with Lord Thornstead, surely? Not if I sit with you as chaperone."

"That is an excellent idea," Lia agreed, doing her best to sound calm, and not to look apprehensively at Charlie. Had he been told that Lia was not to visit his patient? Apparently not, for his face lit up.

"That would be right nice, my lady. His lordship will like that. And I could maybe spend some time with his clothes, if you didn't mind? Everything he had with him was wet, my lady. It has all been through the laundry, but Lord Harrowby said we was not to leave him, so I haven't been able to brush and press things."

Lia had never imagined that folding and ironing clothes was something to anticipate with eagerness, but Charlie's look was pleading. When she agreed, he almost bounced in place with pleasure. "I mean to be a valet one day, my lady," he explained. "This will be really good practice."

Thus, her meeting with the young lord proved to be much easier to arrange than she could have believed. Charlie went off to advise the gentleman that Lady Aurelia would be his chess partner, and to make sure he was appropriately dressed for female company.

Lia rang the bell and ordered refreshments sent to Lord Thornstead's room.

While she did so, Miss Walton picked up her basket of hand-work. She had once made the most beautiful needlework pictures, with stitches so tiny and colors blended so skillfully that they looked like paintings. Some of them were framed and displayed in the schoolroom. She could no longer see well enough for such work, but the bolder stitching she now did, despite her gnarled hands, still gave great pleasure to maker and viewer.

Of course, Miss Walton must be approaching seventy years of age. She had been governess to Father's four older sisters, and then to their daughters, being passed from household to household until Lia left the nursery for the schoolroom and Miss Walton returned to Byrnewick to be Lia's governess.

She was, at Lia's request, going to come to London for the few months of Lia's maiden Season, and would then retire. Father was gifting her with a cottage and a pension, for her forty or more years of service to the family.

Lia was still thinking about all she owed to Miss Walton when the governess knocked on Lord Thornstead's door, and Charlie opened it.

"My lady," he said, and stood aside for her to enter.

Lia's gaze turned first to the bed, but it was neatly made and empty. A flicker of movement had her glancing at the bay of the window, where a tall, thin youth stood beside one of the chairs by a chess table.

He bowed as her eyes met his. "My lady. Thank you for coming to help me pass the time."

Lia bobbed a curtsey. "It is my pleasure, my lord. I am sorry you were so unwell. Are you quite recovered?"

"A little wobbly, Lady Aurelia, but otherwise quite recovered."

He smiled. Lia liked his smile, and she had to concede that he was handsome enough. But he was much younger than she expected. She had assumed her brief glimpse of him when he arrived had been misleading, but he was still a boy. A boy who would grow to a man, she supposed, but still. Lia had understood him to be nineteen. Older than her, not the same age or even younger.

Lord Thornstead swayed, and Lia realized she was keeping him standing. She hurried to the other chair at the table. "Miss Walton, please take a chair so that his lordship can sit down. My lord, this is my governess, Miss Walton. Do sit, please." Before you fall down, she did not say. *See, Mama, I can behave in polite company.*

After a bow to the governess, for which Lia gave him points, Lord Thornstead sat, with a sigh of relief. "Thank you, my lady."

"Perhaps you are not ready for visitors yet," Lia said, doubtfully. "Shouldn't you be resting?"

He was shaking his head before she had finished speaking. "I have done nothing but rest. Please, Lady Aurelia, stay and keep me company. I promise I shall not overdo things."

Lia exchanged glances with Miss Walton, who smiled and

gave a small nod. If her governess thought it would do no harm, then she would stay, and get to know this boy to whom she had been promised by her parents.

The game was set up. Lord Thornstead took two of the pawns under his edge of the table then offered her his fists, clenched fingers down. Lia chose the right, and he turned his fist over and opened it. White. Her move first.

"I play chess with Miss Walton," she told the young man as she moved her queen's pawn two squares.

He countered by moving his king's pawn to face hers. "Do you win?" he asked, a twinkle in his eyes hinting that he was teasing.

"We are about even," she said, as she jumped her queen's knight to the square in front of the queen's bishop's pawn.

"Lady Aurelia is a good player," Miss Walton inserted, looking up from her embroidery.

Lord Thornton matched Lia's move, but with his king's knight. "Excellent. She will give me a challenge, then."

*I certainly will.* Lia narrowed her eyes as she slid her bishop through the space the pawn had made. "Do you play chess with your tutor?" she asked, hoping to find out whether he was still young enough to have a tutor.

Without removing his attention from the pieces, he nodded. "And with my brothers and sisters. Also, with friends. Mostly, I play with Perce. He is older, but we are still evenly matched. In chess, anyway." He made his move.

"Who is Perse?" Lia wondered, as she pondered her own move.

She was watching the board and not the young lord's reaction, until his words captured her whole attention.

"My brother. Percival Versey. Lord Thornstead. Your betrothed. Lady Aurelia? Are you well? Is something wrong? Have you heard from Percy?"

"Lord Thornstead is your *brother*?" Lia asked, the idea slowly seeping into her mind.

The unknown young man was pursuing a thought of his own. "He should be here by now. I hope nothing has happened to him. But Martin would have let me know, would he not? Percy had the ague, you see, and could not travel. I left him at an inn in the care of his valet. Perce insisted. I was to come ahead and assure you he was on his way. I told Miss Hatfield, when I was well enough. *Let Lord Harrowby know that my brother will be here soon*, I said. I thought he would have arrived by now."

*I rather think he has*, Lia thought. *But why…* Just to be sure her outlandish idea was actually true, she asked, "Does your brother, Lord Thornstead, know anything about sheep?"

# Chapter Four

"**B**E YE THE new shepherd, like?"

The question came from a comely wench in a maid's gown and apron, her white maid's cap perched upon black curls.

Percy, who was passing through the kitchen yard on his way to the stable yard, paused to answer the girl. "Temporarily, miss. Until Horace is on his feet again."

"Oi'm Bessie," the girl cooed. "What be yor name, marra?" She fluttered her eyelashes.

This must be the Bessie his coy betrothed wanted to wish on him. Percy had the girl pegged as a flirt from her first words. He knew the type.

Being an honorary marquess and the heir to a duchy, Percy had been chased by flirts and the marriage minded since before he was old enough to shave. Had kissed quite a few of them, too. And more. The flirts, not the marriage minded. Put Bessie in silks and lace and clean up her accent, and she'd fit right in. Not that he would be kissing Bessie.

"Good morning, Miss Bessie. If you'll excuse me, I've been up most of the night and I'm on my way to bed."

The girl moved to stand in his way. "Oi'll let 'ee pass for a kiss," she proposed.

"No kisses, Miss Bessie. I'll not dishonor my betrothed," he told her. Nor would he complicate an already tangled situation still further.

Bessie looked ready to argue, but the voice from the kitchen door put a stop to that. "That's enough, Bessie. Cook is looking for you."

It was Lia, dressed now as befitted her station, and looking even lovelier than ever.

Bessie scurried off, skirting the lady, and disappearing through the door behind her. Percy admired his betrothed as she approached, while thanking his lucky stars that he hadn't given in to the temptation to pay the cheeky maid's toll.

"Lord Thornstead," she greeted him.

Percy bowed. "Lady Aurelia. Or may I still call you Lia?"

She glared through narrowed eyes. "Are you saying you knew?"

"I guessed," Percy admitted. "You sound and carry yourself like a lady. And you?"

"Your brother told me. He is awake and asking for you. He wants to know why you are herding my father's sheep, and so do I."

The lady was annoyed, but Percy did not see what he could have done differently. Falling into step beside her, he said, "When I turned up looking like this, your butler refused to believe that I was me, especially since he had a Lord Thornstead upstairs. I wanted to stay close until I was able to prove my identity."

"You could have told me who you were," Lia insisted, as she led him into the house and along a narrow passage. They passed multiple doors on one side and a single door letting on to a cavernous and busy kitchen on the other. Lia kept walking.

"Pot, meet kettle," he retorted. "Besides, I didn't think you would believe me. *I* wouldn't have believed me."

She glanced back, meeting his eyes. She was too ladylike to sniff, but she came close. The door at the end of the passage opened on to a steep set of servants' stairs, so narrow they were forced to go up in single file up flight after flight. Since her back remained firmly turned to him all the rest of the way up, he could no longer see her face, but the tension in her shoulders and neck was like semaphore, signaling her irritation.

For the daughter of an earl, she was remarkably familiar with the servants' side of the house. Percy could say the same about himself and his brothers and sisters, all of whom had been running in and out of the kitchen all their lives. He would have thought it normal if not for the horror shown by his sisters' governesses over such a social solecism.

At the top of the next flight, she opened the door into a finely decorated and furnished passage.

"Lord Lancelot is in here," she told him, opening the door to a room part way along.

Lance was sitting in a chair by the window. At a glance, Percy could tell his brother had been even more ill than he himself had been. Lance stood, holding out his hands in welcome.

"Percy, you rogue. What's this about you playing shepherd?"

"Not playing, you scoundrel. With you taking over as Lord Thornstead, I needed a new job. How are you, old chap?" Percy caught his brother's hand in both of his own, a lump preventing him from speaking for a moment.

"In the pink, Percy, truly." His protestations were silenced by a bout of coughing.

"Truly, Lance? For you look as queer as Dick's hatband!"

"I'm on the mend," Lance insisted. "I didn't mean to take your place, Perce. I was sick when I got here, and I don't know why they assumed I was you. No one addressed me by name until Lady Aurelia did, just half an hour ago."

The lady who was sitting quietly in the corner offered a comment. "Lord Harrowby found your signet ring in your saddle bags. Or Lord Thornstead's, I should say. Apparently, you asked after Lady Aurelia before you passed out."

Percy was wondering who the speaker was when Lia satisfied his curiosity.

"Oh, Wally. I do apologize. Allow me to present Lord Thornstead. The real one. Percy, Miss Walton is my governess, and my dear friend."

And, at the moment, her ladyship's chaperone. Percy wondered where the elderly lady had been when Lia brought him his breakfast.

A few moments were spent on pleasantries before Lia brought them back to the topic, addressing Percy. "Since then, Lord Lancelot has been nursed by the vicar's sister and two of the footmen. I was not permitted in the room lest I pick up the ague." She added the last sentence with a touch of bitterness. "I must suppose they called you 'my lord' or 'your lordship' when they were talking to you, Lord Lancelot."

Lance nodded. "I suppose that is it," he said. "I do not recall."

*That explained it.*

"I am sorry, Percy," Lance added. "I did not mean to have you refused the door."

"Not a problem, old chap. If I hadn't turned up in a groom's old clothes, they might have believed me when I introduced myself!"

"But why are you dressed like that? And where is Martin?"

That was the question Percy would like to have answered. "I was out of my head with fever for a couple of days, Lance. Perhaps Martin thought I was going to die and that he might be blamed. Or perhaps he always intended to rob us if he had the chance." Percy shrugged. The anger that gripped him whenever he thought about the villain made it hard to appear casual about the man's trespass, but His Grace their father always insisted that a true gentleman did not show emotion.

"I woke up to find he had taken everything I had with me except the shirt I was wearing and another that was in the wash. Everything, including the two horses. I resent the loss of Chiron most of all."

Lia gasped. "The wicked knave!"

Percy couldn't agree more. "The innkeeper was inclined to throw me out in my shirt. He was sure it was all a plot, that the three of us were villains intent on robbing him of my board and keep. Luckily, the innkeeper's wife felt that the food, and her good care of me, were gone for good anyway, and they should treat me kindly on the off chance I really was a lord, in which case, I would pay them by and by. They let me stay another two days to finish recovering, and managed to find some clothing for me. Castoffs from a groom, I believe. Mind you, the quality of the cuisine left something to be desired."

Lance burst out, "Perce, I told you I should have stayed."

"Perhaps you should have," Percy admitted. "If I hadn't sent you off in the rain, maybe you would not have been so sick."

"Or maybe," Lia commented, sounding impatient, "this Martin would have robbed you both, and the innkeeper would have had you thrown into prison until you both died or your father arrived, whichever came first."

Percy wanted to laugh at the tart comment. "You do have a way of putting things into perspective, Lady Aurelia," he told her.

"Your parents are going to be surprised, Lady Aurelia," Miss Walton commented. "I suggest that, since they are away from home at the moment, you speak to the butler and the housekeeper about preparing a room for Lord Thornstead."

Percy protested. "I am hardly dressed to be a visitor in the manor, at least not until our baggage arrives with the coaches." He saw Lia's raised eyebrows and explained, "His Grace insisted on sending several carriages and a barrel load of attendants. Lance and I left them behind the first day out of Versey Abbey. We thought they'd take a fortnight more than us to get here, didn't we, Lance. They cannot be far away now."

"You can share my cravats, Perce," Lance offered. "I don't think you'll fit into anything else of mine."

"You will grow, dear boy," Percy replied, attempting to sound like their Aunt Enid. Lance tossed a pawn at his head, and he ducked and caught it.

"Lord Thornstead," Miss Walton told him, "I am sure we can find some clothing that is more suitable for you until your carriages arrive."

PERCY AND LANCE had, in fact, done exactly what Lia had that morning. Run away from their father's servants. It made Lia feel as if they had something in common, even if she rather resented that fact that, as a male, her betrothed was allowed a longer rope than she ever had. To be honest, since he had aroused her sympathy with the story of his trials, she was feeling kindlier towards him. Perhaps this marriage would not be so abominable after all.

Certainly, it was good to have a betrothed who was older, taller, and all together more grownup than his brother. And she could not forget how he made her feel—uncomfortable, yes, but it was not an unpleasant sort of a discomfort. From what she'd overheard when the maids were gossiping, the tingles she'd felt when they touched were a sign of desire, and that could not be a bad thing, when the man was to be her husband.

He should have told her who he was when they first met, or at least when he realized who she was. He was a knave to deceive her so. Still, he was a handsome knave and she apparently desired him. Perhaps that made his sin easier to forgive. Perhaps.

Though she did feel left out of their camaraderie. Her brothers were the same, teasing and fighting one another, but each ready to protect the other's back. She excused herself and went to find the butler and housekeeper. They were horrified to hear what the heir to the Duke of Dellborough had been through, and the butler, in particular, was mortified that he had turned Lord Thornstead away from the door, and that his lordship had spent the night in a shepherd's hut looking after the estate's gravid ewes.

The butler's stream of apologies dried up when he got a good look at Percy's patched and tattered coat and baggy trousers.

Percy endeared himself to Lia a little more when he said, "Yes, I know. And to make it worse, I was wet through and muddy from clambering over the pass in the rain. The head shepherd's good lady was kind enough to dry my outer garments in front of her range yesterday afternoon, and brush off the worst of the mud. Truly, I do not blame you in the least. I did not look myself yesterday."

The butler straightened and allowed himself an approving smile. "It is very good of you to take it that way, sir. Now let me see what I can find you to wear. And I shall have a bath taken to your room. Those garments, sir, can be burnt."

"But the ewes! I told the head shepherd I would stay until he could find someone else." Another count in his favor in Lia's eyes. He took his promises seriously, even though this one was made to an estate worker. In fact, Percy wanted to go to the head shepherd's cottage and explain himself, but he could not hide his yawns. Miss Walton said firmly that he needed to bathe and sleep, and Lord Lancelot should also sleep. "You have both had the ague, and might easily become ill again if you are not careful," she scolded in her gentle way.

The butler's suggestion that a note would be enough did not find favor with Percy. Lia found herself offering to explain things herself. "Miss Walton will walk over with me, will you not, Wally?"

So it was decided. The butler led Percy away, and Charlie moved up to assist Lance to bed.

"WELL, MY LADY," said the head shepherd, "that's a turn up, that is. He's a duke's boy you say?"

"Yes," said Lia, "and will be a duke himself, one day."

His wife made a remark in broad Northumbrian that Lia took a moment to untangle. *My Dave will be able to say one day, that there duke of Lady Aurelia's worked for me when he was naught but a boy.* "Yes, Mrs. Robson," she agreed. "He will, at that. Mr. Robson, Lord Thornstead is worried about leaving you in the lurch."

"Now then, my lady," said Mr. Robson. "You tell the young lord not to worry. Our Davie will step in, and be glad to do so. I had it arranged with Mr. Pinter, but your laddie turned up looking cold and hungry, so I took him on. It'll be no trouble for our Davie."

Lia knew that *our Davie* was the Robsons' third son. A bright student at the village school, he had been apprenticed to the earl's steward instead of following his father and brothers into shepherding. Not that he didn't also know the family business. "I shall tell his lordship that. He will be relieved."

Mr. Robson chortled. "And tell him if the duke business does not work out, I can always find a job for him." The Robsons were highly amused by that sally. Lia chuckled too, and promised to pass the remark on to Lord Thornstead.

It would be hours before she could do so, however. Both guests slept for the rest of the morning and into the afternoon.

Miss Walton refused to allow Lia to wander the manor, fretting about the slow movement of the clock hands. Instead, they went to the library to review Lia's studies of the peerage. Mama often joined these lessons when she was in residence, enlivening the dull listings from *Debrett's* with personal memories of each family.

It was not that Lia found it hard. Memorizing had always come easily to her. However, it was mind-numbingly boring. She believed Miss Walton, however, when her dear mentor suggested it would all fall into place once she started to meet the people whose names, titles, estates, and family histories she was memorizing. Meanwhile, she was very grateful when Miss Walton suggested that she would benefit from a break.

"Shall we go for a walk, my dear? And then, I think, it will be time for your piano practice."

At least Miss Walton's walks and lessons gave her something

to think about when what she really wanted to do was wake up Percival Lord Thornstead and put him to questions.

How did he feel about marrying her? What sort of a marriage did he think they would have? And above all, what sort of a husband would he be? She supposed that last wasn't a question any person could answer about themselves. She would have to figure it out for herself, but she could not do so if she could not talk to him!

"You are looking weary," she observed at the end of the lesson, as Miss Walton smothered a yawn. "Why don't you have a rest, Wally? I will stay here and work on that awkward fingering in the third movement."

Miss Walton narrowed her eyes, but also smothered yet another yawn. "Not with two young gentlemen in the house, Lady Aurelia. While your parents are absent, I am responsible for you."

"Dear Wally, they are both asleep. What if you send my maid to sit with me? I promise I shall not leave the music room. It shall take me at least an hour to conquer this wretched thing." She stabbed her finger onto the offending music sheet.

In the end, Miss Walton yawned and left her to her practice. Poor Wally. She should be given a generous pension and retired, but Lia dreaded the idea of facing the London *Beau Monde* without her beloved mentor, even if her interesting new betrothed and his family would be there. She imagined Miss Walton would not attend evening events, where Lia would be chaperoned by her mother, but Lia would want Miss Walton during the day. The less time she spent with Mama, the better they both liked it.

Now for this music.

After several attempts, she finally managed the digital athletics required to play the difficult piece. She played it right through, from one end to the other, familiar enough with it now that she didn't need someone else to manage the page turns.

However, about halfway through, a hand came over her

shoulder and turned the page for her. Percy's hand, she was certain, for the arm it was attached to was in a gentleman's coat, not in servant's livery, and who else would it be?

She continued through the plaintive music of the third movement and on into the more hopeful fourth. The music absorbed her, and she forgot all about the identity and even the existence of her page turner.

All too soon, the tempo rose to the triumphant end. As the echoes of the music still sang in the room, she rested her hands on the keys, her heart pounding, a triumphant grin spreading across her face. She had done it!

The sound of applause brought her back to herself. She swung her legs around to face Percy.

"My lady, that was spectacular," he enthused.

"Really?" Lia asked. "Or are you just being polite? I enjoy playing, and Miss Walton says I am good, but I have nothing with which to compare."

"Believe me," Percy insisted. "I have attended more musicales than I care to remember. You are better than good. It is not just that you play well. You feel the piece as you play it, and you made me feel it, too. You make me want to sink into the music— as you did yourself."

Lia considered that. He seemed sincere. "Thank you, then." She felt a relieved smile spreading across her face. "Goodness, that helps! Mama keeps telling me that I must practice, practice, practice, for everyone will judge me on my performance."

"Does your Mama have cloth ears?" Percy demanded, then obviously realized that the remark was improper, for he begged her pardon. "I did not mean to insult your mother."

But his words had Lia giggling, for they were true. Mama could not carry a tune, but was astounded and insulted if anyone pointed this out. She could play the piano, her fingers pressing all the correct keys for the required timespan, but it made no difference to her whether or not the piano was in tune. "I expect Mama had some bad experiences when she had her Season," she answered, diplomatically.

"Are you nervous about London?" Percy asked. "You don't need to be. I shall be there, and I shall help you."

That was reassuring, actually. Lia dreaded that no one would bother to dance with her once it became known she was betrothed. If she could count on Percy, at least she would be partnered for one dance.

She said so, and he laughed, then sobered when she glared at him. "What is funny?" she demanded.

"You are serious." He sounded surprised. "Lady Aurelia. Lia. I haven't known you long, but long enough to know you are beautiful, intelligent, kind, and talented. Well-born, too. Believe me, you will have no problem finding partners."

"Really?" Miss Walton had warned Lia not to believe flatterers, and Mama had said the same thing. But Percy certainly sounded sincere.

"It is true, my lady. Have you not looked in a mirror?"

"I have seen myself, Lord Thornstead," she explained. "I have seen very few other young ladies, so I have no basis for comparison."

"I have seen the London debutantes from the past two years, and none of them are as lovely as you," Percy assured her. "But you are also interesting to talk with."

"My mother says that, when I am in London, I must speak only about the weather and fashion, or people will think I am peculiar. She says that brains are all very useful, but no man wants to marry a lady who is smarter than he is."

"I cannot see why you would want to marry a man who wants a wife who only talks about weather and fashion," Percy commented. "But in any case, you shall not be looking for a husband when you are in London. I know you are not pleased about our betrothal, but our fathers are determined on it."

"Are you pleased?" For he would be a poor creature indeed if he was prepared to marry sight unseen just because his father said so.

"I am now I have met you, Lia," he said. "I'm sorry if you are not."

Lia sighed. "I am not displeased," she acknowledged. "I am cross I was not given a choice, though."

Sorry, too, that she was not to have suitors—Mama had spoken about gentlemen calling with flowers, about compliments and rides in the park, about gentlemen trying to outdo one another in gestures of admiration. *Mama enjoyed the experience. Why am I not permitted to do so?*

"We can agree on that," Percy said. "Can we also agree to make the best of it, do you think?"

Lia was not certain she was ready to give up her discontent. After all, she had been robbed of the experience she had been preparing for her whole life.

"His Grace has bribed me to do this with good grace," Percy admitted. "As my wife, you would share the bribe."

That sounded slightly insulting. "You have been bribed to marry me?" she asked. "So much for your compliments, sirrah."

Percy shook his head. "My obedience to the duke my father was never in question, Lia," he said. "I could go to the altar grumbling or happily. Those were my choices. Lance suggested that, if I would find myself wed either way, I should see if I should negotiate some freedoms for myself and my wife after our wedding. He's a smart fellow, is Lance."

Now Lia was intrigued. "What kinds of freedoms?"

"Our own estate in Berkshire, less than a day's travel from London, and a separate wing in Rutherford House, the Dellborough mansion in London, so we do not have to live with His Grace. His Grace has agreed to settle ten thousand pounds on me, invested so we can use the income to pay for servants and food and so on. He will continue my allowance and double it, and if we manage our estate well, we'll have more income from that. We will be independent, Lia. As long as we do nothing that will cause His Grace to withdraw the allowance, we can live our own lives, without our parents' interference."

That was quite a bribe! Lia found she was staring at Percy with her mouth open, so she shut it.

Her betrothed had not finished. "Of course, once you are married to me, your parents will have no further authority over you, but we shall have to be careful not to upset His Grace. He is quite reasonable in what he expects, though, and he will not interfere in our lives. He told me that, if I am old enough to be wed, I am old enough to know how to go on. I think the same applies to you, Lia. Do you not agree?"

It sounded too good to be true. She had seen marriage as the end of the freedoms of her Season, but perhaps the reverse would be true. *Yes, I am still cross about being given no choice, but I would be a fool to cut off my nose to spite my face.*

"I wonder if my parents would be open to bribing me, as well," Lia said.

"We could try," Percy suggested. "Lia, may I kiss you?"

Lia thought her heart might stop. Certainly, she stopped breathing. He was waiting for her answer, his eyes fixed on her lips. She licked them and his eyes darkened. "You want to kiss me?" she managed to stammer.

"Since I met you in the sheep field," he replied.

Those tingles were rioting. Lia found herself nodding.

"Yes?" Percy asked.

She nodded again. "Yes."

It felt nothing like what she had imagined. He moved closer, cupped her elbow, and drew her to her feet, then put his palms gently on both sides of her face. Then he lowered his face and brushed her lips with his, setting off the strongest tingles so far.

He wasn't finished, though. His mouth settled over hers, and a flight of butterflies took up residence in her stomach. His lips kept moving. Her own began to move in imitation, and then, when she opened her mouth a little, the tip of his tongue swept into the gap.

Her senses reeled and her body melted against him. For a moment, he clutched her in place, his hand against her behind.

Then he withdrew his tongue, then his mouth, then his strong hard body, cupping her elbows again to support her until her knees could hold her up.

"We had better stop." Percy said, and she took heart at the fact that his voice was not quite steady. "The door is open, and if a servant or, Heaven forbid, your governess comes upon us, we will not be given the opportunity to steal any more of those." His eyes gleamed. "And I very much want to."

He was right. Lia cast a glance at the door and forced her mind to focus. What had they been talking about? Ah, yes. "What else will we need, Percy? I have heard a lot about the Season, and I have been taught to manage a country house, but I know nothing about living in Town."

"I imagine it is much like living in York, or Newcastle Upon Tyne," said Percy.

Lia shook her head. "I have not lived in any town, Percy, or even visited. I have seldom left this valley, and when I have, it has mostly been to Outer Byrneham. I have been to Berwick-Upon-Tweed three times, but only for an overnight stay. Mama and Father think girls are better raised in the country."

"His Grace thinks children should be with their parents," Percy commented, "so I have been going to London for as long as I can remember. My sisters, too. His Grace says we pick up a little town bronze just by playing with other children of our own class, and a little more each year as our tutors and governesses take us to the museums and parks. My sister Gwen makes her debut this year, but last year, she went to a number of parties for girls and boys who were not yet on the Town, and my sister Isolde will do that this year."

It sounded wonderful. "We should raise our children like that," Lia suggested.

"I agree," said Percy. "But don't worry about how to go on in London, Lia. I'll help you.

"My parents say I am willful and disobedient," Lia warned him. It was only fair to let him know that she would not allow him to order to her around.

"I don't doubt it." Percy grinned. "I am willing to wager Miss Walton doesn't know everything you get up to, and your parents don't know half of it."

That was rude. True, but rude. She felt her face color, but chose to ignore it.

"That said," Percy added, "what do they expect when they leave you in the country and make you work all the time?"

Lia nodded. She rather thought that she and Percy would deal very well together. Especially if there was more kissing. She had seen people around the estate kissing. By accident, such as when she came around a corner and a footman and maid leapt apart and tried to pretend they were working. Or when she entered the stable without warning and surprised a groom and a dairy maid in a passionate embrace.

At the party that celebrated the end of shearing, too. She was never allowed to stay past dark, but even before dark, drink dissolved inhibitions and propriety, and several couples were less hidden in the shadows than they thought.

She had always thought it looked ridiculous, and she certainly had not felt tempted to try it for herself. Until Percy showed her what it really felt like. Kissing was wonderful.

# Chapter Five

PERCY COULDN'T BELIEVE how lucky he was in the bride the duke had chosen for him. And while she claimed to be merely resigned to the match, he couldn't miss the way she examined him when she thought he wasn't looking. She might not realize it, being an innocent, but the way she pressed against him when they kissed, the way her lips responded to his, showed she was attracted to him, too.

They spent the following day considering what Lia might ask from her father in return for her willing compliance with the marriage he had contracted for her.

It had been Lance who suggested the first item. "It sounds as if you will have more fun once you are married than before, Lia. Why don't you ask your father for the money he plans to spend on your come out, and suggest to both Lord Harrowby and His Grace that the wedding be moved to the beginning of the Season?"

"And that way," Percy said, "you can buy the gowns you want, rather than the ones your mother thinks appropriate for you."

The idea of being in charge of her own wardrobe appealed to Lia. "Mama keeps pointing out gowns in the London fashion magazines, and they are all awful. When I choose anything, she says, 'Those are not suitable for an unmarried girl, Lia. Wait until you are married.'"

"You need to ask for more than that, though," Percy said. "He probably won't give you all you ask for, so you need some things he can take away."

"I understand!" Lia showed she had been listening to her father, or perhaps the head shepherd, when she said, "If you want to pay twenty pounds for a ram, you offer ten pounds to start."

"Exactly," Percy agreed.

The three of them suggested various additions. Lia rejected the idea of a holiday cottage in Outer Byrneham or even Berwick. "Too close to Mama," she said.

"What about Scarborough?" Miss Walton asked. "It is a seaside town on the coast in Yorkshire, so not close enough for a same-day or overnight visit, but not far away in years to come, when your mother has accepted you as an adult and your brothers are grown and ready to be friends."

"How far away is it from York?" Lia asked. "Father and Mama often visit York."

Miss Walton thought it was a day's journey which Lia decided would be acceptable.

A cottage in Scarborough went on the list, but they were interrupted at that point by a footman, sent by the butler to tell Lord Thornstead that his carriages and servants had arrived. Percy went to see them settled, and returned a short while later with Lance's valet.

"You will have to see to us both, Palmer," he said, having explained what happened with Martin. Palmer, having greeted his master and been presented to Lady Aurelia and Miss Walton, bowed his way out of the sitting room that had been allocated to the two guests, saying he would unpack for both his gentlemen.

"We will need a town carriage," Percy said, when Palmer had left. "I do not mind borrowing one of His Grace's if we need to travel a considerable distance, but not to go around in London. And I cannot take my wife to balls in my curricle. A carriage and team, Lia. Do you think your father would agree to that?"

"Put it on the list," Lia decided.

They added two more items before they separated to change for dinner, something they had not bothered to do the night before. "But Lance and I have our clothes now," Percy said. "And I want to make a good impression on your parents." The earl and countess were expected back in time for dinner.

As he washed and changed, he reviewed the list in his mind. The cost of a whole new wardrobe, which would be largely mitigated by the early wedding, for the earl would be paying for Lia's clothes either way. A seaside cottage for holidays in the north. A town carriage and team, and also a cabriolet that Lia could use in the country to drive herself to see the tenants and the neighbors. A riding horse, too. Lia had been using her father's stable, but did not have a horse of her own.

Most of those things they would have to buy if the earl did not agree to provide them. After all, a fashionable young couple needed to be dressed well, and people with houses in town and in the country needed a way to get from place to place. Looked at from one point of view, the cottage in Scarborough was as much for the Harrowbys as for Lia and Percy, since it would bring them to the north of England from time to time, making visits easier.

Percy was quite pleased with himself, and with Lia, too. The only flaw in the day was that they had not had any time alone together, and he wanted to kiss her again. The opportunity would arise, however, and meanwhile, they had learned more about one another while hammering out their list of what Lia continued to call bribes. The next step—persuading the earl to go along with their plans—might be harder, though.

When he returned to the sitting room he shared with his brother, Lance was also dressed for dinner.

"The doctor said you should remain in bed," Percy said.

"I haven't, though, have I?" Lance pointed out. "I was up all morning, and I am well. If I promise I'll come back up to bed if I get tired, will you stop making a fuss?"

With some misgivings, Percy agreed, provided Lance held his arm as they went down the stairs. "You may not think I am responsible for you, Lance, but His Grace certainly does, so hold on to me, for my sake, so I can tell His Grace I did what I could to look after you."

They met Lia on the stairs, in a gown so pale that it muted the loveliness of her complexion and even seemed to take the shine out of her hair. It was somehow the wrong shape, too. Perhaps because of all the ruffles. "Father and Mama are home," she said. "They were running late and asked for dinner to be put back fifteen minutes."

That meant a nervous wait in the drawing room, but at long last the earl arrived, with the countess on his arm. "Welcome to Byrnewick," Lady Harrowby greeted him. "Lord Thornstead, I assume, and this must be Lord Lancelot. I trust I see you well, Lord Lancelot."

Lance bowed. The boy had beautiful manners, and Percy had never met an older lady Lance could not charm. "My lady, it is a pleasure to meet my hostess. I have been wishing to thank you for your hospitality and for the care I received while I was ill."

Lady Harrowby proved to be no exception to the general rule, for she simpered and insisted that it had been no trouble.

Lord Harrowby left his wife to the charmer and spoke to Percy. "This business with your valet is bad, Lord Thornstead. Took everything except the shirt off your back, my butler told me. Poor fellow is mortified that he turned you away from my door."

"No harm done, my lord," Percy insisted. "It was natural, given he thought I was already upstairs. I assure you, I was a common-looking fellow in my borrowed coat. I am grateful for your care of my brother. Lady Aurelia tells me he was so sick that the doctor stayed in the house for several days."

"Glad to do it." Lord Harrowby changed the subject. "So, you have met my daughter. The naughty puss was told to wait until we could make the introduction, but I suppose she rushed in as soon as my wife and I were out of the way."

Pretty much, from what Percy had heard. "I believe her hand was forced by circumstance, my lord," he told her father. "Having heard that my brother was not me, she guessed at the identity of the man turned away by the butler."

Lord Harrowby nodded. "Talking to the servants again," he sighed. *The dolt. Who else was she to talk to when she was left alone with them?*

"To my gain, my lord," was all Percy said.

The butler announced dinner, and Lady Harrowby ordered Percy to escort Lia and Lance to escort herself. Lord Harrowby followed along, leaving Miss Walton to convey herself to the table.

"What about the villain who robbed you, Lord Thornstead?" Lord Harrowby demanded, once they were all seated at the table.

"I have written to His Grace my father telling him about Martin, and asking him to settle my bill at the inn," Percy said. *His Grace would fix it.* Of course, Martin might have taken ship for parts unknown, but Percy doubted that would save him. His Grace had a long reach, and would not ignore Martin's trespass.

"We shall not discuss such dismal matters at the table," decreed Lady Harrowby. "Lord Thornstead, what do you think of your betrothed?"

Percy looked at Lia, who had been silent since her parents entered the room. She stared back at him, her eyes wide with alarm.

"Lady Aurelia is charming and beautiful." He spoke directly to her, hoping she would see his sincerity. Perhaps this was a good opportunity to begin sowing seeds for the coming negotiation. "I hope you and my father will consent to an early wedding, my lord. Six months seems a long time to wait."

Lady Harrowby chuckled. "You young men. Always impatient. But you shall not rush my daughter, Lord Thornstead. She is determined to have her Season."

Lia's jaw stiffened and her nostrils turned white. She opened her mouth. Percy, recognizing the signs from his sister Isolde, spoke before she could say something unfortunate out of temper, "I hope to be able to persuade you that Lady Aurelia will enjoy the Season more as Lady Thornstead, my lady."

Lord Harrowby looked thoughtful. "I will think on it. Lady Harrowby, the lad makes a point."

Percy's betrothed had read the message he had been trying to send her, and had recovered her temper. "Thank you, Father. Now I have met Lord Thornstead, I see you only wanted what was best for me."

The conciliatory remark surprised both parents, giving Percy pause. Exactly how rebellious was his wife-to-be? Mind you, now he had met her parents, he was not surprised. Any person of spirit would be restless in the ill-fitting traces to which they tried to fit her.

The rest of the dinner passed pleasantly. Both Lance and Percy had been expected to attend meals with selected guests since they turned twelve, and Percy had been on the Town for nearly two years. Between his good manners and Lance's natural charm, they managed to maintain the conversation.

Lady Harrowby tended to scold Lia for imagined flaws and minor errors, sometimes asking Percy or Lance for their corroboration of her complaints. Percy hid his shock at such poor manners and instead stepped in to turn the conversation, ably seconded by his brother. On one occasion, Lord Harrowby intervened. "That's enough, Lady Harrowby. Not in front of the guests."

Lord Harrowby, though, was as apt as Lady Harrowby to correct Lia's posture or scold her for speaking too much, or for touching on an inappropriate topic—the examples being the progress or lambing, the lamentable situation in Paris, and the clearances of the Highlands.

Poor Lia. The sooner he got her out from under their baleful eyes, the better. Perhaps he should enlist His Grace, though he did not want to commit any of what he had observed to a letter in case it fell into the wrong hands. His Grace sent his more important business missives in code, but Percy had not yet been taught the code. Perhaps he should ask to learn it.

After dinner, he reminded Lance of his promise to go up to bed, and Miss Walton, too, could hardly contain her yawns.

"I think we would all benefit from an early night," announced Lord Harrowby, to Percy's relief. He had not been looking forward to port with his future father-in-law, nor to leaving Lia to her mother's far-from-tender mercies.

⇒⇒⇒⫷⫷⫷

LIA HAD BEEN grateful to escape to bed. Mama was upset, not only that Lia had met Lord Thornstead without maternal supervision, but that Lord Thornstead had not taken Lia in dislike, as Mama had clearly expected. Mama did not like her predictions to fall flat.

She relaxed too early, for there was a knock on the door just as Pansy was putting her night rail over her head. Her heart sank. She already knew it must be her mother. She hurried into her robe while Pansy answered the door, Mama entered.

"Well, child," Mama said. "I am to tell you that Lord Harrowby and I are pleased. You have not given Lord Thornstead a distaste for you." Mama's tone of surprise and regret was expected but lowering.

"I have tried to please you," Lia answered, which was true. She had spent years and years trying to please her parents and failing. In the last three years she had settled for appeasing her parents and otherwise pleasing herself.

Mama made a disconsolate noise. "Well done," she grumbled, and then cheered slightly. "I wonder how long he plans to stay. If we can encourage him to leave within a few days, and if we can avoid him as much as possible once we are in London, we might be able to get you to the altar."

Lia wanted to thank Mama for the vote of confidence, but

such sarcasm would be punished. Instead, she pushed the hurt down and said, meekly, "Lord Thornstead suggested an early wedding, Mama. Should we consider it, do you think?"

On the other hand, Lia realized, a little opposition might work on her mother's mind. "I was looking forward to my Season, and to you and I attending all of those balls and other entertainments." There. Let Mama consider spending every evening having to chaperone Lia.

Mama narrowed her eyes. "Miss Walton or me," she pointed out.

"Yes, if Miss Walton is well enough," Lia agreed, working hard to appear compliant and not tip her hand. "My Season is not as important as the match Father wishes for me," she added. "I see that now. After all, I shall be a marchioness." Mama had offered that as an incentive several times.

Predictably, Mama finished the quote. "And one day a duchess, Lia." She sniffed. "Your father shall decide what is best. Goodnight, Lia. If you continue to be on your best behavior, the earl and I shall be very pleased." And surprised, said her tone.

She marched from the room, and Lia deflated back on to her bed.

"There's one thing to be said for this betrothal, my lady," said Pansy. "Living with Lord Thornstead is likely to be a nice change."

⇒⟫⟪⇐

LIA HAD BREAKFAST with Percy and Lance. Miss Walton had sent her apologies. She had a cold, she said, but the housekeeper visited her and came out shaking her head. "I fear it is the ague, Lady Aurelia. I blame myself. I should not have allowed her to sit with Geordie a few days ago." Geordie was the footman who had attended Lance with Charlie, and who had caught the ague.

Lia wasn't sure what to do. Mama and Father would not be

up for some hours, but Lia did not have the authority to send for the physician and Miss Hatfield. But perhaps it was risky to wait. The ague was dangerous for the elderly. Perhaps Percy would have an idea.

Percy took charge immediately, and sent one of his own grooms.

Lia fretted until the physician arrived, an hour later. She went up with the doctor, but not into the sickroom, for Mama would not approve. "The doctor says Wally is not nearly as ill as you were, Lance, but she must stay in bed, for any exertion may make it worse. Oh, I do hope Mama does not forbid me to leave my bedchamber unless she is with me!"

"We had better ask a maid to sit with us for the sake of Lia's reputation," Lance suggested, which was a good idea. Mama would see, then, that Lia was taking care. Not that it was likely to make a difference.

Percy, however, took the bull by the horns and approached Father when he came downstairs late in the morning. "May I have a word, sir?" he said. "Miss Walton is in bed with the ague. I wanted you to know I took the liberty of sending for the physician. I understand she is a treasured family dependent."

"Yes, my sisters' governess, Thornstead," Father agreed. "Good man. Can't have old Wally neglected. What did the doctor say?"

"It is not a bad case, my lord, but Miss Walton's age gave the doctor pause. He says she must stay in bed, for any exertion might make the ague worse."

Father made some *tut tut* noises, and told Lia, "It looks like you are to have a holiday, girl. You'll not do anything to upset Miss Walton, now!"

"On that topic, sir," said Percy, "Lady Aurelia sent for a maid to sit with us once we heard that Miss Walton would not be joining us. May I assume my betrothed may continue to join my brother and me when she is not otherwise occupied, provided she has a maid for the sake of the proprieties?"

"I see no problem with that," Father replied.

My goodness, Percy was clever at getting his own way!

Father went off to his study. Lia and her guests retired to the library to play cards and talk, with Pansy along to keep Mama from fussing.

Mama must have heard about Miss Walton with her breakfast tray, which she took shortly after noon, for at a quarter past the hour, a footman interrupted a spirited argument about whether Lance should be handicapped in some way for the next round, since he had beaten them both three times in a row.

The footman offered her a commiserating look as he said, "My lady, her ladyship requires your presence in her bed chamber."

Percy caught her hand and gave it a kiss. "Good luck, Lia. If you are not back in half an hour, Lance and I will launch a rescue."

"I shall copy you," Lia told him. "I shall be polite, pleasant, respectful, and agree to nothing."

Lance gave a shout of laughter. "You have him to an inch, Lia."

She shot him a grin as she looked back from the doorway.

# Chapter Six

"A M I ALLOWED to comment on your prospective mother-in-law?" Lance asked. "No. Better not. Mother used to say, 'If you cannot say anything nice, say nothing at all.' How long are we staying in Northumberland, brother?"

Percy scrunched up the piece of paper on which they had been keeping score and threw it at Lance. Lance was about to return the insult with the wrapping from the new pack of cards they'd opened, but he held fire when the door opened.

"I believe our children are in here," Lord Harrowby was saying, as he walked in the door. A step behind him was His Grace, the Duke of Dellborough.

Both young men shot to their feet, and bowed. "Your Grace," they chorused.

"Here are mine," His Grace said to Lord Harrowby. "Yours appears to be missing. What have you done with your betrothed, Thornstead?"

"You missed her by a few minutes, Your Grace. Her mother sent for her."

"I shall have her fetched," Harrowby announced, and disappeared back out the door.

His Grace approached his sons. "So. You are both here. Thornstead, you are back on your feet, if not quite as hale and hearty as a fond parent might hope. Lancelot, you have also been ill, by the look of you. Sicker than Thornstead, one might even guess."

Lance blushed and Percy felt a stab of guilt. "Did my letter not reach you, Your Grace? I wrote to let you know what happened at the inn, and that I was better."

The ducal eyebrows lifted halfway. A sardonic remark was imminent. "Your letter was—I shall not say appreciated, Thornstead. One struggles to summon appreciation for a letter that explains one's eldest son and heir has been robbed and left for dead by a villain one selected oneself to be that young man's most trusted servant." His Grace their father held it as an important tenet that a gentleman never showed emotion, but apparently even His Grace made exceptions, for cold anger edged every word.

"I survived, sir," Percy pointed out. "Thanks largely to the innkeeper's wife."

"Yes," the duke drawled, "and you will no doubt be pleased to know that that part of your message pleased me. Especially since the previous mail had brought me no fewer than three other messages that left me in some doubt over that agreeable fact."

"I wrote as soon as I could, sir," Percy protested.

"Yes, my boy. And I am glad you did. The gratifying news that you were alive was, of course, a relief to a father's heart. I could have wished for slightly more detail before I set off up the Great North Road at a pace not consistent with my dignity nor, I fear, my age."

Percy, processing that remark, was touched to think his father had ridden north at high speed.

"I am particularly pleased to see you, young Lancelot," the duke added, "since my three letters all mentioned Thornstead, and ignored the existence, or at least the presence, of my second son. And Thornstead's letter was sparse on the details important to a father, saying only, 'I am now heading off to join Lance.' But one was left to wonder, joining Lance where? And why were my sons, who left together, in two different places?" He managed to sound almost plaintive, while retaining his austere dignity.

At that point, Lord Harrowby reappeared, escorting Lady Harrowby and Lia. Lia looked unhappy. No. Subdued was a better word. As if some vital part of her had been extinguished. Lord and Lady Harrowby fussed over the duke, who thanked them politely for their letters. Apparently, both letters had arrived on the same day, one calling His Grace north as soon as possible, for his son Thornstead was seriously ill, and the doctor feared for his life, followed by one that assured the duke that Thornstead was on the mend.

That accounted for two of the duke's three letters, but Percy realized they must have left His Grace with the wrong impression.

"Sir," he said, when there was a pause in Lady Harrowby's assurances they had been delighted to look after the young lord. "Lord and Lady Harrowby did not know their patient was actually Lance, and not me. Lance was too sick to introduce himself when he arrived, you see, and they found my signet ring and assumed he was me."

"Thornstead, one trusts you have no ambition to become a novelist," His Grace replied. "I hesitate to mention it, except that you seem to be beginning the story in the middle."

He bowed to the two ladies. "Perhaps, if Lady Harrowby and Lady Aurelia would permit, we might be seated to hear what happened in its proper order?"

Lia flushed a bright red at the subtle rebuke. Lady Harrowby, whose responsibility it was to make guests feel welcome and comfortable, did not even notice she had been reminded of her duties. "Of course, dear duke. Do be seated, please. I haven't heard this story myself. I wondered why Lord Lancelot was pretending to be his brother, but Lord Harrowby said it was all a mistake and I was not to be concerned. It seemed very peculiar." She frowned. "It *was* very peculiar. Do you not think so, duke?"

"We shall hear what Thornstead and Lancelot have to say,

shall we?" His Grace replied.

Lord Harrowby commented, "Lia has sent for tea and ordered a room made up for you, Dellborough. Ah, yes, and here is the tea."

"I shall pour for us all and the maid shall pass the tea around," Lady Harrowby announced. "How do you take your tea, Your Grace?"

His Grace, whose sons knew he would have preferred a wine, inclined his head in polite appreciation and asked for a cup with tea only, no additions. Percy, who was familiar with his smallest gesture, picked up his impatience from the tap of one middle finger on his thigh, but he said nothing as the lady continued chattering as she poured the tea.

He spoke, however, as soon as Lancelot was served, and the maid withdrew.

"Now, if you please, Thornstead, and in order."

Percy had expected the command, and had been using the respite to organize his thoughts.

"Lance and I stayed at the Green Man in Newcastle, as you suggested, sir. I woke with a sore throat and a headache, but I thought it would pass off once I was properly awake. By the time we reached the Duck and Goose, a half day's travel out of Newcastle, I was afraid I might fall off my horse. When I told Lance and my valet, Martin, Martin felt my head and said I had a fever. He and Lance arranged for us to stay the night, but in the morning, I was worse. I was worried about disappointing Lady Aurelia and Lord and Lady Harrowby, who were expecting us, so I asked Lance to ride on ahead, while I stayed at the inn and Martin nursed me."

He waited to see if the duke had any comment, but his father merely waved for him to continue. The next part of the story, however, was not Percy's. "I don't remember anything much after Lance left. Not for several days. The face of the innkeeper's wife, mostly. Lance, tell His Grace what happened to you."

"It was much the same story, sir," Lance disclosed. "I set off from the Duck and Goose with a sore throat and a headache, and arrived here at Byrnewick so ill that the person who was the first to see me thought I was going to fall off my horse. I vaguely remember coming through the gorge to the valley. Then nothing until several days later. The servants who looked after me seemed to know who I was. They called me *my lord*. It was a few days later before someone called me by my name."

Percy admired how Lance had left out Lia's part in both being first to see Lance, and the first to hear he was not Lord Thornstead.

Lord Harrowby then explained about finding the ring. His Grace nodded gravely. He even listened without outward impatience to Lady Harrowby's interruption, which was all about the good care they had taken of Lord Thornstead and how surprised they were to find he wasn't, in fact, Lord Thornstead, who was instead in Harrowby's sheep fields, with the sheep.

His Grace's eyebrows shot up at that, and his patience ran out. He held up a hand, stopping Lady Harrowby's chatter in mid-flow. "My apologies for the interruption, Madam. I thank you for your kindness to my son, Lancelot. If you would be good enough to allow Thornstead to continue? Thornstead, you did not remember much for the next few days, you said."

Percy described the situation he found himself in when he was once more conscious. A few sentences brought him to Lord Harrowby's door, and a few more to Lady Aurelia stopping him as he walked through the stable yard. Following Lance's example, he left out his first meeting with Lia. He didn't want her parents hearing about that.

"And that is the whole story, Your Grace. For the past two days, I have been a guest here, and have been getting to know Lady Aurelia." Percy smiled at his betrothed. She still looked as if all the joy had been sucked out of her, but she managed a small smile in response.

"They have been fully chaperoned, Your Grace, at all times," Lady Harrowby assured the duke. "Of course, I know they are betrothed, but…" She favored His Grace with a detailed discourse on her opinions about raising females, assuring the duke in the process that her daughter had been trained in all of the womanly arts, and would be sure to make a demure, obedient, and faithful wife.

Percy winked at Lia, and her smile this time was a bit more genuine. *Good.* But he was going to have to get her away from her mother sooner, rather than later. He hated seeing her squelched.

"I had an adventure of my own," the duke said when Lady Bryne ran out of superlatives to describe some boring creature who was definitely not her daughter. "You will be interested in this, Thornstead. My third letter was from an innkeeper in Newcastle."

Ah! The third letter. Percy had almost forgotten about it. His Grace appeared to be waiting for a response.

"I am interested, sir, but bewildered," he said.

"My equanimity was somewhat discomposed by the letter," the duke admitted. "It presented condolences from the innkeeper on the death of my son, and proposed that they send me the body and the baggage, once their bill was paid. Having received three letters that placed you, Thornstead, in Byrnevale, but did not mention Lancelot, I was somewhat concerned."

Percy guessed where this was going. "It was Martin?"

"We might safely assume so." He wrinkled his nose. "He was too short and his hair the wrong color to be Lancelot, and he had your baggage, which is what misled the innkeeper. He also took a room under the name of Lord Thornstead. I suppose he thought you were dead or in jail, and decided he might as well be cosseted as a ducal heir while he was sick.

"He died of the ague. Poetic, in its way. I paid his bill and retrieved your baggage. Also, your horses, which was a disappointment to the innkeeper, who had not mentioned the animals. I also did myself the honor of visiting the Duck and Goose and paying your bill there, then, being close, continued on to

Byrnewick. And so, my sons, my kind host and hostess, my charming Lady Aurelia, our tale is done."

He stood. "I trust, Lady Harrowby, it would not offend if I begged off from your so hospitable company to refresh myself from the road? I am not, I regret to say, as young as I used to be."

"Oh, my. Yes, of course, Your Grace," Lady Harrowby leapt to her feet. "Allow me to show you to your room, Your Grace. I shall have a bath drawn..." She followed him out of the room, still talking, and Lord Harrowby followed the pair of them.

Lia, who had stood when her mother did, collapsed gracelessly back into her seat. "Your father is..." She obviously could not find a word to describe the force of nature that was the Duke of Dellborough, for she fell silent.

Percy wondered what word he could offer. Austere? Sarcastic? Remote? Scary? Fiercely protective of his children? All of those applied.

"He certainly is," Lance said, fervently.

"Are you worried about having him as a father-in-law?" Percy wondered. "We wouldn't be living with him. Our wing is completely separate, with its own entrance. And you will be family, Lia. His Grace is, in his own way, devoted to family."

"Are you worried about having Mama as your mother-in-law?" Lia shot back.

"I'm more worried about leaving you with her," Percy said, "especially with Miss Walton being ill. What did she say to you, Lia? When you came in, you looked as if you had been flattened by a runaway barrel."

"Wally!" Lia leapt to her feet again. "Oh, Percy! I am just as dreadful as Mama said. I forgot all about Wally! Mama was offended I sent for the physician and Miss Hatfield. She said I could hold myself responsible, for she had quite enough to do without being concerned about a servant who had a sniffle. She predicted I would forget poor Wally soon enough, and I did, Percy!"

Percy could not see what the fuss was about. "She has Miss

Hatfield with her, does she not? And your Mama would be the first to say you cannot nurse her yourself. The doctor was encouraging in his prognosis. And the duke is enough to put the most dire of catastrophes—which this isn't—out of your mind."

Lia took a deep breath, which caused her breasts to rise and fall under their ruffles. "That is all true," she said.

Percy managed to drag his eyes back up to her face. "Is there anything you must do for Miss Walton at this exact minute?" he asked. "Or can you sit again and tell me what else your mother said? For you were very upset."

Perhaps it was wrong of him to press her, but he could not help feeling possessive and protective. She might not be his wife, yet. But she was, in some undefinable way, already his, and he wanted never again to see her so empty looking. He wanted to defend her from all enemies, even if one of them was her mother.

Lia flapped a hand—a dismissive gesture that was somehow also one of defeat. "Just the usual. I am a disappointment. I am a disgrace to the family name. I put myself forward unbecomingly. I won't take direction. You will be ashamed of me and will refuse to marry me, or will wed me and shut me away in the country."

The light was draining out of her again, even as Percy watched. Desperate to reverse the damage he had just done by insisting on an answer, he dropped to his knees in front of her and took her hands in his.

"That is all rubbish, Lia. You are clever, creative, intelligent, and interesting. You have ideas and you make things happen. Those are attributes to be proud of." He kissed her hands, heedless of Lance and Pansy. "I want you for my wife, and if you do not want me for your husband, then I shall woo you until you change your mind. We shall have a wonderful life together, and just think—as soon as we are married, you shall outrank your mother!"

The shrinking, pinched look had drained away as he spoke, and at the last sentence, she giggled. "She shall not like me having a higher rank than her, Percy."

For dramatic effect, he lowered his voice to a whisper. "She will not be able to do anything about it. Think of that!"

"If I were you," Lance interjected, "I'd go for a walk before she gets back. It isn't raining at the moment."

An excellent idea, and perhaps he could find the opportunity for another kiss. Percy got to his feet, and Lia said, "I had better check on Miss Walton, first. Will you wait for me, Percy?"

"Remember, Lia, your mother put you in charge of the sick room. When you look at it from a certain point of view," Percy said. "I'll go and ask for rain capes and umbrellas.

Lia stopped on her way out of the door. "Should you be out in the rain, Percy? It has not been long since you were ill."

"How wifely," Percy teased. "We shall not stay out if it rains, my golden girl. The rain cape is just to keep us dry if we have to run back to the house."

# Chapter Seven

LIA WENT UPSTAIRS, the name Percy had called her running through her mind. *My golden girl.* She knew, of course, that Aurelia meant *the golden one*, but nobody had ever before suggested the name was appropriate for her. Her mother had made the name distasteful by the way she said it, as if her disappointment with her daughter began with what she had been christened. But Lia didn't mind Lance calling her *Aurelia*, and Percy's interpretation almost reconciled her entirely.

As she passed the second floor, she stopped to find out where her mother was, adopting the simple but effective tactic of asking the maids. Mama was no longer with the duke, but she and Father had retreated into their rooms. Since they could not be depended on to stay there, Lia hurried up to the third floor to ask after Miss Walton, who was resting and comfortable, or so said Miss Hatfield when she came to the door in answer to Lia's knock.

"Do you or Miss Walton need anything?" Lia asked. "My mother has put me in charge of seeing to your comfort, so please let me know what I can provide to help you." Remembering Percy's twist on her mother's words made her smile again. To think she had been afraid that marriage would just be a move from one prison to another!

Before she returned to the main stairs, Pansy arrived. "His lordship suggested we leave the house by the servants' stairs, my lady. He's a right one, is Lord Thornstead, isn't he, my lady? He and Lord Lancelot will be waiting by the kitchen door."

They were, too, armed with enough umbrellas and rain capes to go around. "Let's check the sheep," Percy suggested. "I have a familial interest in the lambs born while I was in charge. I am, in a sense, their godfather."

Lia didn't mind where they walked. When her mother was in residence, the air inside the house was harder to breathe and knowing her mother might send for her at any moment weighed her down. Stepping outside allowed the weight to roll off her back, and today she was able to take a full breath for the first time since Mama and Father had returned from Berwick yesterday evening.

"We will not stay out for too long," she decreed, against her own wishes. She must remember that the gentlemen were not long out of their sickbeds. "I shall not be responsible for you becoming sick again. What would His Grace say?"

"Something sarcastic," Lance suggested. "Seriously, though, if we choose to walk out in the cold and become ill again, His Grace will blame us. You are not responsible for what other people do, Lia."

"I am apparently responsible for every misstep my brothers make," Lia retorted.

Percy took her hand. "They cannot blame you when you are married to me and gone," he pointed out.

Even through the gloves, his touch set off what she was beginning to think of as "the Percy effect." Every time he touched her, she felt strange. Restless. Tingly. When he had placed his bare hands around her bare hands in the library, and especially when he kissed them, she had had the mad urge to kiss his, or perhaps to kiss his cheek. Or more.

Kissing had something to do with making babies. Mama became distressed and angry when she asked about it, and even

Miss Walton refused to discuss the matter, saying any questions would be better addressed to her future husband.

Lia had been frustrated by the answer, but now she thought it was wise. She would ask Percy at the first opportunity, and she knew he would not laugh at her ignorance, but would give her a proper answer. She could trust Percy.

AFTER DINNER, THE duke excused himself from the company, explaining that his afternoon rest had barely taken the edge off his weariness. "If you would attend me briefly, Thornstead, and then I will leave you to return to the drawing room. Lancelot, you will wish to go to bed. Young people recover quickly, your mother used to say, but she used to prescribe sleep and food, and I can do no better than to follow her example."

"Lance may wait until I return downstairs, sir, may he not?" Percy said, with a worried look at Lia.

The duke inclined his head. Lance picked up Percy's unspoken message and offered Lia his arm. "Would this be a good time to show me the book you mentioned on our walk?" he said. Clever boy. A book of essays and sketches on walking the Roman wall would allow them to hold their own conversation, and not be drawn into conversation with Lady Harrowby.

Percy followed the duke upstairs with an easier mind.

Up in his rooms, the duke relaxed into a chair in the sitting room and sent his valet off into the bedchamber. "Be seated, Thornstead. What is your impression of Lady Aurelia?"

*My golden girl.* "I wish to marry her as soon as possible, Your Grace," Percy replied.

"A change of tone from London, when you discoursed eloquently on the topic of my own tardy entry into the marital stakes," the duke observed.

"I had not then met her," Percy pointed out. "You have chosen her for me, and I am content," he added, politically.

But efforts to turn the duke up sweet seldom worked out as one hoped. This time, only one of His Grace's eyebrows shot skyward. Never a good sign. "Your obedience is gratifying, my son. However, I might return to you your own words, this time in reference to Lady Harrowby. My negotiations were with Lord Harrowby, whom I have known for some time. I had not then met Lady Aurelia's mother. In short, I have reservations about this marriage. Say the word, Thornstead, and I shall put a stop to it. I might point out that the reason that the betrothal was not to be announced until after you and the young lady met in London. I wanted to be able to withdraw from the agreement without scandal. Which we can do, Thornstead, now that you and I have met Lady Harrowby."

"No!" Percy was startled into saying, panicked at the thought of his golden girl being left to have the shine snuffed out of her. "I beg your pardon, Your Grace. I mean, I wish to go ahead with the marriage, sir. I believe Lady Aurelia will make a fine wife for me and an excellent duchess when her time comes, which we hope is not for many years. She is young, it is true, but she is brave, intelligent, kind, and altogether delightful."

"That is not her mother's impression of her," the duke commented.

"I believe I have spent more time with Lady Aurelia in the past three days than her mother has in the past year," Percy responded, with rather more asperity than he intended. However, His Grace's eyebrows did not shift, so he decided to say what he was really thinking.

"Sir, Lady Harrowby does her best to squash Lady Aurelia into the shape her ladyship thinks appropriate, but in doing so— Perhaps I can explain it this way. Did you see the gown Lady Aurelia was wearing?"

"One could hardly avoid doing so," the duke replied.

"All of her gowns are like that. The wrong color. The wrong cut. Too many frills and flounces. They might suit another girl," he added, doubtfully, for he couldn't imagine a girl whose looks would be enhanced by Lia's gowns, "but they are not right for Aurelia. Her mother may look at her, but she does not see her. It is the same with everything else. She berates Aurelia all the time, even in front of me and Lancelot. Nothing Aurelia does suits her mother, and everything she does, from asking after Lancelot's health to ordering a physician to attend her governess, is met with—Calling it disapproval is an understatement, sir."

His Grace nodded his head twice, his lips pressed together. "You wish to rescue Lady Aurelia."

Percy opened his mouth to agree then paused to consider his words. "I wish to *marry* Lady Aurelia. The way her mother treats her is a cause to hasten the timetable."

One eyebrow twitched. Up, then down. "Is it desire that moves you, Thornstead? Useful in a marriage, I will grant you. But a poor reason for a decision that will have lifetime consequences."

Percy ignored his surge of temper. His Grace's children all knew it was possible to change the duke's mind if sufficient evidence could be presented for the point he or she was attempting to make. But to lose one's head was to lose the argument.

"I freely admit the desire, Your Grace, and I believe it to be mutual. However, I also see in Lady Aurelia a woman with the qualities of a life companion with whom I can build the kind of family happiness our mother brought to our family."

It was a low blow, for *Maman* had been His Grace's weakness. Perhaps his only weakness. He had become even more austere, more aloof, since her loss, and never spoke of her. His children knew how deeply he grieved, but to the outside world, His Grace was untouched.

"Perhaps if I tell you about my encounters with the lady?" Percy suggested.

The duke inclined his head.

"May I ask for your discretion, Your Grace? None of what I am about to say reflects poorly on Lady Aurelia, but her mother might not be of the same mind, and I am loath to give Lady Harrowby another reason to punish her daughter."

Father's eyebrow twitched at that, but he merely said, "You have my word, Thornstead." His immediate agreement was then countered by the comment he added, "It is not my affair how the Harrowbys raise their daughter. If I find her conduct unbecoming, I can simply cancel the marriage agreement."

It was deliberate provocation. Percy refused to rise to the bait. Instead, he began with Lia's visit to the sheep fields and continued through the last three days, trying to explain just what it was about his golden girl that attracted him.

The duke was noncommittal. "Hmmm."

Percy thought of another approach. "May I ask, sir, what it is about Lady Aurelia that causes you to question your earlier decision?" He only hoped that, whatever his father said, Percy would be able to talk him round.

The duke gave another slow nod. "A fair question. I find that I hardly know the answer, Percival." A measure of his father's perturbation—while *Maman* had always addressed her eldest son by his given name except in the presence of nonfamily members, His Grace had called him *Thornstead* since he was in the cradle.

One of the duke's tricks was to remain silent, tempting the other person in a conversation to fill the void. Percy tried it now, waiting for his father to expand on that remark.

"I have heard about four Lady Aurelias," His Grace continued, after several moments thought. "Lord Harrowby described a perfectly acceptable young lady, whose birth was unexceptionable, who had been educated in all the ladylike arts including the care of a house and its servants, who was well-read and a good musician besides, and who included amongst her virtues as a wife for my eldest son, a comely appearance. While passing through Berwick late last year, I was able to confirm the appearance, but did not, at that point, wish to raise the expectations of the young lady or her mother by furthering the acquaintance."

Lord Harrowby had given an incomplete but accurate description of Aurelia, Percy thought. He nodded.

The duke steepled his hands in front of his chin. "The second young lady is the one you describe. A lady of spirit, perhaps not always wise—but that is a fault of youth—but well supplied with good intentions and good sense. A young lady who goes beyond well-read into curious and intelligent—which makes her a good match for my son. A lady who cares about those in service to her."

Percy nodded again. "Yes, Your Grace."

"The third young lady was described by her mother. Obedient to a fault, never any trouble, respectful of her elders, accomplished in the ladylike arts, but not to the extent of allowing a devotion to any of them to distract her from her primary purpose which is, I was given to understand, conforming to the wishes of her parents and in due course her husband. In essence, a pattern-card of behavior without a thought in her head except to please."

He held up a hand to stop Percy when Percy would have spoken. "This is the young lady I met this afternoon and this evening. Do you wish me to tell you about the fourth young lady, Thornstead?" His raised eyebrow was a question mark, but Percy was not fooled into thinking the question had more than one answer.

"The fourth Lady Aurelia I also had from her mother, who clearly did not realize she was contradicting herself. The fourth Lady Aurelia is an untrustworthy, disrespectful, disobedient hoyden, a girl, in short, who is bound and determined to disgrace herself, her mother, her father, and—by association—her family. This young woman will be a good wife only if soundly and frequently beaten—a strategy that, I gather, has been imperfectly followed, since Lord Harrowby is too kind for his own good."

"They have beaten her?" Percy was half out of his seat at the thought, though his urge to find someone to pummel was at odds with his wild desire to seize Lia and ride off with her to somewhere safe.

"Be seated, my son. Your lady is currently safe enough. Her mother has been instructed by Lord Harrowby not to beat their daughter." His Grace looked as if he had bitten into a lemon. *Maman* had always forbidden physical punishment for all but infractions of violence against another, claiming that beatings taught a child that—once they were larger—they too could impose their will by force.

All the schoolroom and nursery staff had been instructed that infractions could be punished by the loss of a treat or other such measures, but that violence would not be tolerated. One tutor had been fired for taking the switch to Percy, and a governess who used the back of a hairbrush to punish one of Gwen's misdeeds was also given her marching orders.

His Grace must have agreed, for nothing had changed since *Maman*'s death.

"Please let me marry her, sir. I must take her away from here," Percy pleaded.

"This is what I shall do, Percival. I shall speak with Aurelia alone. If, after our conversation, I am convinced you see her character correctly, and—!" He emphasized the last word and repeated it for good measure. "*And* she is beginning to care for you as you are beginning to care for her, then I shall arrange things so that we can take her back to London with us."

"Thank you." Percy's thanks were fervent enough, but there was one small point he would like to change. "Perhaps, though, Aurelia and I might make our own way back to London? A wedding journey, if you will?"

Both eyebrows made their rapid ascent. "A wedding journey, Percy? Have you reason to believe the lady is receptive to your physical attentions? If so, you omitted the information from your report."

With the heat burning his cheeks, Percy admitted, "Only a single kiss, sir." Inexpertly but enthusiastically received, and returned. He added, "We are never left alone."

For some reason, the duke gave a bark of laughter. "Perhaps

just as well, Thornstead. Now be off with you. These old bones are longing for their bed. In the morning, I shall demand a private audience with my prospective daughter-in-law. Don't tell her beforehand, my son. You will only frighten her."

With that, Percy had to be content. He stood to return to Lia, but the duke did not let him go without having the final word. "By the way, my son. The silence trick?"

Percy could feel his eyebrows jerk up.

The duke chuckled. "And now the eyebrows. Imitation, they say, is the sincerest of flattery. I am touched, Thornstead. Now run along and rescue your young lady from the dragon her mother."

Percy did not run. But he did hurry. On the whole, he was hopeful. If Lia were willing to show her real self, or if the duke could coax her to reveal who she was, all would be well. Percy could not imagine the Harrowbys opposing His Grace. Or not successfully, in any case.

If not, it would have to be a dash for the border, for leave Lia to her mother's non-existent mercies, Percy would not.

# Chapter Eight

LIA HAD HOPED breakfast would be a time for just her, the two young lords, and the mandatory maid. When the Duke of Dellborough joined them, she lost her appetite. She managed to reply to his genial greetings. After that, she sat looking at her plate while he greeted his sons and exchanged a few remarks about the day. Percy offered to fill him a plate, but he disclaimed an interest in anything beyond a slice of toast and a cup of coffee.

Then he addressed a remark to her. "You are not eating, Lady Aurelia?"

"Thank you, sir. I have little appetite this morning." A stupid remark, when she had filled her own plate and had had every intention of eating what was on it.

"In that case," he stood, "perhaps you will bring your tea and accompany me? Just the two of us," he informed his sons, who had stood when he did. "I wish to speak in private with my future daughter-in-law."

Lia cast a desperate glance at Percy, but he did not seem inclined to come to the rescue, instead mouthing something that looked like, "All will be well."

"The maid," Lia gasped, desperate not to be alone with this powerful and unfathomable man.

"Is unnecessary." He fixed her with that sardonic look he did so well. "I have no ill intentions, my dear, I assure you."

Percy nodded at her, and Lance looked between them and said nothing. The maid resumed her seat and her mending. Lia took a deep breath, picked up her cup, and walked through the door that a footman was holding open for them.

"The library?" the duke suggested.

She led the way, her tiny store of courage leaking out of her as she trod the familiar steps.

In the library, she picked the chairs near the window. They were furthest from the door and from any other room. If His Grace wished to say something to her in private, she would prefer the conversation not be overheard.

She stood waiting for him to sit, and he waited patiently for her to remember she was a lady and in some senses his hostess. "Please be seated, Your Grace," she managed, when the thought occurred to her.

He nodded approvingly, as if he had a right to school her. That lit a flame to the tiny fragment of indignation she had been unable to resist when he insisted on seeing her in private. She kept it hidden, determined to present the meek exterior that her mother expected of her.

The duke's next words blew her determination to smithereens. "Lady Aurelia, since my son has made up his mind to marry you, I thought you and I should make the effort to become acquainted."

That remark struck her as exceedingly unjust. "But you did not consider it necessary for us to become acquainted when the betrothal was entirely the idea of you and my parents, and Percy and I had not met?" She snapped the response and then flushed. Her abominable temper! Now he would dismiss her, and the betrothal, and Percy would be lost to her. Her betrothed would be so disappointed that she had shown her true colors.

"Excellent," said the unaccountable man. "Percy assured me you had fire, and here is the evidence of it. You are partially right, Lady Aurelia. I can assure you, however, that the betrothal would not have been announced until I had met you and until you and Percy had had time together. You have always had some level of choice, my dear."

Apparently, she had not upset the duke after all. "I apologize for losing my temper, Your Grace," she said.

"There is no need for an apology, my dear," the duke replied. "I was attempting to provoke you. Tell me, Lady Aurelia, why do you want to marry my son? I assume you *do* want to marry my son? If you do not, you may tell me so. I will put a stop to it, I promise you."

Lia felt as if she was at a tennis match, and she was the ball. His Grace seemed to change direction so quickly she could not gain any kind of a footing in the conversation, let alone turn it to her own advantage, as she had watched Percy do.

"Before I met Percy," she said slowly, searching for the words to express her thoughts, "I would have accepted that offer." If His Grace wanted honesty, she would give him honesty. There was a risk he might tell her mother, but Lia did not think so. He was remote, but for some reason she trusted him. Perhaps because of the speed with which he had dashed north when he feared his son had died. She could not imagine her own parents taking the same trouble if she were reported dead. They would send a courier, and wait to find out whether they should put on their blacks.

That said, she was the unwanted daughter. Perhaps they would make the effort for one of her brothers, especially Father's treasured heir.

She shook off the sour thought and returned to her story. "My feelings about the marriage changed after I met Percy. He told you that, when we met, he was pretending to be the temporary night shepherd."

At the duke's nod, she continued, "I was worried about how much I liked him. He spoke and acted like a member of my own class, but he was a shepherd. I knew I should not have had such feelings for him. Feelings I could not possibly act on. I left the field determined not to go back, because he made me... no, my own reaction to him made me uncomfortable."

His Grace nodded. "I see."

Lia was not sure she wanted to know what the duke could see. Far too much, probably. "Later that morning, Lance—Lord Lancelot, I mean—told me he was not Lord Thornstead. I understood, then. A Percy who was missing, and a newly arrived Percy who didn't seem to belong in a shepherd's hut? It was too much of a coincidence. When I asked him, he told me immediately who he was." She shrugged. "He told you the rest. He took his rightful place in the manor, and we have been enjoying one another's company." And kisses. They had managed another moment of privacy last night, when she had sent Pansy ahead of her to her bedroom and they had said good night to Lance at his room's door. The kiss—or rather kisses—had been even more delicious.

"And these feelings you mentioned?" the duke asked.

With flaming cheeks, Lia said, "They are stronger, sir. But also, I like Percy. I admire how well he manages Mama and Father. I enjoy being with him. I like debating with him, and playing cards, and everything we do together... It has only been a short time, Your Grace, but we have become friends. More than friends, really, because..."

She trailed off, trying to put into words matters for which she had no language. "I like Lance, too. And we are friends, too. But it is not the same. With Lance, I never think about him being a boy or even about me being a girl, but when I am with Percy, I never forget..." She swallowed the rest of her words, unwilling to discuss with anyone, let alone Percy's father, the poorly understood physical needs that tormented her.

Either he understood or he had heard all he needed, for he changed topic. "How often does your mother beat you?"

That embarrassed her even more than the previous subject. "Only when she loses her temper with me, sir." Her voice was a shame-faced mumble.

The duke did not take pity. "Which is how often? Daily?

Weekly? Monthly?"

The answer required a little thought. "When she is in residence? Perhaps two or three times a week, but she is seldom in residence for more than two weeks, and she and Father only come north a few times in the year."

Her own sense of dread about the coming Season had her adding, "That was in the past. Now, she plans to stay until we leave for London, and then I will be living with her until I marry." Lia shuddered. "Percy says we should persuade Father to let us marry early, even straight away. But Mama will not allow it. She says I am finally going to be of some use. A daughter who is marrying a marquess, your heir, Your Grace. She will be welcomed at all the best parties, and everyone in London will be trying to impress her so they receive an invitation to the wedding."

The duke narrowed his eyes. "When you say 'beat,' what do you mean, Lady Aurelia? Does she slap you? Take a switch to you?"

Back to this again. "A slap or a punch. Or whatever is to hand, sir. A riding crop. Her fan, on one occasion, and she broke it, so she punished me for that, too."

"And you wish to marry my son to get away from your mother." His Grace sounded sympathetic.

Lia answered before she had thought his question through. "Yes." But that was not the truth, or not the full truth. "I mean no, not for that reason. I wish to marry Percy. My wish to marry him *soon* is because I wish to leave home."

His eyebrows went up again. "Explain, my lady."

"I do not want to go from the pot to the fire, Your Grace. Marriage will allow me to leave my mother, but only a fool would buy a ram unseen." Her infelicitous choice of words caused the duke's lips to twitch, as if he wanted to smile, and made her face burn worse than ever when she realized what she had said.

"I mean, a husband is just as likely as a mother to beat a person, and one cannot escape a marriage. I like Percy. But more than that, I trust him."

"And you desire him," the duke replied, calling the feelings by their rightful name. "Liking, trusting, and desiring. Many marriages have started on shakier ground. Tell me more about yourself, my dear. Have you spent your entire life here at Byrnewick?"

Had she persuaded him to allow the betrothal to continue? Or was this more of the same interrogation? Lia answered the question. "Yes, Your Grace. I have never been farther away than Berwick-Upon-Tweed, and then only for an overnight stay on three occasions."

One eyebrow flicked up then down. Lia was not sure, but she thought the duke was signaling surprise. Certainly, his face remained impassive as he asked, "How do you spend a typical day?"

She found herself telling him far more than he perhaps intended—not just the subjects she studied, but how she felt about them, and what she did in her leisure time, and even about Miss Walton, who had been with her nearly all her life, since she was first judged old enough for a governess. For such a remote man, the duke was a very good listener.

"Wally was governess to my aunts, and then to their children. She was going to retire when my youngest cousin left the schoolroom, but I had just turned four years of age, and Father asked her if she would come, just for a couple of years. That was more than thirteen years ago, Your Grace. She is coming to London with me so Mama will not be forced to be with me all the time—Wally will be able to chaperone me to daytime affairs and take me to the modiste and places like that."

She screwed up her face a little, letting her worry show. "Wally should be retired to her little cottage, with a cat and little to do except read and play the spinet. She says her cottage will be too little for a piano, but she does love the piano.

"I want her with me for selfish reasons, but I am afraid it will be too much for her. She has been managing by having an afternoon sleep, but that probably won't be possible in London. And now she is ill—perhaps she won't be able to come at all, and that will be a good thing for her, I think."

*But not for me.*

"You are fond of your governess," the duke noted.

Lia bristled. "I love my governess, and I do not care if it is unbecoming for a lady to love a servant. *She* loves *me*. And she is more than a servant to me."

His Grace smiled. "Hold your fire, my dear. You are quite right. She has been, in some senses, your only parent. Tell me, does Miss Walton agree with Lady Harrowby's assessment of your character?"

Her chin jutting pugnaciously, Lia replied, "No. Wally says I am spirited and clever, and as good as I should be. Wally thinks that Mama dislikes me because I was born a girl, which meant she had to try again for the two sons she owed my father. She says I should be patient with Mama, and try to avoid making her angry."

"Good advice," the duke drawled, "but very hard to put into practice for someone who is spirited, clever, and still very young."

While Lia was still wondering whether he was being sarcastic, he said, "Lady Aurelia, you have been very patient with all my questions. I have a proposal that might satisfy both you and my son and resolve your concerns. I shall need to discuss it with your father, but I have no doubt he will agree."

All Lia could do stare at him. Did he mean he would agree to an immediate marriage, as Percy wanted? It would be better than staying with Mama, or at least it would if Percy turned out to be the man she thought he was. But how was she to know? It was not as if she had ever met any other young gentlemen!

But he continued talking and as her mind caught up, a bubble of excitement began to build in her breast.

"My daughter Guinevere is making her debut this year. She is also seventeen, and is very excited. I propose, my dear, that I take you home to London with me, and put you in the hands of Guinevere's chaperone, my sister Enid. The pair of you shall prepare for the Season together, and make your debut at the Dellborough Ball, in five weeks' time."

It sounded perfect. But would Mama agree?

"Your Miss Walton may move to her cottage, your mother will be able to see you in company, but not in private, and you and Percy shall have time to see if your attachment was a matter of propinquity. During that time, your betrothal will remain secret, so that you may step back from it, if that is what you decide, without any public comment. If, after—shall we say six weeks from your first ball?—you are both of a mind to be husband and wife, we shall announce the betrothal and the marriage will follow shortly after. What do you say?"

She tried not to gush like a young girl, even though his idea was more exciting than anything she could have imagined on her own. "Oh, Your Grace, that would be wonderful. If only Mama will permit it!"

The duke issued a small smile. "You may safely leave that to me, Lady Aurelia."

THE DUKE WAS as good as his word. Lia never found out what he said to her parents. She knew her mother would have refused him, but Father, who usually only bothered to put his foot down if one of her brothers was involved, decided that Lia was to go with the duke. Mama shut herself in her chambers, but the preparations for Lia's trip went ahead.

Lia and Percy decided not to risk upsetting the applecart by asking Father for anything from the list they had composed, but Father, of his own volition, gave the duke a draft on his bank to pay for Lia's clothing. "The girl is my responsibility," he said. "It makes sense for her to come out with your chit, Dellborough, but

I cannot have people saying that I left you to pay for it."

Miss Walton, thank goodness, was on the mend, when, several days later, Lia was allowed to see her for a few minutes to say goodbye. "Father says, when you are well enough, he will arrange for your retirement, Wally. And if you are not happy with his arrangements, I beg you to let me know, for Percy says we will buy you a cottage anywhere you wish and pay your pension. After all, it is I who have benefited from your love and the education you have given me. Percy says that what you have done for me, you have done for him, and we owe you more than we can ever repay."

Miss Walton pressed her hand. "I am happy to see you so content with the match, Lady Aurelia. He is a nice young man, your marquess."

Lia's face heated, thinking of the kisses she and Percy had shared whenever they could steal a moment alone, and the sweet words he said to her. "He is. And I shall try to be a good wife to him, Wally, as you have taught me."

"Be yourself, my dearest Lady Aurelia. Trust yourself. You are good person. A little impulsive at times. But you are young, and you have a loving heart."

Miss Walton was the only person who had ever thought so, and Lia was going to miss her.

Then again, perhaps others cared as well. Most of the indoor and outdoor servants managed to find an opportunity to wish her well, and Pansy, who was coming with her, had to find room in Lia's trunks to pack all their presents.

The head shepherd's wife had knitted her a warm hat and gloves. The housekeeper had embroidered a set of handkerchiefs with the initial A in one corner, surrounded by forget-me-nots. The gardener gave her cuttings from her favorite roses, packed in damp sand and with instructions for planting them in London.

"The young lord says there is a forcing house at His Grace's London home, and if you plant them in pots, they will be ready to plant at his lordship's estate once you are married," he explained.

"A little touch of home."

The stable servants had made her a complete set of brushes and combs for grooming a horse, presented in a leather case that had been made by the estate saddler. They, too, must have consulted Percy, for the head groom said, when he presented them, "We thought perhaps you would not be permitted to groom your own horse any more, my lady, so we asked the young lord. He says you are to have a horse to ride in the park like all the other fine ladies, and you could groom it if you wished."

The downstairs maids had pooled their pennies to purchase a fan, "For you to keep cool at those grand London balls, my lady." The upstairs maids contributed a framed sketch of the house, drawn by one of their number who had a decided talent, and framed by the estate carpenter.

As for the footmen, the butler, on behalf of all the indoor menservants, presented a dressing table set that was the finest Outer Byrneham had to offer.

When the time came for them to leave, Father was in the entrance hall to see her out the door. "Be good for the duke," he instructed. "And do not disgrace us in London, child."

Lia dropped a curtsey, her heart sinking. "Yes, Father."

Percy came up beside her, to put her hand on his arm. "Any kind wishes for your only daughter, Lord Harrowby?" he asked, coldly.

Father frowned and his eyes narrowed, but suddenly the duke was there, too. "I am certain Lord Harrowby has only kind wishes for Lady Aurelia," he said. "Is that not so, Harrowby?"

Father's glare evaporated. "As you say, Dellborough. Lia, my dear, I trust your mother and I will see you well when we join you in London. A pleasant journey, child, and I wish you every success."

"Thank you, Father," Lia said. Forced, his best wishes were worth little, but Percy's and the duke's support made all the difference to her feelings, which lightened still further when Percy escorted her down the steps, and she found nearly all the servants of Byrnewick out in the courtyard.

The cook was waiting by the coach, carrying a box. Her assistant and the kitchen maid were carrying a large, covered basket between them. "Food for the journey, my lady," the cook said. "If His Grace permits?"

"With my thanks, Madam," the duke replied. "Whatever it is I am smelling, I am sure it will be up to the standard of the excellent meals I have enjoyed during my stay."

Blushing at the duke's compliment, the cook passed the box to Lance. "This is for today, my lord, and the basket is for the next few days, and could go into another coach."

Other kitchen servants were passing boxes to the servants in the other coaches, or passing wrapped bundles up to the coachmen and grooms. "You are very kind, Mrs. Beddowes," Percy told her. "And you have thought of our servants, too."

Lia wanted to give Cook a hug, and would have a few years ago, before all the lectures about proper behavior. Instead, she tried to put her thanks into words, and if the dear woman had not been able to gather her feelings from what she said, she must have seen the tears Lia could not quite repress. "I shall never forget this. I will miss you all," she said.

"We must go," Percy said. He handed her and Pansy up into the coach and climbed in after them. Lance passed the box of food to Percy and then Lance and the duke followed. A footman closed the door, and a moment later, they were off. Lia leant forward to see out of the window, and to wave to the younger servants who had run across the courtyard to line the archway out to the carriageway.

Then it was the turn of the outdoor servants, who stood on her side of the carriageway to wave her on her way, and after that the estate workers and then the tenants. The villagers lined both sides of the road as they drove through Inner Byrneham, and then the carriage began to climb the hill to the pass.

It was on a wave of goodwill that Lia left the valley in which she had lived her whole life. Stepping out into the unknown was scary, but exciting, too. She wiped the tears from her eyes and treated Pansy, Lance, Percy, and even His Grace to her broadest smile.

# Chapter Nine

TRAVEL, AT FIRST exciting, rapidly became tiresome. Lia, used to knowing every soul she met, found herself overwhelmed by the endless succession of people and places. Newcastle-Upon-Tyne was larger than she could have imagined, and York larger still. When Lance told her that London was five times bigger than York, she almost wanted to turn back home.

It was as well that was not an option, or she might have done it.

Instead, five days passed, as they grew ever closer to her new life. All three men had riding horses, but they took it in turns to sit with Lia and Pansy in the carriage. Pansy, once she got over her awe, peppered Lance and Percy with questions about life in London, and Lia asked about who she would meet at Versey House.

When it was the duke's turn to sit with them, he spent most of the time working on papers that were delivered by couriers whenever they stopped for the night, but he also told them stories about his travels through England and on the continent.

All three men helped Lia to forget her fears and look forward to the adventures to come.

At last, they arrived in London, entering the city from the northwest, where farmland gave way to mansions and parks and then to elegant townhouses, tall and splendid, four to five stories high, row upon row of them, along both sides of the wide and peaceful streets into which they had turned after leaving the highway.

Percy elected to share the carriage for this last stage, while his brother and father rode ahead. He gave her a running commentary as she leaned forward in her seat, her nose nearly on the window. "That is Lady Ravenwood's house. She holds the most exquisite parties. You are sure to be invited. Down that street live the Redepennings. Their son Rick is a great friend of mine. You will like Rick. Ah! Here is Dellborough Square. We shall be home soon, Lia."

The street now had houses on only one side, and formed a square around a central garden. Townhouses, taller even than those they'd already seen and with even more ornate and elegant facades, lined three of the sides. The carriage stopped outside the house that occupied the entire fourth side.

"Versey House," Percy offered, unnecessarily.

*We are here.* And now Lia was to meet the rest of His Grace's family. What would Lady Gwendoline think about having to share her Season and her chaperone with an ignorant girl from the distant north? What of Lady Kirkland, whose opinion had not been asked before her brother the duke offered to double her supervision duties?

Lia wanted to stay in the coach and demand it return her to Northumberland and her beloved valley, but that wasn't going to work.

She allowed Percy to hand her down, and even managed something that she hoped looked like a smile. Someone must have assisted Pansy from the coach, for she hurried to Lia's side, looking nearly as frightened as Lia felt.

Perhaps Percy's reassurance was meant for the pair of them. "No need to worry. Everyone will love you. Come and meet them."

The door opened, and Lance looked out at them. "Come

inside! Everyone is waiting to meet Lia. His Grace and I have been here for an hour already!"

Percy patted Lia's hand where it rested on his arm, and she forced another smile. "I am excited to meet them," she assured him, and allowed him to escort her over the threshold, with Pansy hurrying in her footsteps.

⟫⟫⟩⟨⟨⟨

HER CONCERNS ABOUT how she might be received by the women of the house had been unnecessary. The duke welcomed her to his house, and presented her to the lady at his side—a woman nearly as tall as he, with coloring and features that echoed his in a feminine mold. The Dowager Countess of Kirkland, Lia assumed.

"Enid, allow me to present to you Lady Aurelia. Aurelia, Lady Kirkland, my sister."

The lady's smile had nothing of her brother's cool distance. "Lady Aurelia, we are so pleased to have you here. Lady Guinevere Versey, meet Lady Aurelia Byrne. Guinevere has been in a fever of impatience to make your acquaintance, Lady Aurelia. Guinevere, my dear, is your curiosity about her coloring satisfied?"

Lady Guinevere was golden haired and blue eyed like her brother. Tall, too, and with an infectious smile that drew one from Lia. She crowed, "Oh, Lady Aurelia! You are just perfect! I would have loved you if you had been fair, but I was hoping and hoping for a brunette! We shall knock London back on its heels. Look at her, Aunt Enid, isn't she beautiful?"

Lady Kirkland smiled at her charge's enthusiasm. "Lady Aurelia shall think you very peculiar, Guinevere. I should explain, my dear," she said to Lia, "that Guinevere has friends whose coloring is quite different from, and complementary to, her own, one auburn and the other so fair as to be nearly white. She was quite decided that a brunette was needed to complete the quartet."

"'Though we be mad, there's method 'n'it,'" Lady Guinevere joked. Lia recognized the quote from Shakespeare's *Hamlet*. "You will love Evelyn and Claire," Guinevere declared, "and they shall love you. I am quite determined on it, Aurelia. May I call you Aurelia?"

"Lia, if it pleases you," Aurelia managed.

Gwen clapped her hands. "Lia! Perfect. And you shall call me Gwen. For we are to be like sisters, and share our debuts. Lia, we are going to have so much fun!"

Lady Kirkland touched her niece lightly on the arm. "You shall have time to tell our guest all about what is in store for her later. She has another family member to meet, and will then want to go up to her chamber and refresh after the journey. Lady Aurelia, Lady Isolde? May I make you known to one another?"

The girl who stepped forward was not much younger than Gwen and Aurelia, but she had not yet lengthened her skirts or put her hair up. She had the coloring and height of the other family members Aurelia had met. "I am pleased to meet you, Lady Aurelia," she said.

"And I to meet you," said Aurelia, politely. "Please, do call me Lia, as your sister does."

At Lady Kirkland's command, Gwen and Isolde took Lia up to see her bedchamber, a beautiful large room on the family floor of the house. Pansy was already unpacking her trunks and laying out her things, and Lia made her known to the two Versey sisters.

"My room is next door," Gwen told her. "And look—there is a connecting door, so if we want to have a comfortable chat, we do not need to go around."

Isolde, who was still living on the nursery floor, sighed. "You two are so lucky," she said. "When it is my turn, I shall not have an almost-sister to share with."

Gwen kissed her cheek. "Lia and I shall share as much as we can with you while it is our turn," she promised. "And we shall be there beside you through your turn."

*Lia and I.* Lia liked the sound of that.

WHEN PERCY MOVED to follow the girls upstairs, meaning to go to his chambers and order a bath, Aunt Enid stopped him. "Not that way, Thornstead. Your things have been moved to the relatives' wing."

"Already?" Percy had hoped to spend a few nights in his own bed. "Is the wing even habitable?"

"Thornstead!" Aunt Enid sounded amused. "Mrs. Wright would be most upset to hear you. Dellborough's servants clean the place every month, and do a thorough spring clean once a year, during which they make a list of everything that needs to be fixed. You will be perfectly comfortable, and your chambers are set up as closely as possible to the way you had them set up here. I have assigned one of the footmen to be your valet, and maids will come over to clean. You may, of course, eat your meals here."

Percy was flabbergasted. "I am not even to be allowed to stay overnight? After days of travel?"

"You are not to be permitted to stay in the same house as a young lady who is not your sister. Not when I am responsible for that young lady," replied his aunt, her voice implacable.

He cast a glance at his father, the only person who could countermand Aunt Enid's orders. The duke flicked his eyebrows up and then down. A shrug. No help there, then.

Aunt Enid, though, must have missed that subtle sign, for she spoke to His Grace. "I insist, Dellborough. In the circumstances, she cannot afford the least implication of impropriety. If Lady Harrowby's daughter is going to have a fair chance with the *ton*, Thornstead cannot stay in the same house as Aurelia."

"What circumstances? Why is Lady Aurelia particularly likely to be gossiped about?" Percy wondered out loud.

Lady Kirkland regarded him for a moment before she replied. "Because people do not know her, Thornstead. The Harrowbys tend to go to the lesser towns for their social engagements. York. Cheltenham. Bath. Brighton. Even Edinburgh, I believe. They do not move in our circles, and few of those who do know Lady Harrowby like the woman. I applaud Dellborough's decision to bring Aurelia under his wing for her debut, and if we can introduce her and make a good impression before Lady Harrowby actually arrives in London, I do not expect her parentage to do her harm."

She nodded decisively, and pointed to the front door. "But there shall be no possibility of impropriety. You will leave the main house by the front door and enter by the front door. You will not stay here overnight. You will make it clear to your friends that you are not permitted to stay in the house. Do I make myself clear?"

*Clear as a bell.* Percy had no room for argument. He said so. "I will do nothing to harm Aurelia's reputation, Aunt Enid. Thank you for explaining. I take it I am to be permitted to return for dinner?"

"You may arrive no earlier than half past six for seven of the clock, Thornstead," Aunt Enid commanded, and Percy bowed to signify compliance.

⫸⫷

HIS NEW HOME, the relatives' wing, was not so much a wing of Versey House as a separate townhouse on one end of the mansion. Yes, it shared a connecting wall with Versey House and a door on the first floor allowed access from one side to the other. But the relatives' wing had its own street frontage and back garden, its own mews through the garden gate, and inside, its own kitchen suite, drawing rooms, bedrooms, attics, and all the other requirements for comfortable living.

He had to concede it was clean enough, but it had had no residents and only occasional guests since his father inherited the dukedom nearly twenty-five years ago. Most of the rooms were in dust covers. None of the furnishings or appointments had been updated since the duke first took up residence as a young bachelor. Since the duke was in his early sixties, that must have been forty years ago or more.

Percy had assumed they would go on much as they had at Byrnewick, except that he would be able to take Lia around London to show her the sights. He assumed, too, that she would have to spend an hour or so a day fixing up her wardrobe and the like, and she would need time for her music. But mostly the pair of them—and her maid and perhaps Gwen—would be together.

Undoubtedly, he had thought they would be able to steal a few more kisses, for how hard could it be to step aside into an alcove or behind a curtain when they were both living in the same house?

If he had retained any shreds of that dream after Aunt Enid's lecture on propriety, they were soon lost to the reality of what it meant to prepare for a Season with less than four weeks before the Dellborough Ball and, as Aunt Enid put it at dinner that night, "Everything to do, for nothing the poor child has with her is going to be of any use." She added, to Lia, "I mean no offense to your mother, Aurelia, but her taste will simply not do in London."

As Aunt Enid laid out her campaign plans the evening that they arrived, Percy's image of a leisurely few weeks evaporated. Aunt Enid had already made appointments with three different modistes—for day wear, ball gowns, and riding habits. Also with a shoemaker, a hairdresser, and a milliner. In addition, they would shop for stockings, shawls, and scores of other things, or, at least, it seemed like scores to Percy.

When Lia, somewhat alarmed, asked if there were enough hours in the day, Aunt Enid took her seriously and allowed that it should be possible, if they planned carefully. "We shall focus mainly on your clothing this week," she declared. "After that, we will need to return for fittings, and we will need to order more garments and the accessories to go with them over the coming months, but the big effort will be done." Dressing debutantes was apparently a serious business, and one that took time.

Apparently, though, dressing Lia was not the only task ahead of them. "From what you have told me, you have much to learn before the ball, my dear. At the very least, we need to test your skills to ensure you can feel comfortable in Society. And if any deficiency require amendment, we shall deal with it, for you are a clever girl, and I know you will learn quickly."

A dancing master, a music tutor, and a painting tutor would come to the house. Percy and the other Verseys could expect to be co-opted for role playing in which they would practice conversation and manners at afternoon visits, the theatre, balls, and all sorts of other entertainments.

"It will not do you any harm, Guinevere, to brush up your own skills," she added.

"All of that in four weeks?" Percy commented.

"Less than that, Thornstead," Aunt Enid replied. "In two weeks, we will begin to join informal gatherings to meet the other young ladies and gentlemen who are approaching their first Season. Aurelia and Guinevere must be properly garbed and have the required skills by that time. We will continue to order clothing and take lessons, but time must be set aside for the social gatherings."

"Are they not to have any time off to see the London sights or ride in Hyde Park?" Percy asked.

Aunt Enid's frown was quelling. "Time enough for that when they have been presented at their ball, Thornstead," she told him. "You will want your sister and Lady Aurelia to have the confidence that they look well and know how to behave."

Which was inarguable. With an inward sigh, Percy offered his services as driver and parcel carrier. At least that way, he would see his beloved more than just at meals.

IN THIS HOUSE, the name *Aurelia* was no longer used to berate. Indeed, as Aunt Enid—Lady Kirkland had asked for the more familiar address on their second meeting—took her from one lesson to another, testing her knowledge, she constantly praised Aurelia, even as she pointed out minor areas in which Aurelia could improve.

It was four weeks of constant activity. Fittings for gowns—no more pastels that washed the color out of her skin and no more flounces. Shopping trips for gloves, shoes, fans, bonnets, parasols, shawls, and a myriad of other items that were, apparently, essential.

Sessions with the dancing master. Sessions with the music teacher, who asked for extra time with Lady Aurelia as she had a real talent that should be nurtured, but a number of faults that must be corrected. Visits to families whose daughters were also making their debut. Even carriage rides to see those sights of London that Aunt Enid considered essential so that Aurelia's conversation would not reveal her as a complete novice.

None of this left much time for Lia and Percy. He had moved into that separate part of the great house that would become their home when they were married, and Lia saw him only when in company. He escorted them whenever they needed an escort, and had dinner with them most evenings, but they were chaperoned at every moment.

No more of the kisses that sent her reeling. Not even any more quiet discussions, just the two of them. Her day was planned from the moment she woke until last thing at night. Aunt Enid, when challenged, said that Aurelia would have the rest of her life to be alone with Percy, but only four weeks to prepare for her introduction to the Ton.

With only that one disappointment, the days were wonderful, and they flew by. Lia loved her gowns and how they made her look. She enjoyed the lessons. Most of all, she was thrilled to have friends.

Evelyn and Claire accepted her as enthusiastically as Gwen.

Evelyn proved to be Lady Evelyn Gracie, daughter of the Earl of Portsworth. She was the one whose hair Aunt Enid called *auburn*. In the plain-spoken north, they would have referred to her tresses as red, but that was to do them a disservice. They were a rich color that glinted with shades of copper and gold depending on how they caught the light. Evelyn's complexion was as pale as milk, and she was almost as tall as Gwen, though sumptuously curved where Isolde was as slender as the legendary sylphs.

At least Claire Prescott was not tall. The daughter of a wealthy but untitled landowner whose principal estate bordered Versey Abbey, she was shorter than Aurelia and had hair so pale as to be nearly white. She, too, was slender, something that annoyed her. "I am the eldest of you all," she complained when she met Aurelia. "I've turned eighteen, and I still look like a child!"

"You look beautiful," Gwen had declared. "We all look beautiful, and together we look stunning."

It seemed to be true. At the afternoon gatherings to meet other girls who were making their debut this year, it was impossible to miss the impression the four of them made on the young men present—mostly brothers and cousins of the girls. Many of them had already asked for dances for the Dellborough Ball.

By the time the ball approached, she had already met many of the young people on the guest list. She and her friends went through the list to see who else would be there. Evelyn and Gwen knew most of those listed, and were able to tell Claire and Lia which of the girls were inclined to be spiteful, and which not.

"If Miss Lewis makes an overture of friendship, watch your back," Gwen whispered at one afternoon tea. "That is her preferred spot for plunging her knife." Evelyn nodded at Lia in agreement. "Lady Lydia, on the other hand, is quite capable of knifing you while looking straight into your eyes," she said.

Most of the girls were friendly enough, though. If nothing else, Aurelia was pleased to know she would not be walking into a sea of strange faces when she attended her first ball.

# Chapter Ten

IT WASN'T THAT Percy wanted Aurelia hanging on to his arm as if he was her only support in an uncertain world. He was delighted that Gwen and Aunt Enid took her straight into their hearts. Truly, he was. Still, he had not expected to find himself suddenly excluded from an all-female cabal that included his betrothed but left him out in the cold.

Heavens, even Isolde, who was only fifteen, was welcomed to contribute to their discussions and strategy sessions, and go with them to the modiste. Aunt Enid had taken him at his word and frequently asked him to accompany them to whatever merchant was considered essential to the serious business of dressing the debutantes. But never to stay.

Today was typical. Percy had been asked to escort them to that artist in fabric who had the privilege of making their gowns for the Dellborough Ball. It was less than a week away, and today was for final fittings. Once they arrived at their destination, Aunt Enid gave him a time to return, and he was dismissed. It seemed his only function was to carry their parcels, and even that was a sop to his male pride, since a footman could have done the task just as well.

"It will only be for a few more days," Gwen assured him, which made him cross with both himself and his sister, for she was talking to him as if he was a spoilt lordling who needed to be placated.

It was not as if he was about to have a tantrum. Though he certainly felt like one. Shouldn't a betrothed man be allowed more time with the girl who would be his wife?

Percy was not allowed to be alone with Aurelia even on outings to see the sights. He could be with her only in the company of at least Aunt Enid, and usually Gwen as well. Often Isolde and Lance, too, who should surely be with their tutors rather than getting in the way of a man who missed his beloved.

He could have gone home, if the wing of the house to which he had been exiled could be called home. He thought it might be quite a nice place, redecorated, bustling with servants, and filled with light and flowers. Now, with no permanent servant except his valet (the maids who dusted came through from the main house), and most of the rooms still in dust covers, it was gloomy and unwelcoming.

Once Aurelia had settled in town, his father said, the pair of them might like to discuss hiring servants and redecorating. He would if he was ever allowed to talk to her!

He decided to drop in at his club. He and several of his friends had started their own, being ill-suited to those more traditional clubs patronized by their fathers and too young to be anything but onlookers at the altogether more exciting clubs of the Corinthians, the Bloods, and the Dandies.

The Up-to-No-Good Club had its own premises—not, it was true, in the best part of town. But that was all to the good, for the rent was so much cheaper. They had set the subscription high enough that the payments from the ten of them covered the rent, two servants in the kitchen, three footmen to do the fetching and carrying, and a cleaning lady who came several days a week. They paid individually for food and drink, and for any extra servants needed for an entertainment. If one or more of them used the apartments upstairs, they paid extra for the laundry.

Harold Worthington was there when Percy arrived. He was

sitting in the lounge, reading the newspapers and drinking brandy, though it was only noon. "Percy! I thought you were tied to the apron strings this Season! Did your womenfolk let you out? Do you have a curfew?"

Percy picked up a cushion and hurled it at his friend. "Stow it, Worth."

"Touched a chord there!" Worth noted. "Sit down, my son, and tell Vicar Worthington all about it." None of Worth's friends could figure out why Worth's parents thought their second son would make a good church man, and Worth himself had not yet told his parents that he would rather they bought him a commission in the army.

He had managed to convince them he needed a Season in town to recover from the exertions of his Oxford studies. Percy wondered if he had managed to conceal his academic record from them, for very few of his exertions had anything to do with study.

"Families can be hell," Percy said, with the double aim of expressing the essence of his own problem and diverting Worth's mind to his own problems.

"Worth having problem with his family again?" Rick Redepenning entered the room. He was pulling on his uniform jacket, so he must be going out rather than coming in. Rick was a naval lieutenant on half-pay, waiting for another posting. At the moment, he was the person most likely to be staying nights at the club. That would change when he got his ship.

Rick was a friend from childhood—Percy's mother and Rick's mother had been close, and the boys remained in touch after Rick had joined the Navy.

"Percy is running away from his family," said Worth, who had clearly not been distracted enough.

"Not really," Percy sighed and collapsed into a chair. "It would be more accurate to say I've been ejected."

"Brandy?" asked Worth, lifting his glass.

"A wine," Percy suggested. Yes, it was early, but what else was a man to do when his betrothed was being stolen from him?

"I am collecting my aunt, my sister and my… um… I have to be back for them at two by the clock."

"Same for me," Rick agreed. "It won't do to be bosky when I'm at the Admiralty. I've had word of a possible posting. Someone who knew my grandfather. I'm meeting him this afternoon, but I have time for a wine."

Worth summoned the butler by the simple trick of leaning out of the door and shouting.

"Tell us about Miss Um," Worth commanded, when the butler had been sent to review their modest cellar and produce something appropriate for two gentlemen who had important meetings.

Percy succumbed to the desire to talk about his beloved. "Lady Aurelia Byrne, daughter of the Earl of Harrowby. She is staying at Versey House and making her debut with my sister." He sighed.

Worth waggled his eyebrows. "Staying in the same house! You should be able to do something with that situation, Perce."

Percy had managed to steal a few kisses in her father's house—the most chaste of kisses, but oh, so sweet. No more. "Aunt Enid has insisted on me moving to the relatives' wing. And she watches Aurelia like a hawk. I can't see her for a moment without Aunt Enid or one of my sisters interrupting."

"Aha!" Rick commented. "That pretty, is she? Is she amenable, do you think? When is she out?"

"A wager!" Worth suggested. "The winner is the first to kiss her."

"Kiss whom? If it's a wager, I'm in." The speaker did not enter the room, but leaned against the door frame. Taking an attitude, Aunt Enid would call it, and she was not wrong.

Francis Ballinger, Earl of Alston, was the older brother of one of the founding members of the group, Matthew Ballinger. Percy admired Alston's dash and his ease in social situations, and most of the club did their best to ape his fashionable style of dress and his air of bored tolerance.

Sometimes, however, and never less than now, Percy regretted the decision to open membership to older brothers. Alston was widely admired, and by the ladies as well as by the young gentlemen.

Percy could probably talk the others out of making Lia the recipient of their gallantries by pointing out she was young, an innocent, and a guest of his family. Alston would see those attributes as incentives. There was only one thing that might put him off, and even that was no guarantee, not when Alston was in his devil-may-care mood.

There was only one thing for it. "Lady Aurelia is not a light skirt, gentlemen," he began.

Alston interrupted, his smile dangerous. "You do not, I hope, mean to suggest I do not know how to treat a lady, Thornstead. I am, after all, a gentleman. If this is about that maid at the house party, spare me your middle-class morals."

At said house party just before Christmas, Percy had come upon the earl importuning a maid and had intervened to allow the girl time to choose whether she wanted Alston's attentions or not. She chose to make herself scarce.

According to His Grace, a gentleman never, ever seduced an innocent, regardless of her social status. "Using your knowledge of passion to overwhelm the senses of an innocent is not fair play," His Grace always insisted. "Keep such tricks for those who know how the game is played."

When it came to females, Alston was no gentleman.

Alston had laughed the incident off, but that wasn't the last of it. Percy had dismissed Emily Mabberley, his mistress, when he was first told about the betrothal, intending to be a faithful husband. His Grace spoke with contempt of those who broke their marriage vows, and had kept his own, though he had been a famous *bon vivant* before marrying Percy's mother.

Alston had apparently stepped in to offer her a contract after Percy left for Northumberland. When Mrs. Mabberley refused him, Alston had decided Percy must have warned her off. He had been displeased with Percy ever since, though he had reluctantly accepted Percy's declaration that he'd never discussed Alston with Mrs. Mabberley.

The explanation Emily had given Percy did not convince Alston. He had given her a generous settlement, and she had declared, with delight, that she now had enough to open the shop she wanted.

"What nonsense," Alston had scoffed. "What fallen female would choose the hard work of keeping a shop over being kept in luxury and pampered?" It had bewildered Percy, too, and he had worried about it. Had it been his fault? Had he been a poor lover or deficient in any of his attentions? Emily had not complained. Indeed, she had compared him favorably to previous protectors.

For the first time, he had asked himself how she had entered the demi-monde. Light skirts, he had always understood, liked the lifestyle. They enjoyed sex, and coveted the benefits they could acquire through selling their bodies. Emily's delight over her shop plans put all of that into doubt.

At least it was not something that needed to concern him in the future. He had every intention of being a faithful husband, and given how much he desired Lia, he did not think it would be a problem.

He returned to the point he wanted to make. "It is not common knowledge, and will not be announced for several more weeks, but Lady Aurelia and I are betrothed. The marriage agreements are signed, and we shall be married at Versey Abbey two months from now. I trust you gentlemen not to speak of the betrothal, and..." he turned his glare back to Alston... "not to make my intended wife the object of your gallantries."

Alston bowed. "I shall, of course, as a gentleman and your friend, comply with your request, Thornstead. I shall 'make her the object of my gallantries' once she is your wife, instead." He chortled at his own wit.

"Don't be more of an ass than you can help, Alston," said Rick. "Percy's wife shall, of course, be out of bounds to us all.

Congratulations, Percy."

"Wish you happy, Thorn, if this is what you want," Worth offered, gloomily. "I wouldn't fancy being leg shackled myself, though the mater insists I will need a wife when I'm in holy orders."

"Percy likes his wife-to-be," Rick pointed out.

Worth wasn't convinced. "He wants to shag her. Doesn't mean he wants to be stuck with her for life."

"I very much want Lady Aurelia to be my wife and my life companion," Percy assured Worth. "She is..." He could not think how to describe her. Now she was no longer wearing those awful gowns her mother imposed on her, she was lovelier than ever. He could not wait to see her all dressed for a ball! On the other hand, he was not at all sure he wanted other men to see her. At all. "It is impossible to explain. Just wait until you meet her, and you will understand."

"We shall look forward to it," Alston said. He had a glint in his eye that Percy didn't like, but he was probably making a mountain out of the molehill. Alston might be a devil with the ladies, but he had never seduced a nobleman's innocent daughter, and had, besides, already promised not to flirt with Lia.

⫸⫷

As she dressed for the Dellborough Ball, Lia did not know whether excitement or fear were uppermost. At least she could be sure that she would not be left to sit on the sidelines all evening. More than half her dances were already taken.

Percy would be Lia's partner for the opening dance and the supper dance. The first dance should have gone to Father, but he and Mama had not yet arrived in London. No doubt Mama had manufactured an emergency out of spite. Since she had not been involved in organizing this ball that was partly in her daughter's honor, she would not want to attend it. "Is it awful that I am happy Mama and Father will not be here tonight?" she asked Pansy.

"No, my lady," said Pansy, in a tone that hinted she was surprised Lia even felt it necessary to ask the question. "You will have a much finer time without them."

Pansy had grown in confidence since they arrived. The housekeeper, she had confided, was kind. The other maids were welcoming. And Pansy was being treated with the respect due to the maid of the future wife of the heir to the house—the betrothal was supposed to be secret, but below stairs, everyone had already drawn the correct conclusion.

"And no wonder," Pansy said, "when his lordship wants to be wherever you are, and when the pair of you cannot keep your eyes off one another."

Lia held her gown up before her. It was in two parts, like most fashionable gowns, but Pansy had placed one inside the other to show the final effect. The petticoat part was of embroidered muslin silk in the palest shade of green-blue. Lia had learned it was not all pastels that faded out her complexion, but any tone of yellow, or with high yellow content. The pale yellows and oranges that her mother favored made Lia look ill, and the modiste had forbidden her to consider wearing them. Lia had no problem obeying that edict.

The figuring on her petticoat was little bunches of pink roses, and the skirts ended without a flounce. The bodice had a shawl neckline, the soft muslin of the gown turned in a continuous piece to drape over the over-robe of heavier silk that completed the gown.

The over-robe was striped—a deeper but still pale green with narrow green vertical stripes. Elbow-length sleeves ended in a froth of lace, and the garment was cut away from the bodice and the skirts, except near the top, between her breasts, where it fastened with a ribbon bow, and at the waist where a wider ribbon formed a sash across the petticoat.

She looked into the mirror, trying to imagine what Percy

would see tonight. Even with her hair in curl papers, she looked remarkably unlike the Lia he had first seen in a sheep field.

Pansy must have guessed at her thoughts, for she said, "Once your hair is done, my lady, Lord Thornstead is going to swallow his tongue."

There was a knock on the door, and Pansy went to answer it. Lia turned, still holding the gown in front of her.

It was Aunt Enid. "My, Aurelia, you *are* going to cause a stir. I have brought M. Beaufort to do your hair. Give your gown to your maid and put your dressing robe on, my dear. Then I shall admit him."

Lia obeyed, allowing Pansy to help her into the pretty robe to cover up the undergarments she already wore—the lace-trimmed under-petticoat that would give shape to her skirts, the prettiest stays she had ever worn, and her stockings and garters.

No wonder they started so early. M. Beaufort worked magic, but he took his time. The proof of his skill arrived in the form of Gwen, who had been M. Beaufort's first client of the evening. Before a quarter of Lia's curls had been released, combed out, and pinned, she knocked on the door and came to watch Aurelia's transformation.

"Gwen," Lia said, "you look so beautiful!"

Gwen performed a twirl to bell out her skirts, which were a delicate shade of pink, embroidered with pale blue roses that had never been seen in nature. Her petticoats had a small flounce and rows of horizontal ribbon at the base, and her robe was a figured silk. Even the ostrich feathers that danced above her head had been dyed pink.

And now M. Beaufort was placing the confection of lace that held Lia's ostrich feathers. Three only, pale green to match her petticoat. She was almost ready. She thanked the hairdresser, and he bowed his way out.

Pansy and Gwen helped her into the over-robe. While Pansy was fussing with the ribbons, making sure they sat just right, Aunt Enid handed her a small box. "I told Thornstead that gentlemen did not give presents to young ladies, but he reminded me that the marriage agreements are all signed, and you are, in fact, his betrothed. Which is true, my dear, but I beg you not to tell anyone where you got this until after the betrothal is announced."

It was a triple string of small pearls, holding a gold locket in a heart shape. The heart was decorated with fine incising in curls and scrolls, and inside, a head-and-shoulders portrait of Lia faced one of Percy.

"Do you like it?" Gwen asked, anxiously. "Isolde painted the portraits."

"They are lovely. I adore it," Lia answered, absently. She was reading the inscription on the back. *To my golden girl, who will shine tonight and always.*

"What does it say?" Gwen demanded.

Lia handed it to her, and hovered anxiously until she had it back again.

Perhaps Aunt Enid had seen it already, for she said, briskly, "Gwen, help Lia to put the trinket on. We must hurry up. They will be waiting for us to join the receiving line."

Pansy was there in a moment with Lia's dancing pumps—dark green with pearl buckles. Next came her fan and a dainty reticule, and her costume was complete. She had a moment to admire the fashionable and pretty stranger in the mirror before Aunt Enid hurried them both out of the door.

Percy's tongue did not quite hit the floor, but his mouth certainly dropped open, his eyes widened, and he could not stop staring. His Grace spoke to him twice before he even noticed. "Percy, your sister? She is making her debut, too."

After that, Percy tore his eyes off Aurelia and complimented Gwen. His Grace said, "You both look very lovely and very grown up. I am quite beside myself with pride and fear. If we have enough room in the house for your bouquets and your callers tomorrow, I shall be amazed. And to think that I volunteered to go through this with two young ladies at the same time—and I still have three more daughters to go!"

Lia, though, caught a glint in the corner of one of his eyes, as candlelight caused a glittery reflection in a little moisture there. It was a revelation. His Grace made these sardonic remarks when he was moved by emotion.

"Enid," he said, "they are a credit to you. Shall we ready ourselves for the onslaught?"

The receiving line passed in a whirl of faces and names, with a few people standing out. The four girls had planned their colors together, and first came Evelyn in an ethereal blue. A few minutes later, Claire, in pale mauve, arrived with her aunt, who was her chaperone.

Several young men of the many that Aunt Enid presented assured her that they were close friends of Percy. One of them was Rick Redepenning, elegant in naval blue and white. "Percy—" she glanced at Aunt Enid and saw an admonitory eyebrow— "Lord Thornstead has spoken of you, Lieutenant Redepenning."

"Nice things, I hope," the lieutenant joked. "May I beg a dance, Lady Aurelia?"

She agreed and he moved on to pay his respects to Gwen. What with the dances Lia had already promised at the afternoon gatherings, the first set divided between His Grace and Percy, and the supper set also promised to Percy, she was likely to run out of dances before she left the receiving line.

It was a magical evening, from her first dance with Percy, a vigorous contra-dance, until the last guest made their farewells and Aunt Enid sent her and Isolde up to bed.

Her dances with Percy did not give them a lot of time to talk. In the contra-dance, they had their turn out of the line for just long enough for Lia to thank him for her locket. "I love it, Percy. I shall treasure it always."

"When you are my wife, I can give you—oh, so much more! Everything I suggested, Aunt Enid said, 'That is hardly suitable for a debutante, Thornstead.' It made me wish we had run away after all."

Percy looked so disconsolate that Lia touched his arm, forgetting that it was one of the behaviors Aunt Enid had warned against. "Only six weeks, and then our betrothal shall be known," she reminded him.

Their turn in the dance came again. As he led her down between the rows, skipping and merry, he leaned towards her and spoke under the cover of the music. "And when you are mine, I want to shower you with jewels and see you wearing nothing else."

My goodness! Lia had never heard the like, but the image stayed with her for the rest of the evening, and it was as well that she danced nearly every dance, for it gave her an excuse for the high color that kept sweeping her face.

# Chapter Eleven

For Percy, the ball was one frustration after another. He had been admiring Lia's new wardrobe since her first new gown arrived. He had been right about a different choice of color and less frilly styles. She could not have been any prettier, but her clothes were now a fitting setting for her.

When she came down the stairs that evening, he wished he'd gone to the dressmakers with her and demanded all her gowns be made from black bombazine. Buttoned up to the neck. He wished he had argued harder to convince His Grace to announce their betrothal straight away. He wished he had rushed her to Scotland and wed her before the wolves of London could see her.

It got worse. Yes, he had his two dances with her, but all the other dances were taken by rakes and rogues and scoundrels. Rick Redepenning could be trusted to keep the line, he supposed, though he was not called Rick the Rake for nothing. Worthington, too, would not betray a friend, and nor would Matthew Ballinger. He had Alston's promise to console him, but even so, the earl eyed Aurelia as if she were a tasty lamb. Of even more concern, so did Rick's cousin George, Viscount Longford. For all his youth, Longford was a blackguard, and why Aunt Enid invited him to this ball, Percy did not know.

The list of potential dangers went on, and only the

knowledge that His Grace and Aunt Enid would be sorely displeased kept him from leaping on to the dance floor and declaring that she was his. At least, he had consoled himself, he would have her to himself at supper, but no such luck. Gwen, Lady Evelyn, and Miss Prescott had joined them with their escorts. It was a fun table. But it was not what he had hoped for.

Then, when the whole affair was over and he might have hoped to have a quiet word with his beloved, he found that Aunt Enid had swept both girls off to bed. "She says," His Grace told Percy, "that she expects a houseful of bouquets and suitors tomorrow, and the girls will need a good night's sleep. You will remember to send flowers to Gwen, Percy, will you not? As well as to Aurelia?"

Flowers! He needed flowers for Lia, and they should be delivered in time for her to have them when she woke. It was after three in the morning, so she would probably not rise with the sun, as was her habit in Northumberland. But still, he would have to be fast lest someone steal a march on him.

He had told his new valet not to wait up, but he left a note for the man, asking to be woken by ten so he could go to Covent Garden to select two bouquets. No. Three. He would buy one for Aunt Enid, as well. Might as well turn the chaperone up sweet, even if she was fast becoming his least favorite relative.

It took Percy longer than he expected to select three bouquets so big he had to requisition two of his father's footmen to help him carry them to the main part of the dwelling. It was nearly noon, and the largest and most formal of the drawing rooms already resembled the flower sellers' barrow from which he'd purchased his offerings. He was pleased to note that none were as large as his!

The flower seller had insisted that the ladies would understand the language of flowers. Flowers had a language? He had never heard of such a thing. Still, he followed her advice, buying every white and every pink rose that she had.

White for Gwen. They represented innocence and purity, the woman at the market told him. She surrounded them with some other leaves and flowers whose names he forgot as soon as she had told him, but they meant protection, good luck, and some other stuff appropriate for a sister.

Pink for Lia. That color was a declaration of love, and the rest of the bouquet conveyed that she was beautiful and that he would be loyal forever.

The third bouquet was mainly irises and gladioli. *Your friendship is important to me*, said the irises, and the gladioli declared he was *really sincere*. Aunt Enid, he hoped, would know what he meant, and would also be able to interpret the messages to his sister and his beloved.

Who knew flowers could say so much? That is, if the woman on the barrow was being truthful. After her short tutorial, he wanted to tear the red roses he saw in his father's drawing room out of their vases and stuff them in the rubbish heap behind the stables. Who was declaring their passionate love, and to whom?

He surrendered the pink bouquet to the butler, who took it away to put into a vase, and exercised his privilege as a son of the house to stay in the drawing room and read the cards that were leaning against the vases.

One of the red bouquets was from Alston. The other from Longford. Both addressed their cards to Lady Aurelia. Alston was at least bound by his promise, but Longford would not have honorable intentions. At least Percy was forewarned. Who else might he have to watch out for?

He was roaming the room, reading all the cards, when the butler and his minions returned with his flowers. Percy was somewhat consoled that his offering merited the banishment of two other vases to obscure corners.

The door knocker sounded, and the butler muttered something under his breath that sounded like, "Not more flowers," before leaving to answer it. He popped back in a couple of minutes later, carrying a small bouquet of anemones, and said, "Excuse me, my lord," and then addressed the two footmen, who had just finished arranging the vases.

"You two. Fetch the long narrow side table from the blue parlor, and put it…" he looked around the room and gestured towards a wall by the window. "There." To himself, rather than the footmen, he said, "That should take at least twelve more vases."

Percy suppressed the panic that tried to rise at the prospect of so many people courting his golden girl. She was promised to him. He had nothing to worry about. *Did he?*

"The ladies will be receiving callers between one and three, my lord," the butler told him.

*Hell. Am I expected to come along and watch the other men slobbering over my sister and my beloved?* Actually, when he put it like that, Hell itself couldn't keep him away. Presumably the rule about staying for a mere fifteen to twenty minutes didn't apply to a son of the house, and even if it did, he was not moving unless the duke himself commanded his ejection.

Percy went next door to change into something suitable for calling on a lady, and presented himself at five minutes to the appointed hour. He came in through the private door between the two parts of the house, which took him past the duke's study. As he approached the door, he heard his name.

"…Thornstead thought of me, too." It was Aunt Enid's voice. "The only gentleman to do so, I might add."

"Perceptive of the boy," replied his father. "We have made a good beginning, have we not?"

"I believe Guinevere shall take very well," Aunt Enid said. "As for Aurelia, you and Thornstead between you have made it very clear she is taken. Thornstead's first dance might have been a courtesy to a guest, but your dance with her must have set the gossips' tongues wagging. And then the way Thornstead glared at her later partners, and the way they looked at one another during the supper dance…" She sighed, but the sound was more wistful than annoyed.

There was amusement in the duke's voice when he commented, "Is one no longer required to look at one's partner when dancing, Enid? My, how times have changed."

"You know perfectly well what I mean. People will be talking, Dell. I thought you meant this period for the children to decide whether their *tendre* is real."

"People may talk as much as they wish," His Grace said, dismissively. "As long as there is no impropriety, then a change of mind will harm neither of them, and any talk will be forgotten."

Percy, frozen in the passage outside, resisted the urge to burst through the doorway and declare there would be no change of mind.

Aunt Enid said it for him. "I do not believe that Aurelia is likely to change her mind. She admires Thornstead greatly. And he has been most attentive, and rather cross that she has not had more time to spend with him. But we had such a short time to prepare, Dell. Also, it was not appropriate for a young man like Thornstead to be seen with a schoolgirl."

"She is a debutante, Enid. Not a schoolgirl. You shall allow Thornstead the same opportunities as any other suitor, while ensuring that both young people are still protected from stupidity. Drives in the park. Strolls with other couples. That sort of thing. Aurelia deserves to enjoy being a debutante, but she also deserves to be courted. Allow Thornstead to court her."

Percy nodded his agreement. And if his father was making an edict of it, Aunt Enid would fall into line. "Are you sure allowing them to be alone together is wise, Dell?" Aunt Enid asked. "Thornstead has a reputation…"

"Thornstead is first and foremost a gentleman, sister," His Grace said. "Yes, he has lived the life of a wealthy single gentleman. But he will not treat a gently born innocent with anything but the greatest of respect. Especially one he means to make his wife. Aurelia is not being bullied into this marriage, and nor is Thornstead an aging roue. Am I asking too much of you, sister? Will it comfort you to know he has paid off his mistress and declared he will be faithful in his marriage?" And what was that about, Percy wondered. Was Aunt Enid bullied into marriage?

Aunt Enid sounded subdued. "You are right, Dell. The situations are not the same. Thornstead has always been a sweet boy, and certainly, his thoughtfulness with the flowers..."

"Well, then. Do as I say, if you please."

Aunt Enid conceded. "Yes, Dell. I must go. There may be gentlemen arriving even as we speak."

Just in time, Percy concealed himself beside a tall whatnot against one wall before his aunt swept out of the room and along the passage in the direction of the drawing room.

"You may enter, Thornstead," said the duke.

*How on earth...?* But even as he asked himself the question, Percy saw his shadow, cast before him across the doorway. He entered the room, no doubt looking as sheepish as he felt. "I was just passing, and I heard my name," he explained. "I should have announced myself and kept walking. I beg your pardon, Your Grace. I shall also make my apologies to my aunt."

"No need to confess all to your aunt, Thornstead," the duke told him. "I shall shrive you for the pair of us. I cannot have you undoing your good work with the flowers. Well done, by the way."

"It was your idea, sir," Percy pointed out.

"Not the bouquet for your aunt. Excellent strategy. And hidden messages in the flowers! I had no idea, but your aunt was most impressed."

"Me neither, sir," Percy confided. "But the flower seller insisted when I told her one was for my sister, one for the woman I hope to make my wife, and one for their chaperone. She told me I was being very thoughtful, and that the chaperone, at least, would know what the flowers and their colors meant. I half thought she was telling me a taradiddle to encourage me to spend more, but do you mean Aunt Enid understood the messages?"

"Oh, yes. And described them to me and, I have no doubt, both young ladies. I daresay you shall be greeted with delight when you join the company. I believe I can trust you to build on my own good work, Thornstead?"

"I shall ask if I can take Lia for a drive," Percy assured him.

"No, Thornstead." The duke sighed, but his eyes twinkled. "You shall ask Aurelia if you might be permitted to take her for a drive, and then Aurelia will ask your aunt for her approval. You had better hurry before someone else asks first."

Percy bowed, offered his fervent thanks, and hastened to the drawing room.

THE LONDON SEASON was everything Lia had dreamed it might be. In her dreams, she had had beautiful gowns, attentive escorts, dear friends, and one special suitor who held her heart. She had never expected her real season to be like this.

She might perhaps have been permitted to make her debut in London, for Father had decreed it to be so, though Mama preferred the smaller towns. However, her gowns would have been chosen by her mother, and her mother would have chosen the events they went to, the men who were allowed to dance with her, and the ladies to whom she was permitted to speak.

Now she was living her dream, and it was even better than she could have imagined. The one thing she had missed, time with Percy, had been restored to her after the Dellborough Ball. The very next day, he asked for—and received—permission to take her for a drive in Hyde Park.

Every day after that, they managed some time together. A drive. An excursion with friends to a museum or an exhibition, a stroll with a group at a garden party, a table for supper with room for only one other couple who were also courting.

Aunt Enid insisted that she also accept invitations from other would-be suitors. Lia was reluctant to encourage gentlemen to think she was open to their courtship. It was all very well for Aunt Enid to say that she was free to choose another husband than Percy, or not to marry at all. His Grace, Aunt Enid said, would make it right with her parents, but Lia wanted Percy, and the more she knew of him, the more she was sure of her choice.

She turned to Percy in her dilemma. He was the one who had rescued her from her mother after all, and he was the reason she did not want to be courted by anyone else. She described the problem as they strolled along the Serpentine, Pansy a good ten paces behind.

As Lia had hoped, Percy came up with a solution. His good friends would be pleased, Percy said, to squire her around. "You won't have to worry about breaking their hearts, Aurelia, for I have already told them that I mean to marry you." He made a face. "I know I was not meant to do so, but they have promised to keep it a secret."

"I have told my friends," she assured him. "Aunt Enid annoyed me. She said that I need not regard myself as betrothed even though the marriage agreements are signed." She shrugged. "I was so cross, I found myself telling Gwen, Evelyn, and Claire everything." Except about the kisses. Her cheeks heated at her memories. "They promised, too. Not to say anything, I mean."

Percy's eyes darkened, and he turned to meet her eyes. "Everything, my golden girl?"

Her cheeks were burning. Had he guessed what she was thinking? "Perhaps not every little detail." He had guessed, for his eyes had shifted to her lips.

Pansy coughed. She was closer, only a couple of paces away, and Lia realized that she and Percy had stopped walking and were leaning toward one another. He was about to kiss her, and she was about to allow it. Right in the middle of Hyde Park, where anyone might see them!

If Aunt Enid heard about this, she would not allow Lia to go out with Percy ever again.

"Shall we walk on?" Percy asked. His voice might sound calm enough, but his color was high, and he was avoiding her eyes. How nice that he was as discomposed as she was! Aurelia nodded her agreement. "Yes, of course. And you will speak to your friends? It will only be for a few weeks."

His answer thrilled her to her core. "Four weeks and five days." He had been counting.

⇒⇒⇒⇐⇐⇐

PERCY'S FRIENDS WERE very kind. That very afternoon, Mr. Worthington invited her to drive with him, and Mr. Ballinger asked if she and Lady Guinevere had seen the Royal Academy exhibition at Somerset House, and if not, whether he and his brother might be privileged to escort them later in the week.

Percy used the excuse that he was merely obliging his sister to convince Aunt Enid that he should be their most regular escort, but it was with Worth that they first went to the new millinery Evelyn had found.

It was a sunny Spring day, and Worth brought a brougham for the expedition—an open carriage with enough seats for the four friends, Aunt Enid, and Worth himself. Evelyn told him the address, and he frowned, but gave it to the driver.

The milliner had opened her shop only a few weeks ago, and it was on the outskirts of the fashionable shopping area. However, several members of the *ton* had discovered it, and had attracted attention to her exquisite hats by wearing them in Hyde Park and at the Pot and Pineapple in Berkeley Square during the fashionable hours.

The millinery shop was in a quiet street on the ground floor of a modest building, surrounded by other buildings of a similar nature. Worth, who had been covertly staring at Evelyn, roused himself to comment, "Not quite tonnish, but respectable enough."

"It must be that shop," said Aunt Enid. "Look at the queue!"

Sure enough, half a dozen carriages waited in the street, and three fashionably dressed gentlemen stood talking outside the shop with the signboard that said, "Divine Hats."

"I shall ask the driver to drop us as close to the shop as he can," Worth said. "He can wait around the corner. I am sure I can find a boy to send for him when we are ready."

When Aunt Enid nodded her agreement, he leaned over the back-facing seat to speak to the driver, and moments later, he was able to hand each lady down to the paving outside the shop. The door was open, and they could see into a large room that was full of people, mostly ladies. To one side of the door, a window displayed a single bonnet on a tall stand that was draped with a light cloth.

"We shall wait for someone to leave," Aunt Enid said, decisively.

"Lady Kirkland!" said one of the loitering gentlemen. It was Percy's friend the Earl of Alston. He bowed to each of the ladies. "Lady Guinevere, Lady Aurelia, Lady Evelyn, Miss Prescott." Almost as an afterthought, he acknowledged their escort. "Worth."

"Good day, Lord Alston," said Aunt Enid. "Is your mother..." She peered through the door.

Alston looked uncomfortable. "I am not... That is to say... I came here with my friends." He glanced quickly at the two men he was with. They were waiting expectantly. "Lady Kirkland, may I present Mr. Hurley and Lord Bentham?" Alston asked.

Aunt Enid gave the two gentlemen a chilly nod and did not present them to Lia and her friends. Instead, she stepped to one side out of the way of a party of ladies who had just left the shop. "Mr. Worthington," she said, "perhaps you would care to wait here, since the place is so crowded, and there can be little there to interest you."

As Lia passed Lord Alston, she heard him say, "You would be

surprised."

⇒⟫⟫⟫⟪⟪⟪⇐

PERCY HAD BECOME a regular fixture when Aunt Enid was at home for afternoon calls. Alston and Worth were usually there as well, presumably to support Percy. He hoped it wasn't to ingratiate themselves with Lia.

He was ashamed of his own suspicions when his two friends took him to one side. "Did you know that the Divine Mrs. Mabberley intended to open a hat shop to serve the *ton*?" Alston asked.

"I knew she planned to open a shop," Percy replied. "You did, too, Alston. I told you, remember?" He felt a twinge of embarrassed shame that he hadn't asked more about it. He should have—she was so excited about the prospect, and he had shown only the barest minimum of polite interest.

Alston gave an angry grunt. "You mean you knew she was going to sell hats to your sister and your betrothed and you did nothing to stop it?"

"She *what*?" Percy had a sudden vision of a conversation between his former mistress and his future wife. This could be very bad. But on the other hand, what could he do about it? And what right did he have, in any case, to interfere?

Worth explained. "The ladies asked me to escort them to a new millinery, Divine Hats. And no need to glare at me, Alston. I had no idea. The ladies still don't, and why should they? Apparently, Mrs. Mabberley—she is calling herself 'Maxwell' now—makes wonderful hats. They all made purchases, and we are to go back for the ones that needed new trimmings. The shop was so crowded, they had to wait to get in, and everyone was coming out with boxes."

That sounded... acceptable. "She is doing well, then. Mrs. Maxwell, that is." Good for Emily.

"Very well, I would say," Worth commented. "Lady Kirkland said that her hats were Bond Street prices, but worth every penny."

Which left the question, what was Alston doing there? "Were you part of the shopping expedition, Alston?" Percy asked.

Alston was staring at the ladies on the other side of the room, as if he wished he was part of their conversation. "Eh? Oh. Divine Hats. No, I was there with Hurley and Bentham. Hurley wants the Mabberley as his next mistress and thought to make his case. But Thorn, back to your sister and Lady Aurelia. What do you plan to do?"

"Nothing." Percy had decided that his initial gut reaction had been unfair and unreasonable. "Mrs. Mabberley, or Maxwell, has every right to sell hats to anyone she likes. And if they are good hats, why shouldn't my sister and Lady Aurelia wear them? My only worry is that people like Bentham might ruin it for her by telling people she used to be a courtesan." Hurley was bad enough, but Bentham could be vicious when thwarted.

"That's your only worry?" Alston looked horrified and offended. "Your betrothed is buying hats from your mistress, and you are worried Bentham might ruin her business?"

"Keep your voices down," hissed Worth, with a worried glance at the rest of the room.

"My ex-mistress," Percy pointed out. "What is wrong with her selling hats?"

Alston shook his head in disbelief. "She is a courtesan," he insisted. "It just isn't right."

"What are you three discussing?" Aunt Enid asked, approaching them in the corner. "Thornstead, this is no place for a private conversation."

Percy apologized, and avoided answering her question. He was afraid Aunt Enid would take the same view as Alston, and he didn't see why Emily's previous profession should prevent her from selling hats.

Alston and Worth took their leave, having stayed longer than the polite twenty to thirty minutes. Percy spent a few minutes speaking to Gwen and each of her friends, finishing with Lia. "You are looking very fine today," he told her, and she was. It was not just the fashionable clothing. She was more relaxed. Happier, even. "Is that a new gown?"

She leaned towards him. "I shall let you in on a secret," she said, in a low voice. "Pansy changed the lace on one of my robes, and I am wearing it over a different petticoat. Aunt Enid said that no one would notice, but that she did not understand why I was practicing economies, when my father had given the duke such a large sum for my wardrobe. But truly, Percy, why should I wear garments only two or three times? It seems wasteful." She giggled. "Mind you, I might have spent rather a lot on hats today. Evelyn found the most delightful new shop."

Some of his mixed feelings must have showed on his face, for she said, anxiously, "They were rather expensive, but Aunt Enid agreed that they were excellent quality, and suited me wonderfully. The milliner guarantees that each hat is different to every other, and that she will not make an exact repeat of any design. All the best milliners do that so there is no possibility of arriving at an event to discover another lady in the same hat."

"That does sound like a good idea," Percy said. He added, with a laugh, "Which explains why you practice economies, my lady. So you can have unique headwear!"

She did not take it as the joke he intended. "I am at no risk of outrunning my allowance. Indeed, I do not see how I am to wear all the garments Aunt Enid considers necessary. I cannot see the point of waste, but I understand it is important to dress to do you credit."

Somehow, without in the least intending it, he had offended her. "Lia, I do not mind how you spend your dress allowance, where you spend it, or even whether you spend it. I trust you."

That proved to be the right thing to say, for she gifted him the smile he adored. The one he would move heaven and earth to win.

## Chapter Twelve

THE FOLLOWING MORNING, Percy found himself walking to the address Worth had given him for Emily's shop. The more he thought about the idea that the rakes were gathering outside the more it bothered him.

The shop door was shut and locked, but a peek in the window confirmed that lamps were lit inside, so he knocked. When no one answered, he knocked again, and this time he heard bolts being drawn back. The door opened a crack and Emily's voice spoke from the other side. "I am sorry. We are closed. Please return after noon."

The door began to close again, and he said, "Emily, wait. It's me. Thorn."

The door froze, then slowly inched open far enough that he could see his former mistress, neatly and demurely dressed in a modest gown and a matronly cap. "Lord Thornstead," she said, coldly. "I trust you are not here for the same reason as Bentham and his ilk. If so, you may take yourself off."

*Ouch. That was hurtful.* Didn't she know him better than that? "I am here because I am worried about Bentham," he said, swiftly.

She narrowed her eyes for a moment then nodded. "You had better come inside. Just a moment. I need to close the door to undo the security chain."

The door shut, and when it opened again, it opened far enough for Percy to step inside. Emily shut the door again, slid the bolts, and attached the security chain. While she did that, Percy surveyed the shop.

The wall to his right was dedicated to display. Against a dark blue fabric background, a dozen pillars of various heights were grouped, each bearing a single hat stand holding a bonnet or a hat. Even Percy, ignorant though he was about ladies' fashion, could recognize the quality and beauty of the millinery. He could even make a guess at the events to which a lady might wear most of them. A garden party. A walk in the park. Riding. An evening event.

To his left, a long counter fronted a wall of shelves that held hat boxes. The boxes were all in the same dark blue with the name Divine Hats stamped in gold. Straight ahead was an internal door, either side of which a row of gilded chairs faced mirrors large enough for a lady to see her head and the hat upon it.

"What do you think?" Emily asked.

Percy turned to see her watching him.

"It looks beautiful, Emily," he told her. "Very elegant, and practical, too. I'm amazed at what you have accomplished in— what is it? Two months? Not three, certainly."

"Six years, actually," she confessed. "I have been making hats and planning my shop for six years. I thought it would take another two years to save up for the lease and the furniture, but you were so generous—I am very grateful, my lord. You cannot know what it means to me."

How had he not known about this? She had been his mistress for eighteen months, and he had had no idea! Did she have a room in the house he rented for her filled with headgear in hat boxes? Had she spent her time making hats when he didn't visit? He had always imagined her waiting anxiously for him to call, but perhaps she resented the interruption to her real work!

"I had no idea," he said. "I am glad you can have your

dream." If it put into question all that he had believed about their relationship, that was hardly her fault.

"You said you were concerned about Bentham," Emily said.

"All of them, really. But Bentham is the worst of the lot. He is not accustomed to people telling him 'no.'"

"Females, I suppose you mean," Emily commented, but he had really meant people without titles, wealth, or powerful connections. He didn't correct her, for there was no doubt that women were more likely to be powerless than men.

"As soon as you began serving the *ton*, it was inevitable the rakes would find you," he told her, trying not to make it sound like a scold.

As his mistress, she had never argued with him. Apparently, those days were over. "I didn't intend to, Thorn. The traders in this street serve the middle sort, who have enough money for a fancy hat but who would never dream of shopping on Bond Street. But when one of your sort found my shop and told her friends, what was I supposed to do?"

"Serve them, of course," he sighed. She made a fair point.

"Are you angry that I took orders from your sister and your intended bride?" she demanded. The edge of irritation in her voice had strengthened.

"No," he protested. "You are selling hats. You cannot turn away customers. Indeed, I would think you would want the *ton* as customers. They buy more hats than the middle sort, I am certain."

She grimaced. "They cannot be trusted to pay, however. I would rather have less prestigious customers and fewer of them, but be certain of the money I need to buy new materials."

He hadn't thought of that. Percy knew any number of people who would not hesitate to keep their tailor or their bootmaker waiting for payment while they wore out their coat or their boots. His Grace did not approve of such behavior, and Percy had been raised to pay all of his obligations on the spot, or at worst, at the end of each month.

At that moment, they were interrupted. The internal door opened. "Mama," said a little girl. "Clara has gone out to the markets, and I cannot reach my buttons."

*Mama?*

Emily muttered something under her breath and hurried to the child, kneeling to button the back of her pinafore and tie her bow. The girl looked to be about the same age as Elaine, the youngest of Percy's sisters. Five or six, then. He knew Emily was twenty-three, so Mabberly must have married her when she was sixteen or perhaps seventeen. If there had ever been a Mabberly. He had never asked, and she had never said.

"Did Clara give you your breakfast before she went to the markets, Marigold?" Emily asked the child.

"Yes, Mama, but I spilt some on my pinafore, and she told me I would have to change it. Only, I could not reach the buttons."

Emily kissed the little girl's forehead. "You tried, and that is good. Would you like to sit on the counter and sort the ribbons? I haven't done that yet, this morning."

"Yes, please, Mama," was the answer.

She sat happily with a basket, and Emily led Percy to a corner where they could talk. "This business was my chance to have my daughter with me—to allow her to grow up with me and without shame. And now, thanks to Bentham and his like, it is about to be spoiled. You know your kind will not buy from a fallen woman, and if they shun me, I will lose my other customers, too. I don't know what to do. If you have any ideas, I am open to them."

Alston's response showed that Emily was correct. Even Worth had said that, if she wanted a new life, she should have tried it in a new town. No point in telling her what she must already have realized.

"I can try speaking to Bentham and the rest," he offered.

Emily was not happy. "Do you think you can stop Bentham and the rest from spreading my shame all over the *ton* and ruining my business, Lord Thornstead? For if you can, I wish you would try. Otherwise, I do not know what I will do. I cannot just pack up and start again somewhere else. I have paid a five-year lease plus money on fitting out the shop, and I cannot afford to do it all again.

She sighed. "I knew I should start in another town, where there was less chance of meeting someone who knew me as Emily Mabberley, but Marigold... She has lived with my friends all her life. I couldn't just pick her up and move her away from everyone and everything she has ever known."

Her reflections agitated Emily so much that she was marching in a diagonal across the corner. Marigold called out from the counter, "What is wrong, Mama?" Emily hastened to her daughter to reassure her that the gentleman had told her a sad story, but nothing was wrong, and nothing could be wrong, for Mama would look after Emily and they would be together now.

"For ever and ever, Mama, like you promised," said the child.

Emily—or whatever her name really was—sent him a pleading glance, and he took it that she meant him to leave. He bowed. "I will be off then, Mrs. Maxwell. Thank you for receiving me this morning."

"Goodbye, Lord Thornstead," she said. "Thank you for your call." She smiled, but it didn't reach her eyes. "It was kind of you to take an interest."

Dismissal. And who could blame her? Percy was looking back at eighteen months in which she had listened patiently to everything he wanted to tell her, and he had made no effort to learn anything about her. He had thought she was his friend as well as his mistress, and perhaps she was, but he had clearly not been a friend to her.

He would try to be one now. He hunted up Huxley, who was a good-natured if careless fellow, and easily agreed that Mrs. Maxwell should be allowed to make a fresh start if she truly wanted to. Bentham, though, was not as agreeable. "She is a light skirt, Thornstead. A barque of frailty. A harlot. She has no right to be selling items to ladies. She is not fit to be in the same room as them, let alone fitting them with hats."

"In your view, then, she is fit only to rut with," Percy commented.

The other man lifted a single eyebrow. If he was trying to be sardonic, he wasn't as good at it as His Grace. "She is a whore, Thornstead, as you know full well, since she was your whore. Her place is on her back. I made her a perfectly acceptable offer when you cut her loose, and repeated it this week. Instead, she is making bonnets for your sister and the lady that rumor says is your betrothed." He looked Percy up and down and sniffed. "You disgust me."

"The feeling is mutual," Percy told him. "Leave Mrs. Maxwell and Divine Hats alone. If you put word about that she is Mrs. Mabberley, my former mistress, I shall make sure the world knows you are taking revenge on an innocent widow because a woman who looks like her refused to be your mistress."

"But that's a lie!" Bentham accused.

"Is it? I don't have a list of every milliner and seamstress you have bedded, Bentham, but I know of a few, and you've made no objection to them selling hats and gowns to the *ton*. So you must have another motive. As to Mrs. Maxwell, if I say she is not Mrs. Mabberley, who is to say I am wrong?"

Alston's words to him proved to be useful. "After all, what barque of frailty would choose to make hats for other people rather than be kept in luxury? Mrs. Maxwell must be someone else."

Bentham's only response was a snarl.

"I'm glad we had this chat, Bentham," said Percy. There. He hoped that would be enough to deter Bentham from spreading wounding gossip. If it wasn't, Percy would have to think of something else. Perhaps he should speak to Emily's previous lovers. If they would also deny that Mrs. Mabberley and Mrs. Maxwell were the same person, they just might be able to spike Bentham's guns.

LIA ENJOYED THE delights of having six handsome and well-born gentlemen all apparently courting her with the added benefit of not having to be in the least concerned about their intentions. Five of them had none, and the sixth was soon to be her husband.

And if some of the other debutantes were displeased that Lia was gaining so much attention, she could do nothing about that. It was not as if the other maidens had lost by it. None of Percy's friends showed any interest in settling down.

A week after Percy volunteered his friends, she mentioned the ladies' disgruntlement to Lieutenant Redepenning. They were strolling on the terrace of the ballroom at the Duke of Winshire's townhouse, cooling down in the night air after a particularly vigorous dance.

The lieutenant echoed her own thoughts. "I cannot see what they have to complain about. If we had not wanted to support Percy, we would not be here. We usually avoid these affairs like the plague. Not that I don't enjoy dancing, and lawn parties and the like, Lady Aurelia, but it gives the marriage-minded maidens thoughts I'd rather they didn't entertain. I am far too young to take a wife, and I could not afford one on my lieutenant's pay even if I found a lady who tempted me to change my mind."

Lia immediately felt guilty, but when she apologized, Lieutenant Redepenning reassured her. "It is great fun, and safe enough, for they all think we are interested in you. Once you and Percy are wed, we shall return to our useful pursuits, so do not feel you need to apologize, Lia."

"There you are!" It was her mother's voice, and Lia had no time to react before her mother had her by the ear and was dragging her towards the house. "I knew how it would be. Out in the night with a known rake! I no sooner let you out of my sight than you disgrace us all."

"Madam," said Lieutenant Redepenning. "Unhand Lady

Aurelia. She is living in the charge of the Duke of Dellborough, and he will be…" He put a hand over Mama's, and she swung her reticule at him, clouting him on the side of the face. It was a poor return for his courage in defending Lia, but she could see in his eyes that he was prepared to make another attempt.

She opened her mouth, though she had no idea what she could say to calm Mama down. For one thing, she did not know what Mama thought she had done. For another, she was the last person on earth Mama would ever listen to. "Mama—" she began.

Mama ignored her, still focusing her ire on poor Lieutenant Redepenning. "The wicked girl should not be out here with you, but you are older and should know better."

A slim figure stepped from the shadows. "Lady Harrowby. I did not know you had arrived in town."

Thank goodness. Percy had come to her rescue.

"Thornstead," Mama greeted him. She shook Lia by the ear. "I am horrified at my daughter's behavior. Horrified! I cannot hope you will forgive her. It would be best if she just goes home by me." She shook Lia again, and this time Lia could not resist a squeak of pain.

Percy grabbed Mama's wrist and he suddenly sounded very much like his father, ice dripping from his words as he said, "My betrothed was taking the air on the arm of my best friend and was always within my sight, Lady Harrowby. Please take your hands off her."

The last sentence was a command so potent that Lia could almost see generations of dukes standing shoulder to shoulder with this most recent representative of their line, nodding their approval. So potent that Mama let go of Lia's ear, and Percy drew her back from Mama's reach and stepped into her place.

Mama looked about to argue, but another voice intruded on the scene. "Betrothed, Thornstead?" Lia glanced toward the doors that let onto the terrace from the ballroom. Half a dozen people were watching them. It was Lady Sutton who had spoken. The daughter-in-law of the Duke of Winshire, she was the evening's hostess. "Did I hear correctly? You and Lady Aurelia are betrothed?"

"It has been private within the families," said Aunt Enid, smoothly, as she skirted the growing crowd to join Lia. "My brother plans to announce it soon. We are all very pleased, are we not, Lady Harrowby?"

Mama, watched by the avid eyes of some of the worst gossipmongers in the *ton*, mumbled an agreement.

"Lady Harrowby had just arrived in Town," Percy said, smoothly. "Perhaps we might take this reunion between her and her daughter to a more private location, Lady Sutton?"

*Not alone*, Lia wanted to shout, but there was no need. Percy offered her one arm and Mama another, keeping them apart by the width of his own body while he followed a footman to the parlor Lady Sutton offered them. Aunt Enid trailed them, after sending Lieutenant Redepenning to tell Gwen where she was.

"I will stay with her until you return," he offered.

Aunt Enid's thanks were said with a hard glance at Mama. "Thank you, Rick, dear. I know I can depend on you to keep her from harm."

Lia could not see Mama's expression from where she was on the other side of Percy, but she could imagine a fiery glare, and sure enough, Aunt Enid was the first object of Mama's attack once they were inside the parlor with the door shut.

"What kind of a chaperone are you, Lady Kirkland?" she demanded, letting Percy's arm go to march up to Aunt Enid and snarl in the lady's face. "Letting this hoyden walk on the terrace with a known rake. I know what Lia has been up to. Shaming Lord Thornstead and my family with her light-skirt ways. And her chaperone nowhere in sight."

She turned on Lia then, her hand already in motion to slap. "Shaming me," she screeched, but Percy had caught her wrist again.

"You are mistaken, Lady Harrowby," he said. His voice was

calm, but Lia could feel his muscles quiver under his arm as he held his own temper in check. "Lia has never been out of sight of her chaperone or some other trusted person. Such as my dearest friend Lieutenant Redepenning, who would die before dishonoring Lia."

She sneered. "That is not what my friends report in their letters. She has been making a fool of you. It was no more than I expected. Bad blood. Bad blood will win out. You mark my words."

"You have been drinking," Aunt Enid observed. "Thornstead, I suggest we call for your coach and take Lady Harrowby home."

"Is Lord Harrowby here?" Percy asked, but none of them knew and Mama had gone into a sulk. It would not last. She was not skilled at silence. But while it did, she would say nothing.

"I will send a footman to find out," Lia offered, wondering what bad blood she had. There was no point in asking Mama. Not while she was in this condition.

Father came quickly enough, but started with the assumption that this was all Lia's fault. "What have you done, you wicked girl," he demanded.

Percy intervened, quickly. "Nothing at all. Lady Aurelia was strolling on the terrace with a friend of mine, with her chaperone's permission and under my eye. Lady Harrowby came upon them, and immediately began abusing both Lady Aurelia and my friend. I had been with them the entire time, and I had to intervene to stop Lady Harrowby from striking her daughter."

With a suspicious look at Lia, Father said, "That is not the gossip that is going around the room. Are you covering up her behavior to protect her, Thornstead? For I can tell you that a lying jade is not worth the bother, no matter how pretty. If you came across her in the gardens with her skirts up and a bounder beneath them, then I'll not blame you for calling off the wedding. It is what I should have done."

Mama flared into temper, but this time at Father. "You had a choice, Harrowby. And I have given you two sons. I have done my duty."

The private quarrel was interrupted by Percy. "I am not a liar, sir, and neither is Lady Aurelia. Any gossip you've heard has been inflamed by Lady Harrowby's intemperate behavior. I suggest you take her home, and we shall discuss this tomorrow, when Lady Harrowby is sober, and tempers have calmed."

"I'll not have you telling me what to do, you young pup," Father growled, setting his shoulders and fisting his hands in an attempt to loom over Percy. From her place of safety behind Percy, Lia could smell the brandy fumes rolling off Father's breath.

Since Percy had a good ten inches on Father, the attempt to intimidate failed, but it succeeded in further abrading the leash Percy had on his temper. "Then, sir, do as you please. Come, Lia."

"I should make you come home with me," Father said to Lia as she was leaving the room. "But I cannot be bothered with you tonight. I shall come and get you tomorrow, once Dellborough hears what you have been up to and decides to throw you out. Like mother, like daughter."

The sound of flesh on flesh shocked them all, even, perhaps, Mama. Lia turned back to look, and Mama was looking up at Father, her hand still raised.

Lia felt Percy's hand on hers and realized he was shifting her from his arm to Aunt Enid's. "Take Lia away. I'll see my future parents-in-law don't cause a further scandal tonight. If you see any of my friends, please send them to help."

Should she offer to stay? To see if she could help? She had seen her parents like this before, and had always retreated—not just because her presence made things worse, but because they frightened her when their resentment of one another boiled into open hatred.

"Go," Percy told her. "You cannot help them."

He was right. She followed Aunt Enid meekly from the room. They sent for Gwen and their coach, and Aunt Enid asked

Lieutenant Redepenning to stay with the two girls for a few minutes while she had a word with Lady Sutton.

"She is going to make certain that the true story is spread, Aurelia. But for us, for tonight, the ball is over."

## Chapter Thirteen

PERCY HAD MANAGED to maintain a modicum of civility, though the obnoxious pair tempted him sorely. He could ignore their insults to himself, but what they said about Lia made his blood boil.

His Grace had taught Percy to cram his anger down where it could not cloud his thinking, or to leave the situation. "Never make a decision in a rage, Thornstead," he had said so often that the instruction was written in Percy's bones. "Keep your anger under control, decide your reaction in cold blood, and then use the stored anger to fuel your response. You will be a duke. Rage makes people stupid. Dukes cannot afford to be stupid."

Never had it been so hard. He managed to keep his tongue between his teeth during the frustrating hour it took to persuade his future in-laws not to return to the party. Rick and Alston tried both charm and logic, Matthew Barrington ran to fetch first Lady Sutton and then Rick's father, to lend their persuasions, and Worth parked himself in the way of the door, clearly ready to stay there for the rest of the night.

It looked as if it might come to that, for Percy was determined the drunken pair would not be released into the assembled *ton* to spread their calumnies. Finally, however, they consented to being put into their carriage and taken home. Percy borrowed a horse from Winshire's stables to accompany the pair and to see them safely into the hands of their butler. The cool night air had sent the alcohol to their heads. Lady Harrowby was barely awake, and Lord Harrowby needed to be half carried into the house. They would not cause more trouble tonight.

Percy returned the horse and walked home. Whatever he said, the Harrowbys were convinced that the letters they had received from gossiping friends told the truth—that Lia was developing a reputation for being fast.

Lia no more knew how to flirt than how to fly, and she treated Percy's friends as if they were the older brothers she'd never had. Besides, Aunt Enid never left her alone for a moment unless she was tucked up in her bed chamber at night. Witness how quickly she intervened tonight! She must have been standing just inside the door. His protestations had fallen on deaf ears, but perhaps they would be more sensible in the morning.

As he walked, his mind evolved schemes to mitigate the damage the Harrowbys had done and to prevent any more. His chief worry was that Lord Harrowby had every legal right to take Lia away. He was Lia's father and guardian. And if some of what the pair had said this night placed some doubt on the first relationship, the second was beyond question.

Perhaps the man would wake in a more pliant mood tomorrow—no, later today. If anyone could persuade him and his bitter snake of a wife to leave Lia in the duke's house and their ancient scandals in the past where they belonged, it would be the Duke of Dellborough.

However, the danger of a relapse would persist until Percy and Lia were wed. This night had demonstrated that the pair seethed with hatred—for one another, and for the innocent child who was unwittingly at the core of their discontent with one another. Anything could precipitate another crisis—a drink too many, some perceived insult, a misinterpreted action by Lia or Percy.

The safest move, then, would be to bring the wedding forward. By the time he arrived at Dellborough House, he had determined that his best course of action would be to elope tonight. For a fleeting moment, he thought of Emily and the trouble looming over her, but Lia must be his first priority. He would ask his friends to keep an eye on Emily.

There would be scandal, of course, but they could live that down. Few people would risk offending the Duke of Dellborough or the Dowager Countess of Kingswood. There might be whispers, but they would fade away when the *ton* saw Percy and Lia living as a married couple with all propriety.

It would pay to be away before the Harrowbys woke and came calling, but he could not, of course, take such a step without warning His Grace. With that in mind, he went in at the main door of the house and asked the night porter to have his father woken.

"His Grace is in the library, my lord," said the porter, "and has asked that you come to him as soon as you arrive."

His Grace was one or more jumps ahead of Percy, as usual. Percy presented himself, as commanded.

The duke did not bother with greetings. "I take it the Harrowbys are safely at home."

"Yes, sir. Eventually. We managed to prevent them from speaking to anyone else before they left the ball."

"'We' being your friends Redepenning and Alston."

"Also Barrington and Worthington, sir. And we called in Lady Sutton and later Sir Henry Redepenning as reinforcements."

From the pursed lips and the steepled forefingers tapping said lips, the duke was not as relaxed as he would like to appear. "A lot of people to keep a secret, but Grace Sutton and Henry Redepenning are not blabbermouths. Can you rely on your friends?"

"I can, Your Grace." Percy was certain of that.

"From what Enid said, the Harrowbys were drunk and loquacious. I take it they continued to leak hints at an ancient scandal?"

"More than hints, Your Grace," Percy acknowledged. Lest the duke mistake where he stood on the matter, he added, "A scandal which reflects poorly on Lady Harrowby, but not on Aurelia."

The duke shrugged. "Not even on Lady Harrowby, or not as much as you might think. A very young woman betrayed by a practiced rake. The blame lies with the man who got her with child, surely? Some would say that Lord Harrowby is the only one who comes out of the matter with honor."

Percy disagreed. "Some might. Except their quarrel tonight made it clear he was paid to marry his betrothed when he would have withdrawn. And he has held his so-called honorable actions over his wife ever since. And that he and his wife have made Lia pay for their actions all her life. There is no honor in that. Did you know, sir?"

"That Lady Harrowby and the Duke of Haverford had an affair after she was betrothed to Lord Harrowby and before the wedding? That, after Haverford and the lady were caught together in a very compromising position, Haverford bribed Harrowby to marry her, probably to stop her family's wailing, since Haverford doesn't have a conscience or a sense of responsibility? That Aurelia was very probably the consequence of that affair? Yes, I have known that all along, Thornstead. Like you, I do not hold Aurelia to account for such ancient history. And one cannot deny that her blood lines are fit to mix with ours. For all the man is a monster, the Haverford bloodline is one of the oldest in England."

The duke grimaced. "I was not aware until I came to Byrnewick that Lady Harrowby hates her daughter and her husband, and that Lord Harrowby resents them both. I was not surprised, however. They are not likeable people. But I have friends who assured me that the girl had been raised by her governess as a gentlewoman, and was well liked by those who knew her. My personal impression confirmed that estimation."

Percy managed to stay calm as he said, "You did not think it important to tell me, Your Grace?"

The smile the duke directed at Percy was rueful. "I am sorry to destroy my reputation for omniscience, Thornstead, but I did not foresee this direct attempt to sabotage Lady Aurelia's future, even at the cost of damage to their own. It was ancient history, I thought, and did not need to dredged up again."

Percy let his father's unlikely admission of mortal failings pass. "Sir, my present concern is to protect my betrothed, and to that end, I wish to elope. Tonight, for preference, so Harrowby does not have time to take her from this house."

Those expressive eyebrows shot up, accompanied by the subtle twitch of the lips that told a careful observer that the duke was amused. "You were coming to ask my permission for this elopement?" he asked, his voice so carefully controlled that only one who knew him well would see the subtle signs of laughter underneath.

Percy's temper, still none too steady, flared. "To inform you, sir, as a courtesy. Because I will be leaving you to manage the Harrowbys."

"Very proper, Thornstead," said the duke, his voice shaking slightly. "It may be the first time in history that a young man has informed his guardian of his intention to abduct the lady who is in that guardian's care. But I appreciate the—ah—courtesy."

"It is your privilege to mock, sir," Percy told his tormenter, his voice rigidly polite. "In all things but this, I am your obedient son."

"I think you must be my obedient son in this, also, Thornstead." He put up a hand when Percy was about to make a hasty answer. "Step down, my son. I agree with your reasoning, but I believe we might manage a hasty marriage without an uncomfortable journey and the stigma of an elopement. Have a seat, and I shall explain what I have in mind."

LIA SPENT THE night fretting. What would her parents do? Could the duke stop them? Would he even want to do so? Mama, and

Father too, had hinted at an old scandal.

She knew her mother had been with child when married, for the day of Lia's birth was less than seven months later. She was not at all certain about how a baby came to be planted in its mother, but she knew it was planted by its father, and took around nine months to grow.

Servants' gossip and her own observations gave her those facts. Shearing babies followed the celebration of the end of shearing by around nine months, whether the parents were married at shearing time, in the months after it, or not at all.

She had never suspected, until last night, that Father was not her planter, as it were. Would that change the duke's mind? Would it change Percy's?

She would not, could not, return to her parents'—no, the Harrowbys—untender care. What would she do if the duke refused to allow her to stay, if Percy no longer wanted to marry her? She could not imagine that the Harrowbys would pursue her if she ran away, but where would she go? And how could she afford to get there?

She lay in her bed staring upward, then got up and walked the floor, then lay some more, coming up with ever wilder ideas about how she might support herself. She would make a terrible seamstress. She could play the pianoforte, but was that something people would pay for, and how could she find such people?

She knew how to keep house, but she also knew she was far too young to find work as a housekeeper, and house maids were paid a pittance and subjected to what Pansy called "annoyances" from male guests and even the gentlemen of the household.

Pansy said a maid could supplement her wages by submitting to such annoyances and pretending to enjoy them. Kisses and more, Pansy said. Aurelia enjoyed kissing Percy, but could not imagine kissing anyone else.

Which meant that she could not be a mistress. She had heard the rumors about Percy's mistress, who had opened a hat shop, one Lia had bought hats from. Some said that Mrs. Maxwell was a different woman entirely, who just happened to look like Percy's Mrs. Mabberley. Either way, all agreed that Mrs. Mabberley had been given her quittance and no longer worked as a mistress.

It must be just a coincidence that Mrs. Maxwell looked rather like Lia, all but for the milliner's dark brown eyes. Percy had not chosen Lia and had no idea what she looked like. If Lia was indeed an imitation of his mistress, however fortuitous the resemblance, might she be able to use that now?

If Lia had to be a mistress, she would rather be Percy's than anyone else's. She imagined a scenario in which she asked Mrs. Maxwell about what it was like to be Percy's mistress, but she could not see how such a discussion would end in anything but embarrassment, even if Mrs. Maxwell was, in fact, Mrs. Mabberley.

In any case, the gossipmongers agreed that Percy had made it clear he would not keep a mistress and a wife, so that would not answer. For if the Duke of Dellborough dismissed Lia, she was certain he would find Percy another lady to take her place.

Lia nearly asked her maid for suggestions when she arrived to dress Lia for the day, but in the end, she decided that talking would just lead to crying, and her eyes were already red and swollen.

Catching her mood, Pansy was subdued, and said little. She did not ask what had upset her mistress but just offered to fetch some cucumber from the kitchen to soothe Lia's eyes before she went down to breakfast.

"I will take a tray in my room," Lia decided.

With a pitying look, Pansy replied, "His Grace has said he wishes to see you at breakfast, my lady."

*He is going to throw me out. Or at least return me to my father.*

She refused to succumb to another bout of tears, swallowing hard several times and blinking rapidly. At the very least, she would go bravely to her fate.

"Then pin up my hair, Pansy, and I shall go down."

In a rose-colored round gown, simple in cut if in richer materials than she'd worn at Byrnewick, she went downstairs, covering her reluctance with brisk steps.

In the breakfast room, the duke and Percy waited for her. One worry was removed directly. Percy stood up at her entrance and strode across the room to enfold her hands in his. "My love. How are you this morning? Did you manage to sleep?"

She shook her head, unable to speak for a moment as she once again fought back unwanted tears.

"You are not to worry, Aurelia. All shall be well," said the duke. "Come and sit down, my dear, and Thornstead and I shall tell you what we have in mind."

"Allow me to fetch your breakfast," Percy said, then, to the footmen who stood ready to serve, "Thank you. We shall call if we need anything."

"Just toast and a cup of tea, please," Aurelia said. She would not be able to choke anything down until she knew what the two men had planned, but tea would be welcome.

The bread must have been toasted within the past few minutes, for it was hot, crisp, and lightly browned. Percy also brought her a pat of butter, a small dish of fruit preserve, a dish of cut fruit, a personal pot of tea, and a jug of cream.

Once he was seated again behind a heaping plate that included several different types of meat, fruit, and bread, the duke said, "Thornstead believes, and I agree, that bringing the date of the wedding forward will be the best way to manage this situation with your parents. Are you willing to have your betrothal acknowledged today to Society's busybodies, and your wedding within the next two weeks?"

Lia put down her knife. Could a heart race with joy and sink with dread both at the same time? Apparently so. "I am willing, Your Grace." Eager was a better word. Still, she had to be honest. If she began to hope and it was all torn away from her, she feared she would be broken beyond all repair.

"But Your Grace, I fear you are not in possession of all the facts. I am not certain, but if I understood what Lord Harrowby and Mama said last night, I am not Lord Harrowby's daughter. I am a walking scandal, or will be if anyone finds out. If my mother and fa—Lord Harrowby, that is—if they speak like that before others."

The duke nodded and smiled. "Well done, Aurelia. It is always for the best to speak unpleasant news bluntly, rather than wait for it to be discovered. People always find out what you want to hide at the worst possibly moment. Far better to be in control of the rumors!"

"His Grace already knew, my lady," Percy told her. "He doesn't mind, and neither do I. You have been acknowledged by Lord Harrowby, so if he makes a fuss at this point, it will rebound to his discredit, and your mother can only be hurt by any scandal. Besides, by the time there can be much talk, you will be a married woman and a Versey. Wife, furthermore, to His Grace's heir. The gossip shall not affect you."

"Much," His Grace cautioned. "The gossip shall not affect you much. People may stare and talk behind your back, but none shall cut Lady Thornstead. Provided you and Thornstead live with propriety, it will all blow over by next Season."

Aurelia felt the tension seep away. "How soon may we be married?" she asked.

"It would be as well," the duke told her, "to have a few days between news of the betrothal and the actual wedding. People will understand why it is being done in haste, but too much haste will make us look guilty, and those with a taste for such things will invent a reason for our supposed guilt."

Lia would not feel secure until she was actually married. She thought her shudder was an emotional thing rather than physical, but perhaps she was wrong, for Percy said, "His Grace will speak to Lord and Lady Harrowby. If he believes there is likely to be danger from either one of them, we can marry immediately."

"But how can we wed so quickly? The banns...?" Did they not have to have the banns read? In their respective parish churches for at least three Sundays?

"His Grace has a common license for us, my love," Percy explained. "If our wedding is here in Town, you and I have already met the requirement to live here for four weeks, and I am a parishioner at the church near Versey Abbey, so we can wed there, instead. We don't have to have the banns read."

*Thank goodness.* Even so, Aurelia's soaring elation had an underpinning of dread. Could Lord Harrowby stop the wedding? Would he want to?

✦

# Chapter Fourteen



*Six days later, Versey Abbey*

LIA WAS DRESSING for her wedding in the guest bedchamber at Versey Abbey where she had spent the previous night. Or, to be more accurate, she was being dressed, for she had so many helpers there was hardly room for them all, though the bedchamber was enormous.

All of Percy's sisters, for a start. Gwen, Isolde, Nineve, a precocious eleven, and sweet little Elaine, just turned six and full of opinions.

Gwen was going to be one of Lia's attendants, of course, together with Evelyn and Claire, who were also present to help dress the bride. Aunt Enid, too.

Lia was currently wearing all her undergarments and had a large pinafore over them to protect them while her hair was being dressed. The serving women would then carefully finish dressing her. What would Percy think of her gown?

Lia's own maid Pansy was being assisted by—or was assisting—Aunt Enid's dresser. At the moment, the two of them were in earnest discussion by the bed.

Seven people, all focused on turning Lia into a beautiful bride.

Mama's arrival chilled the atmosphere. "Your Mama looks as if she has swallowed something very sour," whispered Claire. Mama was almost bursting with the unkind remarks she did not dare say.

"Shush," Evelyn murmured.

Lia told them both, "As long as she does not cause trouble today, she may think anything she likes."

"Shush," said Evelyn again, and just in time, for Aunt Enid's dresser emerged from the group by the bed to say, "If it pleases you, Lady Aurelia, I shall do your hair."

"Thank you," Lia replied. "Please go ahead."

How the duke had done it, Aurelia did not know, but Mama and Lord Harrowby had given her up to the Dellboroughs without a murmur or a complaint. And without berating Lia in front of other people after the terrible scene at the Sutton ball. Lia was very careful not to be caught in private with Mama.

She had failed on one occasion. She was in Dellborough House, so felt safe. She was on her way to the library when Mama had darted out of one of the parlors, grabbed her wrist, and dragged her inside, shutting the door to prevent her from leaving.

"Now, you listen to me, my girl," Mama had said. "You think I have been hard on you, and you are right. I look at you and I see me, as I was. I did not want you to have the life I had, so I did my level best to make you perfect. You hate me for the beatings and the scoldings. I know that. But if it's true that you've behaved yourself here in London, it will have been worth it. They say that the letters I got were lies, and perhaps it is true. But you are not out of the woods yet, Aurelia. Even with his ring on your finger, you cannot afford to stray. He has the power to shut you up in the country, or even in an asylum."

"I don't want to stray, Mama," Lia pointed out.

Mama's look was of resigned contempt. "Do you suppose I wanted to be seduced by the Duke of Haverford? Our wants are seldom of any importance, you young fool."

Lia had never thought she might feel sorry for Mama and angry with her both at the same time. "I shall not go apart into the garden with a known rake," she assured her mother. Mama looked as if she was about to slap Aurelia when Aunt Enid opened the door and told Lia to go on her way.

What Aunt Enid had said to Mama, Lia never heard, but the pair of them had been at daggers drawn ever since. After that, the duke had instructed everyone, but especially Mama, Lord Harrowby, and Aunt Enid, that no arguments, insults, or even cutting remarks would be tolerated on Percy and Lia's wedding day. Any and all perpetrators of discord would be ejected from the wedding.

"Are you going to wear the crown?" Elaine asked, pointing to the tiara on the dressing table.

"She is," Gwen answered for her. "But not until her hair is nearly done. Come and sit with me, sweetheart, and we shall count the hairpins as they go into her hair."

The ruse kept Elaine amused for a while, and then Nineve took the child to read her a story. They stopped after three stories to watch the dresser lower the tiara into place and pin it securely, then shift a couple of curls to hide the fastenings.

"There," the dresser said.

"Lovely," Aunt Enid proclaimed, and Lia's friends also chorused their approval.

"Now, the gown," Mama ordered.

"We have an hour," Aunt Enid pointed out. "I suggest refreshments, and a visit to the water closet before Lia puts on the gown. Ah! And here is the tea."

Lia's maid led in a procession of parlor maids carrying trays. Aunt Enid must have sent her for the tea as soon as the dresser began fiddling with the tiara.

For once, Lia agreed with her mother. She could hardly wait to see herself in the wedding gown. But Aunt Enid was right. She did not want to risk spilling anything on it.

Soon. Very soon. In an hour, she would begin her walk down

the stairs and through the house to the Versey Abbey chapel, where Percy would be waiting for her.

What would he think of her gown?

⇒⟫⟫⟩⟨⟪⟪⟸

PERCY PACED THE little parlor that was next to the chapel. "Surely it must be eleven by now," he said, for perhaps the fifth time.

"Perhaps another minute," Lance told him, after he had peered out of the window to check the clock in the tower over the stable block.

"She might be late," Rick offered. "Brides often are, I'm told."

"I did not think you knew any of the marrying kind of girl," Alston teased. Alston certainly knew very few of the marrying kind of girl, and expressed himself astounded that Percy was looking forward to his wedding. Though one or two remarks he had made hinted he was reconsidering his position. Because of the time he had spent with Lia? Percy tucked the small suspicion away. He was the one marrying Lia, not Alston. If it had been a contest, Percy had won.

Worth popped his head around the door to the hall then sidled into the room. "She is coming," he reported. "Lady Kirkland and Lady Harrowby have just taken their seats, and so have your younger sisters. Better get in there."

Lance opened the other door, the one to the chapel, and Percy stepped through, followed by his friends and his younger brother.

The chapel was full, mostly with Dellborough relatives and Percy's friends. The Harrowbys were represented by Lia's mother and her two brothers, taking leave from Eton to attend the wedding. Percy had met the two boys yesterday, and they had impressed him as much as their parents, which was to say not at all. They were self-absorbed bullies, and not terribly bright, either, for they had had the nerve to kick Tris's feet out from under him and to push the youngest Versey, little Artie. They did it where Lance and Percy could see, and then went on to pull Nineve's plaits before Lance could intervene.

Lance was the same age as the older of the two brothers, and while Lance was teaching young Hadrian better manners, Nineve punched Justinian's nose. At twelve to Justinian's eleven, and having four brothers, she was more than capable of holding her own against a single foe, especially one who collapsed into tears when his nose began to spout blood.

Percy then had a severe word with the pair about bullying a girl and a pair of much younger boys—Tris was nine and Artie was only eight. Not that either one was impressed. Percy could understand their nonchalance when his future mother-in-law came breathing fire over *his* bullying of *her* precious sons.

He didn't want to think about that now. He had dealt with it at the time, and this day was for him and Lia.

Even as he thought of her, she was there, coming down the aisle towards him on her father's arm. He forgot to breathe at the sight of her. Her dark brown hair was dressed high on her head and ringed with a crown of pearls set in gold filigree work.

High, that is, except for several curls trailing down her long neck to lovingly kiss her decolletage. He could barely tear his eyes from the expanse of fair skin, lower than any gown he had ever seen her in, though still modest. The pearl set he had given her hung from her neck, the locket just dipping into the top of the crease that showed above her gown and hinted at her breasts.

And what a gown. The robe was layers of gold net trimmed in lace and embroidered with gold and silver thread, and more pearls. The bodice was a fabric in a darker gold, also heavily embroidered. Perhaps the petticoat that showed between the sides of the robe was of the same fabric, for something prevented him from seeing straight through the net, which was just as well considering they had an audience. Nonetheless, the shifting layers gave the impression that she was clothed in nothing but clouds.

"Your jaw is dropping," Rick whispered. Percy snapped it

shut. She came up beside him, still on her father's arm, and the Bishop of Gloucester, who was officiating, began the words of the service.

Though no one would face his father's wrath by daring to stop the service, still Percy felt a thrill of alarm at the challenge to the congregation to speak of any impediment to the marriage. Not that there was one, but he felt on the verge of wonder and had an irrational fear of losing Lia at this last minute.

"Who giveth this woman to be married to this man?" the bishop demanded.

Lord Harrowby spoke up. "I do," and he passed Lia's hand into that of the bishop, who offered it to Percy.

Percy stepped forward as if in a dream to take Lia's hand in his. His golden girl, dressed all in gold. And after a few vows that they would make in just a moment, his to have and to hold. He heard himself speak those vows. This time, the thrill of awe was tinged with triumph, which grew as she made her own vows to him.

Rick handed him the ring he had chosen from the Dellborough jewels—gold, with diamonds and a pale sapphire almost the color of her eyes, in the shape of the heart that was now hers forever.

It slipped easily on to her finger.

He lost himself in her eyes, and had to be recalled to himself by the bishop, who indicated that he should drop the bride's hand. Just for a moment, he remembered from the rehearsal. He did so, warmed by the way her fingers clung to his before she, too, remembered herself.

Two more prayers and their hands found one another's again as the bishop proclaimed the words, "Those whom God hath joined together, let no man put asunder."

He pronounced them man and wife, gave the final blessing, and it was done. Lia and Percy were man and wife, marquess and marchioness, lovers sanctioned by the church. She was safe from the Harrowbys, and she was his. If only he could carry her away this minute, but the wedding breakfast awaited, and their family and friends.

Wishing them to Jericho, Percy strolled back down the aisle of the church with Lia on his arm, smiling as if he was delighted to see those who thronged behind him to follow him to the grand dining room, where the wedding breakfast was set out.

# Chapter Fifteen

WHEN THEY STOPPED for the night at an inn halfway to Thornstead Hall, Percy suggested they wait to consummate their marriage until they arrived at their own home. "I should not take you for the first time in an inn, Lia," he had protested. "In a bed that I know-not-how-many people have slept in and with a long day's travel tomorrow."

"Should not" was not the same as "shall not." Lia thought that Percy's protests were half-hearted at best.

She gave her own opinion on the matter. "We are sleeping on our own sheets. After what Mama has told me about what will happen, I will only get more nervous if we delay. Miss Walton has often said I should discount anything Mama said, and Aunt Enid only said I should ask you to show me what to do. Please show me."

And so he did, and it was wonderful.

The following day, she found the carriage ride a little uncomfortable. The part of her that took her weight when she sat was not painful, exactly, but aching a little. Well-used, she supposed, was the appropriate term. The thought made her smirk, and when Percy asked why she was smiling, she told him.

He groaned. "You are a wicked minx, Aurelia Versey, and you have had your revenge. I ache, too, now." He took her hand

and showed her where.

One of the mysteries disclosed the night before was that Percy's desire for Lia gave her power over him, and she gloried in that now, pressing and gripping until he kissed her fiercely and told her she must stop.

"I will not take you in a carriage, my golden girl. You are already sore."

She kissed him back, all the while unbuttoning his falls. "Achy, not sore. And I can sit on a cushion, or your lap. Can we really do it in a carriage?"

He groaned again and capitulated. "Come and sit on my lap and I shall show you."

It was certainly a new and delightful way to while away the hours of travel.

In the late afternoon, the carriage pulled up at a lookout point where Lia could take her first look at her new country home. "It is magnificent, Percy. I had no idea it would be so large!"

Percy shrugged. Lia supposed that Thornstead Hall seemed modest to him, which it was if compared to Versey Abbey. But Thornstead Hall was at least as big as Byrnewick.

It was built of brick, with window surrounds of a contrasting light-gray stone and the same stone used for corners and the gable above the central third of the front facade. She estimated the front facade at seventy or more feet across, and the side of the building she could see was a similar size.

The two principal floors were topped by a steeply sloping roof well provided with attic windows, and the whole building rose above a basement level that must contain the kitchen and other household necessities. From this vantage, she could see people, made miniature by distance, hurrying down from the main doors and up from the basement level. They were forming into lines. "They must have been keeping watch," Percy said. "They are waiting to meet you, my love."

"Percy! I must look dreadful. My clothes are all in disarray, and my hair! What will they think?"

"They will think the young marquess cannot keep his hands off his wife," Percy suggested, but he helped her straighten her clothing and repin her hair in some semblance of order. "The hat will cover the worst of it," he assured her as he made repairs to his own appearance.

She was certain her color was high and her clothing rumpled, but she was an expert at hiding her feelings. Perhaps every servant gathered to greet her would guess exactly what she and Percy had been doing in the carriage, but they would not see anything in her demeanor to confirm their suppositions.

Percy introduced her to the housekeeper and the butler, who then took her down the line of servants, the housekeeper introducing the women and the butler the men. She smiled and inclined her head, accepted good wishes for her happy marriage, and said a few words to each person, trying to keep the names straight in her head.

Everyone appeared delighted to meet her, and the butler gave a short speech, in which he said he knew he spoke for them all when he said how delighted he was to have Lord and Lady Thornstead in residence. "I know, my lord and my lady, that this is your honey time. You can depend upon your servants to respect your privacy during your two-week stay with us. However, I hope I do not speak out of turn when I say that I hope—that all your servants and tenants hope—you will be returning to us after the London Season. In the meantime, my lord, we all offer you the heartiest of congratulations, and to you, my lady, we express our very best wishes for your continued happiness."

He bowed, and the servants all clapped. Some of the footmen cheered, but hushed when the butler frowned.

"My wife and I thank you for your good wishes, Merrivale," Percy said. "In reference to your hope, you may tell those who are not here today that Lady Thornstead and I mean to make Thornstead Hall our principal place of residence. We hope that the day we must take up residence in Versey Abbey is many,

many years in the future. Perhaps, by that day, our son will have a wife of his own, to be chatelaine in this fine manor." He winked. "I can promise you we shall do our best to produce a son as soon as possible."

Aurelia gasped. "Percy!" The servants would be shocked!

The servants, though, were less prim than Aurelia had been raised to be. They were chuckling at her husband's innuendo.

"I have embarrassed my darling wife," Percy acknowledged, "which was ill done of me. Rest assured, in short, that we will spend much of our time here, though His Grace my father will expect me to visit his other estates from time to time, and we will attend at least some of the London Season. I am glad you plan to hold my wife and myself excused from our duties in the next two weeks. It will be a privilege to take them up in a couple of months, and in the meanwhile, I know I can depend on our senior servants to see that all is done efficiently, well, and with kindness."

That speech, too, earned enthusiastic applause. Then, at last, the formal welcome was over, the servants were dismissed, and Percy was able to carry Lia over their own threshold.

※

HOW NICE LIFE would be if one could be on holiday in the country the whole time. When Percy expressed this thought, Lia suggested he would become bored, but Percy did not think he would ever tire of the life they led for those two weeks after their wedding. Each day, they woke not long after first light, came together in love, washed, and broke their fast.

After that, the program varied according to the weather. It had been a wet year, and May was no exception, with the weather keeping them inside more than half the time. They explored the house, played chess, and took full advantage of the library, which was well provided with books from which they could read out loud and with nooks and comfortable seats in which Percy could indulge his craving for his wife and hers for him.

The house had a billiards room, installed by the current duke when he was Marquess of Thornstead. Percy taught the game to Lia, although his tutoring often turned into a different kind of game altogether, so that the baize surface of the table frequently required ironing. A fortnight was not long enough for her to learn more than the basics, but he promised to play her again when they returned to Thornstead Hall from London.

"How I wish we did not have to go," Lia mourned, and Percy could not agree more. But the duke had decreed that they should see out the Season to kill any lingering gossip, and Aunt Enid had agreed it was necessary.

Percy did not want people speaking ill of Lia, so back to London they would go. While they were here, though, they enjoyed Thornstead Hall and their freedom to the full.

If it was fine, they took horses out to explore the estate and the surrounding countryside. Percy, who had visited here during his childhood, was delighted to show her his favorite places, and discovered uses of the estates various follies he could not have imagined nor understood when he was only seven years old.

In the evenings, she played to him on the pianoforte he had had tuned in preparation for this very joy. Then bed, together. Intimacy with his wife, Percy found, was very different to his previous experiences. Her untutored but enthusiastic responses excited him way beyond the most skilled caresses of the professionals who had given him his first lessons in the pleasures of the bed.

Perhaps, he thought at first, his perceptions were skewed by his extended period of celibacy. Three and a half months was by far the longest he had been without a lover since he was introduced to carnal pleasures at the age of sixteen. But his celibacy was well and truly over. Since they had arrived at Thornstead Hall, he and Lia had exercised their marital privileges several times a day and at least twice more each night, and every time was more wonderful than the last.

He had never been married before, and had never been in love. That must be the missing ingredient in previous relationships. Lia loved him, too, and that was a greater aphrodisiac than all the rest.

# Chapter Sixteen

THEY RETURNED RELUCTANTLY to London, to the neglected relatives' wing of Dellborough House. The trip from Thornstead Hall was only four hours, and they arrived shortly after noon. While they had been away, their new London home had been dusted, scrubbed, and polished to within an inch of its life. A team of servants from the main house had descended on it, said Percy's valet. "My lady shall find everything clean, at least," he said, doubtfully.

Lia agreed with his unexpressed opinion. It was shabby and old-fashioned. "Do you think we might redecorate?" she asked, when Percy showed her around.

"I think we must," Percy declared. "We'll need to hire more servants, too. Except for my valet and your maid, all the servants are borrowed from His Grace."

Panic was definitely a temptation. *There is so much to be done, and I don't know how to do any of it. Not here in Town.* Lia did her best to stay calm. Except when her mother was in residence, she had been in charge of Byrnewick. Surely, here in London, the same principles applied?

At Byrnewick, if they needed furniture or curtains or wallpaper, they would make a list and send it to merchants who sold what they wanted. If the house needed another servant, she would mention it to the housekeeper. Or the butler, if a man was required. Or the steward, for outdoor servants, though that would not apply here.

"We should find a butler and a housekeeper first," she told Percy. "Then they can interview and hire the lesser servants. Let me fetch paper and we shall make a list of what needs to be done in each room." She always felt more in control if she had a list.

He raised his eyebrows in admiration. "I am glad you know what to do, my golden girl."

"Not really," she admitted. "I only know how I would have done things in my parents' home."

"Which is more than I know," he insisted. "How do we find a butler and a housekeeper? Do you think His Grace's people might know of someone reliable?"

An excellent idea. The duke's excellent housekeeper and admirable butler would only recommend people they trusted to their master's heir. "I think we should ask," she said. She hesitated for a moment.

Percy knew her well enough by now to see she had more to say. "Come on, Lia. Tell me what you are thinking."

"It is about your aunt," Lia warned him.

"I would rather not involve her if we can avoid it," Percy confided. "She would love to help, but you know what she is like. She would take over. I want this to be our place. We can do it ourselves, can we not?"

Lia was amazed that he felt exactly as she did. "That is precisely what I was thinking!" She hugged him, and one thing led to another, and they left the list making until later.

By dinner time, they had a new butler and a new housekeeper, both of whom would start tomorrow. The butler was the nephew of the butler in the main house, and had been the duke's head footman. "He is ready for the responsibility, my lord," the butler had assured Percy. "If His Grace has no objection, I am sure my nephew would be ready to start immediately. The thing is, he is married, my lord. To the assistant housekeeper. If you and my lady would accept a married couple as butler and housekeeper, it would be a perfect situation for them."

The duke's housekeeper agreed. The assistant housekeeper, who was a relative of hers, had almost lost her position when she and the head footman were found in bed together. When they disclosed they were married, it did not improve matters, for they had taken the step in secret and without permission

Their family connections would not have saved Mr. and Mrs. Marsh, but apparently Percy had heard of their plight and had intervened on their behalf, which had led to grumbling of favoritism by the other servants.

The duke's senior servants were pleased to have such an amicable resolution to the problem.

"Most households are not willing to hire a married couple except as butler and housekeeper, and the Marshes do not have experience in those positions," the housekeeper explained to Lia. "Della is not ready for a ducal household, Lady Thornstead, but she can easily manage a household of the size you will have here in Town."

Both candidates were delighted at the opportunity, and both assured their new employers that their positions in His Grace's household would soon be filled, with their own understudies moving up a step in the household hierarchy, and a new place made at the bottom of the pecking order.

They were also very grateful to Percy for intervening on his behalf, and assured Lia not once but half a dozen times that they would demonstrate their gratitude in their service.

It showed immediately. As soon as Lia took her new housekeeper next door, and began to talk about the planned renovations, Mrs. Marsh explained that she, her husband, and her aunt had lists of craftsmen who could repair, paint, and paper for them, and of merchants who sold carpets, curtains, wall paper, furniture, and ornaments.

Lia could barely wait.

SHOPPING FOR FURNITURE proved to be fun. Draperies and paint colors, Percy was happy to leave to Lia. After three days, Percy began begging off and spending his time at his club while Lia was negotiating with merchants and tradesmen, and that became the pattern of their mornings. They greeted each day with love making, then rose to be washed and dressed, and broke their fast together. Lia would tell Percy about whatever room she was decorating and consult with him on the decisions that needed to be made, and then they went their separate ways.

Percy visited Emily twice, but she had had no further difficulties with would be lovers, and her *ton* customers must have decided her hats were worth a rumor or two, for they continued to throng the shop.

Percy was always home by two in the afternoon, which was the hour they had decided to be available to visitors on Tuesdays, Thursdays, and Saturdays, and to return calls to others on the other days. After visiting hours, they would go up to the guest bedchamber they were using while the painters and carpenters stripped their rooms and refurbished them.

His desire for her had not abated, nor hers for him. Their late afternoon interlude, followed by a brief nap, set them up for the evening, which was increasingly spent apart. If Lia was going to a ball, Percy would escort her there and dance with her once. He would have stayed and commandeered her every dance, but convention frowned on a man dancing with his own wife.

Rather than stand on the sidelines and watch other men enjoying that privilege, Percy would check that one of his friends or his family were present to help if Lia needed it. Whatever His Grace had said to the Harrowbys to persuade them to agree to the change of timetable for the marriage, it was still functioning. They were distant but polite should they chance to meet either of the newlyweds, and Lia and Percy were polite in their turn.

Percy was waiting for one or both of them to start drinking again. Meanwhile, there were others who would make mischief if they could. Once he'd checked that Lia had an ally standing by to come to the rescue, Percy would retire to the card room, or go to his club where he would meet up with one or more of his friends for a game of billiards and a drink.

When Lia realized how much Percy despised musicales and routs, she insisted that he did not need to come with her, while he argued that he did not want her to be stuck at such an event without support while the Harrowbys were still in London.

The compromise they agreed to was that either Percy or one of his friends would escort her. Slowly, that came to be their accepted practice for the theatre, too, and for dinners to which Lia was invited. Of course, if the invitation was for Percy or for them both, Percy had to go, but somehow, over the weeks, they were spending most of the day and evening apart. Until they met again in bed, for they had resolved they would share a bedchamber and a bed. Percy found solace in going to sleep with her in his arms, and waking up with her sleeping peacefully, curled up against him.

Slowly, over a matter of weeks, it dawned on Percy that he was only truly happy when he was with Lia. The rest of his activities—which had made up his whole life before his golden girl—appeared trivial and boring by contrast.

"I am looking forward to returning to Thornstead Hall," he said to Lia one day. "Not for a holiday, this time, but to live. I have been reading about agriculture, and studying our steward's reports. I'd like to adopt a couple of the innovations he has suggested. And when we were there, you talked about a school for the tenants' children. We could make a start on that."

"I'm looking forward to it, too," Lia agreed. "I am certain I can finish the redecorations by the middle of July. That's when the contracts for the temporary servants run out, and we will leave Marsh and Mrs. Marsh here to care for the house, of course."

The middle of July! That was still four weeks away! How could he bear to share his wife with the whole of London for that long?

⇶⇷

LIA LOVED ALMOST everything about being married. Her list of benefits was not committed to paper, like her lists of paint colors, window dressings, rugs, occasional furniture, and other details, all sorted by room.

It was very real, though. If she had written it down, the page would be most unbalanced, with benefits close written all down one side and the other side almost blank.

Living without constant criticism. That would be a huge one. Living with Percy was part of that, for his compliments, his courtesies, his thanks for even the smallest of services had become nearly as dear to her as he was himself. Percy was a dear person, and her friend, as well as her husband.

Husbands really were the most marvelous people to live with for all sorts of reasons, mostly to do with intimacy. Not just that ultimate form of intimacy to which Percy had introduced her, but touching!

Lia had seldom been touched. Not deliberately, and not with affection. Percy held her hand for no reason at all, set it on his arm when they walked, patted it when it lay on the arm of her chair within his reach. He put a hand in the center of her back when they were queued for a reception line or the theatre.

When they were alone, he hugged her for no reason except an excess of affection, and dropped chaste kisses on her cheek. He invited her to sit on his lap and put his arms around her. After they had taken their pleasure of one another, he held her—often until she fell asleep.

He was not the only one, either! Her new friends also liked touching. She had become accustomed to walking arm in arm or hand in hand, and to be greeted and farewelled with a hug and a peck on the hand or the cheek.

Her friends were also on her list of benefits of marriage, for she would not have been allowed friends had she remained under the Harrowbys' roof, and she would never have met Gwen at all.

Her household servants were on the list. Marsh and Mrs. Marsh had not known her since she was in clouts. They were not thirty years or more older and more experienced than she was. At Byrnewick, she always had the sense that the servants were humoring the child she had been until recently. Here, she was the mistress, and all her servants except the driver for her personal carriage were in their twenties or younger.

The list went on and on. Her house, decorated and furnished to her and Percy's tastes. Her tastes, mostly. Percy had enjoyed choosing furniture for their bedchamber, his study, and the billiard room, but he had mostly left the rest of the house to her.

Every few days, he came home with something he had noticed and decided to buy. None of the items fitted her plans and every item, she found a place for. The large copper urn was in the entrance hall, ready to receive wet umbrellas. The delicately woven oriental rug was hanging on the wall in the small parlor, adding a splash of color and pattern to a room that was otherwise fairly austere.

A fantastically carved bookshelf was relegated to Percy's study to join the desk he had also purchased. Lia blushed every time she looked at the desk, for she could not see it without remembering the use to which they put it on the day it was delivered.

One item that she received with joy, even though she had not chosen it herself, was a beautiful piano. "I ordered it as a wedding present," Percy confided, "but then we married earlier than initially planned. Do you like it? Will you play it for me?"

It was a visiting day, but Lia forgot all about going out as she played for an enthusiastic audience of one on the prettiest pianos she had ever seen, and then furthered the celebration of its arrival once on the piano stool and second time upstairs in their bed.

She also enjoyed having a wider circle of friends—not just her sister-in-law Gwen and Evelyn and Claire, but also Percy's closest friends, who treated her like a favorite sister. Was that a benefit of marriage? She couldn't imagine she would have even met her new friends if she were not betrothed to and then married to Percy.

Matthew Barrington and Harold Worthington were faithful escorts on her shopping expeditions. Barrington disclosed a talent for decorating and furnishing houses, and Worth was courting Evelyn, who was usually found with her, Gwen, and Claire.

Rick, who was still in London waiting to be assigned to a ship, and the Earl of Alston volunteered themselves to escort her to any social engagements where an escort would be useful.

Life was fuller and pleasanter than she could ever have imagined. Still, she wished Percy spent more time with her and less at his club or out with his friends. Recently, he had even began leaving her to receive guests alone, though he still arrived home in time to join her in bed in the late afternoon, which relieved her unreasonable suspicion that he had taken up with a mistress again, either Emily Mabberley or someone new.

She shook off her momentary melancholy. Percy had promised to be faithful. Men and women lived separate lives—it was the way of their world, at least in London. As soon as the redecoration was far enough along that she could leave the workmen under the supervision of her butler and housekeeper, she could go home to Thornstead Hall with Percy.

# Chapter Seventeen

"DEAL ME OUT," said Percy, as Viscount Longford finished shuffling the cards and began dealing. He turned away the offer of cards and waved vaguely in the direction of the clock. "I have an engagement." One he had missed several times in the past couple of weeks, leaving Aurelia alone to welcome visitors or to go visiting.

"A wife, you mean," said Alston, grinning. "Say hello for me to the lovely Lady Thornstead."

"Tell her yourself," Percy retorted. "You are escorting her to the Haverford charity ball, I believe." He might look in himself. He didn't know whether Lia knew that the Duke of Haverford had sired her, but the more he thought about her being anywhere near the man, the less he liked it.

"She must be quite an item, your wife," Longford mused. "She has Barrington and Worth dancing to her tune in the mornings, Alston and our brave sailor at night, and she doesn't even need to jerk your leash, Thornstead, and you're running home to be her afternoon man."

At the libelous insinuation, Percy was briefly overcome by a surge of rage, and it was through a red haze that he heard one of the others at the table tell the viscount to stubble it, and Rick Redepenning say, in the lazy drawl he used at his most dangerous, "Drunk already, Cousin George?"

"Hey," Longford complained. "My drink!"

Percy was busy forcing his rage back far enough to get his mind to work, and while he remained silent, Alston had shoved the table in his haste to get to his feet. That caused Longford's brandy to slop over the side and onto his cards. "You will meet me for that remark," Alston said.

Like hell! If Alston and Longford dueled over Aurelia, everyone who didn't know her would be certain Longford's nasty guesses were true. Percy didn't know where the words came from, but he suddenly knew what to say.

"There will be no duels, Alston. Everyone knows Longford is a stupid drunk who believes all women want him in bed, when we all know that the few women who chase him do so for money or his title. He doesn't believe in friendship or faithful wives because he has no friends, and the faithful wives want nothing to do with him."

Longford looked up from the cards he was trying to dry with his handkerchief, and did what drunks the world over have done. He took bad and made it worse. "Come on, Thornstead. The whole world knows her mother was caught making the beast with two backs in a garden with the Duke of Haverford when she was betrothed to old Harrowby. Her parents had to take her home in disgrace, and pay Harrowby to marry her before she whelped. Like mother, like daughter. Women are all whores, and only a fool will fight over them. You know this. You and Alston are still friends, even if you are both tupping the same harlot."

Alston went to lunge at the viscount, but Percy put a hand on his shoulder and forced the man back into his seat.

"Here is what I know," Percy said. Sometime later, he would realize he had spoken in his own father's voice—low, lethal, and so cold it was a wonder those around the table did not get frostbite. "You, Longford are no gentleman, and therefore I owe you no gentlemanly courtesy. I will not duel with you and nor shall Alston."

Alston opened his mouth as if to object to Percy speaking for him. Percy put a hand out to stop Alston speaking and continued, his voice dropping even lower. "But if I hear you have repeated these allegations or even see the least indication you have thought them, I shall beat you to a pulp, strip you to your skin, dress you in rags, and hand your unconscious body to the press gang. Rick, your cousin might not remember this discussion when he sobers up. I should be obliged if you would remind him."

"I'll do better. I shall mention the matter to Aunt Amelia and Mama," Rick offered.

Longford, who had already wilted, shrunk some more at the threat of his aunts. "You wouldn't!"

"You can tell him that the Duke of Dellborough made the threat," Alston commented. "It certainly sounded like it. I had to look twice to see whether it was him or Thorn!"

"If I tell my father about it, I am sure he will come up with something more creative," Percy commented.

Longford's alarm increased. "You don't need to do that!" he insisted. "I withdraw my remarks, Thornstead. I had no idea you were going to be so sensitive."

"You shall not repeat them," Percy insisted.

"I shall not," Longford agreed. "Your relationship with your wife is your business."

"Lady Thornstead is a virtuous woman," Alston growled.

"If you say so," Longford agreed, nodding anxiously.

Was there any point in making Longford eat his obvious opinion? Percy was very tempted, but he figured it would not change Longford's mind and would only prolong the agony.

He gave a single decisive nod and walked away. He sent the footman for his curricle and left to wait outside for it to be brought around. Alston and Rick fell into step, one each side of him, as he descended the short flight of steps.

"George is an idiot," Rick said of his cousin.

"You were right to stop my challenge," Alston acknowledged.

"I thought about the gossips and realized it would just give credence to these rumors about Lia—Lady Thornstead, I mean."

The heat threatened to bubble up and consume Percy. He forced it back again. "Rumors that my wife has taken my friends as lovers, I take it. And you knew about these rumors and did not see fit to tell me?"

"They were mainly about Lady Harrowby," Rick explained. "Apparently, all the grandmothers know the old scandal. After the incident with Lady Harrowby, it was the talk of the Town, but by the time you arrived back from Thornstead Hall, they had blown over. They have started up again in the last week."

"We have been trying to find out why, Thorn," Alston explained. "It doesn't make sense. Why attack you and Lady Thornstead? But we haven't been able to track them back to their source."

The club's groom drove Percy's curricle up and stopped in front of them. "Keep looking, would you? And do not mention this to Lia," Percy asked his friends. "She is loving it here in Town. I don't want to spoil it for her."

Alston held his lips shut, signally his willingness to keep silent, and Rick shook his head. "We will not say a thing."

"I will have a word with Aunt Enid, and see what she can find out," Percy mused. "Alston, I'll be escorting my own wife, tonight. If you want one, find your own."

He was halfway to his townhouse, still seething over the lies about his wife when it suddenly occurred to him that Alston's reaction to that last remark had been peculiar. Normally, he would repeat his oft-stated intention to remain single into his thirties, "like my father and my grandfather before me." This time, he had colored and looked away. How odd.

Not that there was anything between Alston and Aurelia. Alston's words from when he first told his friends about his betrothal repeated in his mind. *I shall wait to make her the object of my gallantries when she is your wife.* It was nonsense. Just their usual teasing. Alston had been nothing but respectful of Lia. And even if he hadn't, Lia loved Percy, and he could trust her implicitly.

Couldn't he?

The doubts he was not prepared to entertain evaporated at his wife's delighted greeting. She was coming down the stairs as he opened the front door, and she hurried the rest of the way, her hands held out for his. "Percy! I did not expect you!"

"I decided I would rather be with you than with Rick and the others," he admitted. "I hope I am not *de trop*."

She giggled. "Of course not, silly. Oh, but you are joking."

He had not been. Not entirely. To cover his own confusion, he kissed her. Not holding her, but just claiming her lips. As always, she melted towards him, and gratified him with a small moan of disappointment when he withdrew.

"I must not mess your hair or your clothing when guests might arrive at any moment," he explained, though as a strategy it had a major flaw, since he was as aroused as Lia.

She did not argue the point, but instead gave him a sultry smile. "Later, then." A comment that sent his ardor up another notch.

One thing was certainly true. His wife desired him. And the rest of his imaginings were nonsense.

A knock on the door had them hurrying into the drawing room ahead of the first guests, and Percy braced himself to be polite, when what he really wanted to do was turn them all out and have his way with his wife.

The mood didn't last. Had Percy not already heard that Lia was the topic of gossip, he might have missed the innuendos from some of the visitors, not all of them aimed at Lia. Some of the remarks were obvious. "How nice to see you here, Lord Thornstead," said one lady.

"I live here," Percy pointed out.

"Well, yes," said the vixen, with a sly smile. "Lady Thornstead must be gratified that you remember."

Percy resorted to His Grace's eyebrow trick, which sufficiently disconcerted the lady that she turned her attention to another guest.

"Are you attending the Haverford ball this evening?" another guest asked Lia.

When Lia answered in the affirmative, the guest, Lady Cunningham, widened her eyes, batted her eyelashes, and looked around at the others present before asking, "And which gentleman has the honor of escorting Lady Thornstead this evening?" Her slight inflexion on the word *escort* would have passed Percy by before today.

"I have that honor," he said, before Lia could speak, and she smiled as if he had fetched down the sun at her command. She was pleased to have his escort, and he felt a rather large twinge of guilt at deserting her side so often.

Lady Cunningham looked disappointed, but rallied. "I believe His Grace of Haverford is a family connection," she purred.

Lia sent Percy a puzzled look, clearly not understanding the reference. Percy decided that he had had enough. "My wife and I are related to a number of the foremost families of the United Kingdom, Lady Cattingham." His deliberate mangling of her name and his invocation of his bloodlines was enough to silence the woman, and shortly after that, she took her leave.

As more people came and left, he heard more insidious remarks, including a couple of broad hints from so-called gentlemen who had come to visit his wife and were clearly disappointed to find him there. "I thought you'd tired of this sort of thing," grumbled one.

"I'm tired of afternoon visitors, if you do not mind me saying so," Percy said, bluntly. "A lot of gossip to no purpose. I imagine I'll be old, dead, and in my grave before I tire of giving my support to my wife when she chooses to entertain."

The rake gave him a narrow look. "Not what I'd heard," he declared.

"Then you heard wrong."

Meanwhile, his friend was trying to engage Lia in private conversation, despite her obvious discomfort and her efforts to include others. Percy went to her rescue. "Haddow, my wife has other guests. You will excuse her."

"Excusing her is your job, old chap." Haddow chortled at his own poor joke.

"Anything to do with my wife is my job, old chap." Percy emphasized the last two words.

Haddow sneered down his long nose. "A bit selfish of you, old chap. Lady Thornstead and Mrs. Mabberley?" Emily Mabberley? What was Haddow implying? Whatever it was, the man was misinformed, or just trying to make trouble.

He cast a quick glance at Lia, who had taken advantage of his interruption to talk with Gwen. Even so, he lowered his voice, though it was probably a waste of time. Anything one said to Haddow would be around the *ton* within hours. "Whatever you may have heard, Haddow, my wife and I are devoted to one another. Whoever is saying otherwise is attempting to cause trouble, but when I find out who it is, the trouble shall be theirs."

On second thoughts, it was no bad thing for the troublemaker to be on notice. Perhaps they would go to ground and leave him and Lia alone.

Haddow grimaced. "A bad thing for me, Thornstead, but good for you and Lady Thornstead. I might as well go, then."

He couldn't have been much blunter about his intentions in visiting. Was Lia going through this every visiting hour? Clearly, Percy was going to have to spend more time with his wife.

LIA COULD GUESS the target Lydia Cunningham intended to hit with her hints. *Cattingham! Hah!* Thanks to that catty woman, Lia had the answer to the question Lia had refused to ask any of that generation who might remember. The question to which she did not want an answer. Who had been discovered in a London garden compromising her mother to the point that Lia was the result?

Truly, she should not be surprised that the rest of London knew. It must have been the talk of the *ton* eighteen years ago. Indeed, several remarks that had slid past her now made sense. The rogue who had ruined her mother was the Duke of Haverford. It was a status, by all accounts, that her mother shared with scores of others. The man was a rake of the worst kind, using his position and his power to take any women he wanted from among the lower classes and to seduce any lady who caught his roving eye among the upper classes.

Undoubtedly, if Lia were his child, she had an untold number of half-brothers and half-sisters, beyond those known to the so-called Polite World. Even in his own home, his nursery and schoolroom boasted not only two legitimate sons birthed by his duchess but also the ward whom everyone said was the duke's baseborn son.

The gossip that bothered Lia far more was the mention of Emily Mabberley. Was Percy still seeing that woman? Surely not. It was, as Percy said, someone trying to cause trouble.

After everyone had left, she waited for Percy to say something about either of the two topics, but he held out his hand and said, "Lady Thornstead, you mentioned at breakfast that our new bedchamber would be ready for us to move into today. Shall we go up and see?"

"Is this why you came home early?" she asked.

A flash of chagrin shot across his face, but he pasted on a smile. "Do I need a reason to come home early?" he asked. Perhaps it was irritation rather than chagrin. Certainly, he sounded annoyed.

She forced herself to smile back. "I am glad you are here," she said, instead of the angry responses that first came to mind.

"I am, too." He lifted her hand to kiss it. "Is it always so bad?" he asked. "Harpies and trolls? Why let them in?"

He sounded honestly bewildered rather than accusing, so she tried to answer him in kind. "If I am at home to visitors, I must be at home to all visitors. I might not like Lady Cunningham or Mr. Haddow, but I cannot refuse to receive them during visiting hours without good reason."

She shrugged. "In any case, one meets them and others like them wherever one goes. Every word a pin prick or a knife. Aunt Enid says I must learn to match their wit with my own. I find myself thinking of the perfect response two days after one of their insults. And even if I do think of something to say at the time, they laugh as if I am an amusing baby. I *am* a baby when it comes to the games these people play."

Percy pulled her to him and tucked her head under his chin, putting his arms around her. "I am glad you don't play such games," he declared.

"In some ways, the ones who don't come are worse," she mused. "The ones who don't send me invitations or who refuse the invitations I send. Who pretend they have not seen me, or look me up and down as if I am something slimy from under a rock and then turn away."

"You are being cut?" Percy exclaimed. He sounded outraged. Had he not noticed.

"Only by some," she reassured him.

"Does it help if I am with you? Or does it make them worse?"

She pulled back to examine his face. What answer did he want to hear? She opted for honesty. "They are much worse when you are not with me. Alston is their match, and Rick nearly so. But Barrington has no more idea what to say than I, and Worth does not notice what is going on."

"Alston is much in your company, is he not?" Percy asked.

Did he want her to say she did not need him to dance attendance on her? "Alston is very good about keeping me company," she said. "If you have better things to do, Percy, I am sure Alston will continue to offer me his escort."

It was the wrong thing to say, though she did not know how or why. Only that his face clouded over. "I will look after my own wife," he declared, and kissed her so passionately that she lost all track of the conversation.

She almost thought he was going to take her up against the drawing room door, and she would not have stopped him, but a procession of servants came into the room, on their way to tidy up the remains of the afternoon's refreshments.

Percy let her go when they were interrupted, but kept hold of her hand, and drew her out of the drawing room and towards the stairs. "The bedchamber, Lady Thornstead. And quickly!"

Blushing at what the servants must be thinking, she hurried with him up the stairs.

## Chapter Eighteen

Haverford House was a few miles outside of London beyond Chelsea. The event was a subscription ball to raise money for the loyalists displaced by the revolution in America. When the war was lost to the rebels nine years ago, those who had remained loyal to the Crown had been threatened with retribution by the winning side. Tens of thousands had fled, leaving behind their homes and, in many cases, the means of their livelihood.

From what Lia had heard, those who remained had not been treated as poorly as feared by those who fled. But by then, those who had spent everything they had to escape could not have afforded to return if they wished to do so.

Lia, Percy, and the rest of the Dellborough party arrived late, after the reception line had finished. The Duke of Haverford was speaking to the assembled company, welcoming them, and explaining the plight of the loyalists.

Many had settled in other English colonies, but those who had come to the United Kingdom faced extra barriers in reintegrating with the communities that they or their ancestors had once left behind. The British government and people were still smarting from the loss of the American colonies. Americans who had been unwelcome in the nascent United States because they supported the king were now regarded with suspicion in that king's kingdoms because, to the English, they represented the people who had successfully rebelled.

The duke spoke quite eloquently on the topic. He and his wife had set up a fund to which loyalists could apply for money to start again in the businesses or apprenticeships they had left behind when they fled.

Lia had to admit that he was still a handsome man, although he was in his forties—she had visited her father-in-law's library with the express purpose of looking him up in *Burke's Peerage*. Even now, she could see what might have attracted her mother more than eighteen years ago.

As well as his attractive physical appearance, he had a charm that showed in the way he spoke, coaxing the audience, almost flirting with them as he explained the cause and encouraged them to sympathize with the poor loyalists, who had lost all for England's cause.

The duchess, who was much younger than the duke, spoke next, explaining there would be raffles throughout the evening, subscription books available on a set of tables that she indicated, and that the entire proceeds of the tickets would be dedicated to the fund.

She then invited people to enjoy the evening, and signaled to the orchestra to begin the music for the first dance.

Percy went to lead Lia out onto the floor, but his father forestalled him. "Aurelia, will you do me the honor of dancing with me? I am sure my son will step aside in my favor."

Lia cast Percy a helpless glance and placed her gloved hand lightly on that of her father-in-law.

He danced well—better than Percy, though she felt a traitor for the mere thought. She had looked him up in *Burke's*, too. He was born in 1731, though he looked not much older than the Duke of Haveford and danced with no sign of stiffness or tiredness. Even as she had the thought, he led her to a halt, for it was their turn to stand out while another couple took the lead.

"I need a rest, Aurelia," he confessed. "Do not tell my sons, but I am not as young as I used to be."

"No one could tell, Your Grace," she said, honestly, but he laughed and called her a minx.

"If I am spared long enough, I will be in my seventies when Elaine makes her debut," he told her, his voice somewhat wistful. Then his tones grew crisper. "Aurelia, I wanted a moment's privacy to warn you. I have asked Haverford to extend his protection to you, as a person of particular importance to him. That shall put any gossips on notice that two dukes acknowledge you, and should help to scotch these wicked rumors."

Lia inclined her head in agreement, though she had no idea how confirming the rumors would stop them. And if they were true, were they wicked? However, she did not have His Grace's grasp of Society politics, so she would bow to his wisdom. "Whatever you think best, sir," she said.

That amused him. "But you will reserve judgement until you see what happens," he finished for her. "Quite right, Aurelia. Your husband told me you would make a magnificent duchess one day, and I want you to know that I quite agree with him. You need confidence and a full grasp of what we might call the politics of Polite Society. But you will gain both with time."

"Are you sure I can, sir?" she asked. Sometimes she thought that she understood the so-called Polite World less the more she saw of it.

"I am certain of it," the duke reassured her. "Anyone as proficient as you at chess can learn to play the *ton*, Aurelia. Both follow predictable rules."

It was time for them to enter the dance again, and Lia felt a new vigor as she moved smoothly through the paces, the dips, and the curves. If the duke had confidence in her, perhaps she should trust herself a bit more. After all, according to his children, His Grace was always right.

She felt her confidence slip two dances later when she and Percy stood out with his family for a dance, and the Duke of

Haverford approached, escorting his wife with a raised hand under hers, as if they were about to approach the king or enter the dance.

"Lady Kirkland, Dellborough," Haverford greeted them. The gentlemen all bowed, and the ladies curtseyed. Gwen and Lia dropped into a full court curtsey in honor of the duchess. Even Aunt Enid's curtsey was a little deeper than usual.

"This little puss must be yours, Dellborough," said Haverford, putting his hand under Gwen's chin and forcing her to look up at him. Lia, who was always conscious of her husband, saw him stiffen with outrage.

"Lady Guinevere Versey, my treasured eldest daughter." The Duke of Dellborough's voice was pure ice and Haverford withdrew his hand.

There was a glint of mischief in his eyes as he commented, "I do not know which is more likely to wound, on my oath, Dell. Your voice or your minx's eyes. Both are cold enough to be lethal." Then, in a change of mood, "You look like your mother, Lady Guinevere. She was a fine lady. Loyal and true, as well as beautiful. You can be proud to be her daughter."

"I am, Your Grace," Gwen said, with another beautiful curtsey.

Haverford turned his attention to Lia. "And whom have we here?"

Percy spoke up, addressing the Duchess of Haverford. "Your Grace, may I make known to you my wife, Lady Thornstead."

Lia curtseyed again, and looked into kind hazel eyes.

"Lady Thornstead, I am pleased to meet you," said the duchess. "I was a friend of your mother-in-law and have long taken an interest in her sons and daughters. From this day, I shall count you as one of them."

The glint in her husband's eyes sparked brighter. "The relationship is closer than you might think, my dear. Since you have seen fit to bring one reminder of my peccadillos under my roof, you can hardly object to me acknowledging another."

At the flare of alarm in the lady's eyes, and in her own father-in-law's, Lia realized that the Duchess of Haverford had not been warned about the proposed announcement, but it was too late. The duke had already signaled the orchestra, and the room had fallen silent. They were close to the bottom of the stairs, and the duke leapt up three of them until he could be seen across the room.

"My friends, I have another announcement to make tonight. I am speaking particularly to those of you who have been tossing gossip around for weeks about one of this year's debutantes— some would say this year's most successful debutante, since she was the first married and to the undoubted catch of the season. Aurelia, come here."

He held out his hand, and Lia saw no choice, but was glad when Percy clasped hands with her and came too.

"Ah! I get two for the price of one," said the Duke of Haverford. "When my old friend Dellborough asked me to extend my influence and friendship to this charming lady, I wondered at the relationship myself, for a man of my age has many pleasant memories to look back over on a quiet evening." He grinned at the audience, who were leaning forward in their eagerness to hear more.

"Some are unforgettable, however." He kissed his hand towards the left, and Lia saw, to her horror, that her mother and Lord Harrowby stood there, a gap widening about them as the crowd drew away.

"So, it is my pleasure to announce that I freely acknowledge my special interest in this lovely young lady, daughter-in-law to the Duke of Dellborough and wife to Lord Thornstead here. The particulars are of no importance to anyone except those in-volved." He stopped for the murmur that washed through the crowd as Mama's face whitened and Lord Harrowby's reddened.

Haverford changed mood again, the mischief disappearing and the arrogant autocrat rising to the surface. "That being the case, know this. Speak ill of this young lady or her husband, and face the wrath of two dukes, a marquess," he pointed to Percy, and added in a confiding tone, "—who is a pup, but pups grow and so do their teeth—and an earl." The last gesture was to Lord Harrowby.

"Not to mention the distaff side," he added, nodding to Lady Harrowby, and then to Aunt Enid. He also held out a hand to Her Grace.

The duchess took the challenge, climbing the stairs and allowing the duke to bow mockingly over her fingers. "A wise man, or woman, would not discount the distaff side," she said, her voice ringing clearly over the ballroom as her husband's had before her. She then kissed Aurelia on the cheek, murmuring, "Welcome to the family."

Dellborough and Aunt Enid joined them, adding their visual weight to the message. Defy the Haverfords and the Dellboroughs at your peril. As far as it went, that was a good thing, but the Duke of Haverford was a chancy ally. Lia could see he had used the opportunity to settle scores with the Harrowbys and his own wife. Probably with the Duke of Dellborough, too.

At least the Duchess of Haverford did not seem to hold Lia accountable for the announcement and the manner of it. The same could not be said for the Harrowbys. They were leaving the ballroom, but the looks they turned on Lia as they left would have had her trembling with fear in the days before Percy rescued her.

"Fools," Percy commented. "They would have been better to stay."

"After the Duke of Haverford claimed me as his daughter, thereby confirming what people have been saying about Mama?"

"Thornstead is right," Aunt Enid said. "Everyone over the age of forty knows Lavinia Bryson was caught with the Duke of Haverford and two months afterward married Lord Harrowby. And everyone who can count knows you were born seven months after the wedding. But in our world, as long as no one repeats a fact, it does not exist. The duke stopped short—just short—of confirming the rumors, so what they know is one thing. What they are prepared to say, given that two dukes support you, is quite another."

Lia could see the point, but she did not like the hypocrisy of it. "So, Mama should have looked people in the eyes, smiled, and dared them to disdain her."

"Yes, she should," said the Duchess of Haverford. Her husband had stalked off, his mischief accomplished, but Her Grace had stayed with the group on the stairs. "Half the people in this room—more than half, probably, if truth were known—have anticipated their vows or broken them. They claim to be moral, upstanding people, but they are on shaky ground to point the finger at others. Lady Harrowby is a fool to think her former folly was ever a secret, and more of a fool to think it matters. What counts with the *ton* is how she behaves now. If she had done as you say—stayed and smiled—most people would be satisfied that there was no more scandal to be had, and would move on to a new victim."

"Sometimes, I do not like the *ton* very much," Lia observed.

The duchess chuckled. "Then you are very wise, my dear. Come and have tea with me on Monday afternoon, Aurelia, and I shall introduce you to my sons."

THE HARROWBYS COMPOUNDED their folly by fleeing London. They must have left the day after the Haverford Ball, for when Percy heard about it three days later, they were long gone. He was concerned that their defection would undo any good that might have accrued from Haverford's announcement, but perhaps the opposite happened. Without Lady Harrowby's glower to feed the rumors, they lacked sustenance and began to wither.

As for those who had begun to treat Lia coldly and those who had made her the butt of their jokes, they did an about-turn in the face of the support from two powerful dukes. Lia was relieved, but also, she told Percy, tired of the social scene.

"I shall be delighted to go home to Thornstead Hall, Percy," she said. "I suppose we will have to come to town from time to time, but I do not care if we never spend another full Season in London."

"We shall have to come up from time to time," Percy confirmed. "If only to take advantage of all the hard work you have done."

Lia looked around their new bedchamber with every evidence of satisfaction. Their suite was finished, which was more than could be said for the rest of the house. "I am pleased with this room," she admitted.

"The Marshes are pleased with theirs," said Percy. Lia had insisted that the servants' quarters be renovated along with the rest of the house, starting with the Marshes' rooms. Marsh and Mrs. Marsh had been occupying the housekeeper's quarters downstairs while workmen repaired, decorated, and furnished the butler's quarters as a bedchamber for the pair. Once they moved in there, the housekeeper's quarters would be done over as two offices, one for the housekeeper and one for the butler.

The Marshes were thrilled that Lia had insisted on high-quality materials for their rooms. "It is only sense, Percy," Lia had said when he commented. "Good materials last longer."

"Most of it just needs to be finished," she said now. "Mrs. Marsh knows what I want, and will ensure it is completed to our standards."

"Your standards," Percy admitted. "I would have no idea whether a paint color was autumn sunrise or spring dawn." The painters had been required to strip and repaint the morning parlor only last week, because they had used the wrong pots of paint. When Lia had held the painted reference board up against the wall, Percy had seen it was wrong, but he wouldn't have questioned it otherwise.

She didn't argue. "We could leave as soon as you like."

Percy grimaced. "His Grace thinks we should wait another two weeks, so that we don't look as if we are running away."

Lia sighed. "I suppose it would be a shame to undo His Grace's hard work," she acknowledged.

"Would you mind if I went away for a few days?" Percy asked. "I have business in Birmingham, and if I get it over and done with now, we can head off to Thornstead and spend the summer there, without interruptions."

"Shall I come with you?" Lia asked. He stiffened, hunting for a way to explain his trip, but she answered her own question. "No. I have accepted a couple of invitations that I ought to keep. I would not wish the nasty-minded to think I am ashamed to show my face."

"Do you need me to stay and escort you?" Percy was reluctant to depute someone else to what he regarded as his job, but Lia came first with him, always.

"I prefer you, of course, Percy," she said, "but with the gossips muzzled and the rakes frightened off, I shall be fine. Go and do what you must. What is it? Something to do with that canal you mentioned?"

Percy wondered if he should tell her the truth. He hated keeping things from her, but he was afraid she would be upset. "Just some old business that I thought I'd finished with. A few loose ends to tie up."

While Lia's situation had improved, Emily's had deteriorated. She was losing more business than could be accounted for by the exodus of the *ton* from London, and both she and her shop had been attacked. A rock through the window. The word "whore" in red paint, repeated across her front wall. A break-in that appeared to have the sole purpose of destroying the shop's stock.

And most recently and most frightening, an attempted abduction, foiled by passersby only after she had had a bag shoved suddenly over her head and had been dragged, kicking and screaming, almost into a carriage.

She had decided to take advantage of the offer, presented by Percy but funded by all her former lovers, of a shop in Birmingham, where she could focus on making hats for the wives of tradesmen and merchants, as she had originally intended, well away from the eyes of the *ton*.

If it had not been for the attempted abduction, Percy would have sent her off with a hired courier. But he could not be easy in his own mind unless he saw her settled in Birmingham himself.

"Lia? Could you keep my destination to yourself? I do not mind people knowing that I am away on business. Just not where I am going." If Emily's persecutor connected his trip with her disappearance, he did not want them following her.

"Of course," said his darling wife. How he hated to go away from her!

Two days to get there. One to see Emily settled and begin his journey home. Today was Monday, so, "I will leave in the morning, early, and will be back on Friday," he promised.

"And then in two weeks, we shall go home," Lia agreed.

# Chapter Nineteen

THE FIRST DAY was not so bad. Lia could easily imagine that Percy was at his club or off with his friends watching a horse race or a boxing match. Even in the afternoon, when he normally came home for at least long enough to race her off to bed, she coped by extending her visit to Gwen and arriving home with just enough time to prepare for her evening engagement.

Then came the night. Lia had not slept without Percy in her bed since the day of her wedding and she did not sleep now. At least, not well. She tossed and she turned, lay awake, dozed a bit, tossed some more. Several times, she pulled the bed curtains to see if it was time to get up, and at last it was, or nearly.

The dawn was filtering in through the drapes. It was far earlier than she had woken since coming to London, but undoubtedly the servants were up. With a robe over her chemise, she made her way to the kitchen which was, sure enough, already bustling with activity.

"My lady," said one of the maids, and the entire kitchen stilled.

"Please carry on," Lia told them. "I just came down for my cup of chocolate and my toast."

The cook handed a spoon to her assistant. "Stir that," she told the girl, and stepped away from the pot she had been tending.

"Immediately, my lady," she said to Lia. "Will you have it in your chambers or in the breakfast parlor?"

Lia opened her mouth to say, "In the kitchen," but this was not Byrnewick, and she was no longer a child. All around her, activity had ceased as the servants waited for their mistress to leave. "Carry on with your work," she said to them, her tone carrying more irritation than she intended. They jerked back into action as if they were clockwork dolls, suddenly released into a simulacrum of life by the turning of a key. "In the parlor, please," she told the cook. "In about ten minutes. Ask Miss Kirsop to meet me in my chamber." Pansy could help her into day clothes and put up her hair—something simple, since she had no husband to impress over the teacups.

The day continued to throw up reminders that Percy was away. The butler brought her the mail and the newspaper, since Percy was not there to receive it. Worth appeared to escort her and Evelyn on a shopping expedition for fire screens for the house. Percy had agreed to the trip a week ago, but she had assured him that she was happy to accept Worth as a substitute.

And she was. Percy would be back soon, and he did not find this kind of shopping nearly as much fun as she, Evelyn, and Worth did. Still, it made her mournful to watch Evelyn and Worth continue the courting dance in which they'd been engaged almost from their first meeting. To be a third to their romance made her miss Percy more than ever.

It was her afternoon to return calls, and she had a few that she might as well get over—people to whom she owed the courtesy but whose company she did not like. Barrington agreed to be her escort, though he raised his brow at one of the names. "Lady Cunningham, Lady Thornstead? Must we?"

Lia agreed with his reluctance, but the viscountess and her husband were accepted everywhere in Society. Lia's uneasy sense that the couple were dangerous and distasteful was based on little except her instincts and Lady Cunningham's propensity for catty remarks—insufficient to excuse her from the conventions that covered visiting. "Lady Cunningham called on me. I am obliged to call on her. You don't have to come, Mr. Barrington. Nobody is making rude remarks to my face anymore."

"I'll come," Barrington said, grimly. "Lady Cunningham is a snake, her husband is worse, and heaven alone knows whom you might meet at their house. The worst reprobates that are still accepted in Society, beyond a doubt. Alston told me I should always watch my back with them, and never be with either one of them alone."

On the first appearance, however, it seemed like any other parlor in London on the hostess's afternoon at home. Over-dressed people sat straight-backed on the edge of fashionable chairs making small talk about nothing at all and attempting not to be seen looking at the clock to find out if they had stayed long enough to be polite.

None of Lia's particular friends were present, except for Barrington. She was grateful he had insisted on coming with her.

"Lady Thornstead," Lady Cunningham said, "I thought you might have left town. I am sure someone mentioned that Thornstead was away in the country somewhere."

"We intend to remove from London soon," Lia said, not that it was any of Lady Cunningham's business. "Thornstead has some business to attend to, but will be back in a couple of days. Do you and Lord Cunningham continue in Town, or are you bound for the country?"

"For the country, I regret to say, now that Parliament is in recess. Chipping Longford, my dear. So dreary."

"But your little girls are there, I suppose, Lady Cunningham," said Barrington. "That must be a comfort."

Lady Cunningham glared at him, but her lips formed a smile. "A comfort, Mr. Barrington. Yes. Do excuse me, dear Lady Thornstead. I think Lord Greenham wishes to have a word." She hurried away to the other side of the room.

"You've let old Thorny off the leash, have you, my lady?" asked Lord Longford. Lia had not warmed to him, even if he was

Rick's cousin. For that matter, Rick didn't seem to like Longford either.

"Good day, Lord Longford," she said, ignoring his rude remark. "I trust you are having a pleasant day?"

"Not as pleasant as Thorny, I'll be bound," Longford chortled.

Barrington jerked to his feet. "Excuse me, my lady," he said politely, but through gritted teeth. He grabbed Longford by the arm. "A word, if you would, Longford."

Lia stared after them as Barrington stalked to a corner of the room, not precisely dragging Longford, but certainly giving the impression that dragging was still an option.

"Is there a problem?" Lady Cunningham asked, her attention on Lia. Barrington answered. "A disagreement over a gambling debt that we are about to settle amicably, Lady Cunningham."

The conversations that had stopped to watch Barrington's angry passage across the room started up again. Lia took a sip of her tea and smiled vaguely, watching those around her but straining to hear the conversation in the corner.

"Shut your mouth in front of Lady Thornstead, or I shall shut it for you," Barrington told Longford.

"What did I say?" Longford whined. "It's not as if I mentioned the Mabberley."

"*Sshh!*" Barrington's urgent shushing made Lia listen harder. "Thornstead is on a business trip. It has nothing to do with Emily Mabberley."

"You are out there, Barrington. And I thought your brother Alston had keyed you up to all the rigs. Saw them myself, in a carriage outside the strumpet's shop, getting into a coach." He giggled. "Bentham is beside himself. Has a bet on in the books that Mabberley is going to be his. And now Thornstead has taken her off somewhere. Probably setting her up close to his country place, don't you think?"

"Nothing of the sort. You didn't see Thornstead, and he isn't with his doxy. His former doxy, I mean. You were probably drunk, Longford."

Lia didn't think Barrington believed a single word he was saying. Except for the last sentence.

She stood to say goodbye Lady Cunningham, relying on her training to behave like a perfect lady, speak like a perfect lady, take her leave like a perfect lady. She could manage if she focused on being an automaton, all perfect actions and words, and no thoughts or feelings.

Inside, a howling storm raged. She wanted to swear like the shepherds did when they forgot she was there. She wanted to throw things. She wanted to collapse into a huddle and weep. She felt all hollowed out, as if the careless words Longford had spoken had ripped her heart from her chest, but that wasn't true.

She was the one who had taken her heart and given it into the keeping of her husband, and now he had thrown it on the floor and trampled on it.

The voice of reason said that Longford was an unreliable witness, that Percy had promised to be true, that she should wait and talk to him before jumping to conclusions. The voice of reason was losing against all the small pieces of evidence that Percy had been hiding something from her, that he didn't have time for her anymore, that he had lost interest in her.

The last was a step too far, for he was certainly interested in her body, but perhaps Mrs. Mabberley had been refusing him and he'd been forced to slake his lusts with his wife. That thought made her angrier than all the rest. How dare he! How dare he make her love him and then take up with another woman?

"Aurelia, are you well?" Lia became aware that this was the last in a string of such enquiries. Barrington was peering at her in concern. Also, she thought, a little bit of guilt. If he were in her husband's confidence, then he ought to be guilty.

"Barrington," she said sternly, "is my husband off somewhere with Mrs. Mabberley, or Mrs. Maxwell, as she is calling herself?"

Barrington groaned. "I was afraid you might have heard us," he mourned. "It isn't what you think, Lady Thornstead."

"Then what is it?" Lia demanded.

But Barrington wouldn't—or couldn't—say. All he could do was tell her to talk to Percy. "Percy will explain everything," he kept saying.

Lia asked to be taken home. She had no appetite for more vacuous conversation with people she hardly knew and people she did not like. Barrington did not argue. He was probably relieved to escape her company.

She managed not to cry before she was upstairs and locked in her bedchamber. Their bedchamber, where everywhere she looked was another reminder of Percy. Once she let the tears go, she wept and wept. She had been married not quite two months, and she had already been abandoned for another woman.

*If Longford were telling the truth,* cautioned an inner voice that sounded like His Grace. Perhaps she should consult with her father-in-law. He might know what business had taken Percy to Birmingham. Or he might be able to tell her for certain that her husband was once more engaged with his former mistress.

Percy would not like her involving his father in their affairs. If Percy were having an affair, he deserved no consideration from Lia. She went back and forth on the matter, but eventually dried her eyes and sent for Pansy. It would not hurt to walk over to the main house through the internal doors. She did not have to talk to the duke. She probably did not even have to see him, at this time of day.

As it turned out, she saw him, but was not given the opportunity to speak to him. Before she even reached the gallery that, on this floor, circled the entry hall and the two-story void above it, she had to stop twice to avoid bumping into scurrying servants, some carrying trunks or other travel items.

From the gallery, she could see the duke standing as silent as the center of a storm while the chaos swirled around him. He was going somewhere. She had a moment of relief as she realized she would not be able to talk to him either, and so had a good reason not to find out what he knew.

Such cowardice, she scolded herself, as she hurried down the curving staircase.

"And there *is* Aurelia," he said, when he caught sight of her. "I was just telling Lady Kirkland and Guinevere that they must pass on a message to you, my dear. And here you are, saving them the errand."

"Are you going away, Your Grace?" she asked, and immediately wished that she had phrased it differently. He was standing there in a cloak, pulling on his gloves, with servants rushing past him with luggage and out the door, presumably to load the bags, boxes, and trunks onto the carriage she glimpsed each time the door opened. His valet stood by with his top hat. He was obviously about to take a trip.

She braced herself for one of the duke's sardonic remarks, but he only said, "Sad news from France, Aurelia. The king and his family have attempted to flee Paris, and have been captured and returned. His Majesty has asked me to see if anything can be done for my cousin." His Grace's grandmother had been a minor member of the French royal family.

"Will it be safe, Your Grace? I know we are not at war with France, but..." She trailed off, wondering how to say that the revolutionaries did not like the English or aristocrats.

"I am traveling as a private citizen, and I will be careful," the duke promised. "Aurelia, I want you to know I am glad to have you as a member of my family. Be patient with my son, please. And promise me you will always talk matters through before jumping to conclusions."

Lia's mind jumped to the assumption that he was talking about Percy's trip to Birmingham—or wherever else he went, for if he lied about the purpose of his trip, he might also have lied about his destination.

"Aurelia," the duke said. "You love him, do you not?"

A nod was the only answer she could manage.

"Trust that he loves you. Love is worth fighting for, my daughter. And tell him from me that he is an idiot."

He possessed himself of her hand and kissed the back of it.

"Stay well, my family. I shall return as soon as I can."

He turned with a swirl of his cloak and strode away out the door.

"What has Percy done?" Gwen wondered.

Lia burst into tears.

# Chapter Twenty

Percy arrived back in London on Friday, as promised, but far later than he expected, and much, much muddier. The trip out had been easy enough. He had taken an unmarked traveling carriage of his father's to the second stop on the North Road, then changed to a hired carriage, with Percy on a hired horse, the easier to lose anyone who attempted to track Emily's journey.

The change meant that all Emily's stock, as well as her luggage, had to be loaded on the new carriage. Thankfully, she had left behind the furnishings she had had made for the shop, though not without a tear or two. Her safety and that of her daughter took priority over a few sticks of furniture and a few drapes, though.

They had arrived at their destination late on the following afternoon. Percy had seen Emily, her daughter, and her serving maid to their new home and had taken a bed at the nearest inn. The following morning, there were papers to sign, and a land agent to intimidate when he thought he could renegotiate the terms with a young widow.

The next on the list was to open an account with a bank, pay in the letter of credit that would pay to furnish and decorate the new shop, and brow-beat yet another person who felt that the pretty widow he had introduced as his sister should not be managing her own bank account. After that, he accompanied her on a visit to a carpenter and builder, recommended by the bank, who could do the work.

He left for London in the late afternoon, satisfied he had done all he could for Emily and her daughter, and eager to see Lia. He made good progress that night, but the following morning hit a run of bad mounts—one with poor wind, one that threw a shoe, and one that shied at everything that moved and needed to be coaxed out of its fidgets.

Once he was in His Grace's coach with His Grace's horses, he covered the rest of the distance smoothly. He had to pass the club, so he decided to stop and write a note to each of Emily's other supporters letting them know that she was safe and well. Lia was probably at a ball or the theatre, and this was not a task he wanted to do at home. Anyway, he was anxious to put the whole matter behind him. Though he had not reignited his relationship with Emily—had not even been tempted—he would feel better about seeing Lia again once it was done and dusted.

He let himself in through the door, and was on his way to the club's little library and writing room when he heard his name. "…don't see why Thorn would object," said Alston. "He has encouraged me to go about with them." Percy froze, his mind leaping immediately to the conclusion that Alston was talking about Lia. No. Surely not.

"At least you have a chance with the lady," Worth said, mournfully. "What do I have to offer?"

"You are a good fellow, Worth."

"Yes, but I do not have a title," Worth argued. "You do, and can expect a better reception as a result."

Another voice spoke up. "What are you two talking about." Longford. And from the far side of the club's sitting room, from the sounds of it. "Is it Lady Thornstead? Which of you is comforting her while Thorn is off with his light of love? Or is it both of you."

Thorn was wondering the same thing. Never mind writing

letters. They could wait. He had to see Lia.

He left the carriage at his father's mews, and hurried in up through his back garden to the kitchen door. "Lady Thornstead?" he asked, as he passed Marsh, the butler.

"Not here, my lord," Marsh said.

"She's out?" Percy had assumed she would be at home, if Worth and Alston were both at the club. But perhaps Rick Redepenning was her escort this evening. "Order me a bath and send my valet to our chambers. Also, something quick to eat, please. I shall join my lady at her evening entertainment. Do you know where she has gone?"

"She is not here, my lord. She left here yesterday morning. She has taken her luggage and her maid and gone to the country."

Marsh made no sense. Percy must be hearing him wrong. But when Percy asked him to repeat what he said, he said the same thing again. "Gone where?" Percy asked.

But Marsh didn't know. He said, "Lady Thornstead said you would see to closing up the house, my lord, and you would deal with any correspondence."

Percy sat on the nearest chair, his legs suddenly too weak to hold him up.

Where had she gone? And why? He told her he would be home on Friday. "Was there a message? Perhaps something from her parents? Was she upset?"

Marsh hesitated.

"Spit it out, man," Percy commanded.

"She came home from afternoon visits and shut herself in her bedchamber. She was crying, my lord," Marsh admitted. "She did not go out that evening. Yesterday morning, she went next door to visit Lady Guinevere, and when she came back, she ordered the carriage."

Percy stood up. "I'll ask Gwen."

"The ducal household has gone to Versey Abbey," Marsh volunteered. "Not the duke. His Grace went to France yesterday. But the rest of the household left for the Abbey this morning."

Percy sank back down in the chair. "Lady Thornstead came home upset the day before last, went to see my sister yesterday, then ordered the carriage and left for the country. Had His Grace left for France before my wife visited? Why is my father going to France. No. Leave that. I do not care. My wife has gone to the country. The rest of my family has also gone to the country, to the Abbey. Has my wife gone to the Abbey? Did she leave me a letter? Did anyone leave me a letter?"

He was becoming more bewildered the more he knew. *Lia. Where are you? Why have you left me?*

Marsh shook his head. "Not that I've heard, my lord. I shall ask Mrs. Marsh and my uncle."

"You do that." He stood, weary beyond belief. "I shall still change to go out. Someone must know something."

By the time he had washed and changed, and forced down some food that tasted to him like sawdust, so little did he want to eat, Marsh had turned over every stone. His words. "But no one knows anything about a message, my lord," he said.

Percy, meanwhile, had had a new idea. "Did one of my friends escort Lady Thornstead on afternoon calls that day?" If it was Alston, Percy was going to punch him first and ask questions afterwards.

"Mr. Barrington, sir," Marsh replied.

"Right. I am going to find Barrington, then. He might know what upset my lady."

Barrington was usually still at the club at this time, unless he had gone off to a *ton* entertainment or a gambling hell. Percy made haste to the club, hoping to catch him there. He arrived in time to hear Alston complaining, "She has just up and left London. She didn't mention going so soon last time I saw her. What am I to do, Worth?"

The plaintive note in his voice set a flame to Percy's temper. He burst into the room, fist first, and had the satisfaction of landing Alston on his rump. "Come on, you bastard," Percy jeered. "Get up and fight like a man! How dare you even think about her. We were friends, you bastard!"

Alston launched himself at Percy. "I love her!" Punch. "She's the only woman I'll ever want!" Punch.

Percy punched back then went for the neck. "Even if she wasn't mine, you wouldn't deserve her."

Alston was turning blue.

Worth and Barrington grabbed Percy's arms and tried to pry his hands off Alston's neck. "Let go, Thorn. You'll kill him," Worth said.

"I should," Percy retorted, letting them peel him off Alston. "You, too. You knew and you didn't stop him. Didn't tell me."

Worth shook his head. "He's an eligible *parti*, Percy. An earl you know. Don't know why you are as mad as fire."

Percy couldn't believe his ears. "She's my wife, you idiot."

"Lady Thornstead?" Alston choked out, his voice hoarse. "You think I am talking about Lady Thornstead?"

To Percy, the question didn't make sense. But when he was a child, he'd had a picture puzzle of blocks that could put together in several different ways, depending on which way up the blocks faced. Slowly, the picture pieces in his mind began to turn. "Not Lia?" he asked.

"No, you fool," Alston said, scorn thick in his voice. "Do you think I would touch your wife? Do you think she would let me?"

"I didn't, only… I beg your pardon, Alston." He shook his head to try and clear it. "I am half mad, I think. Lia has gone."

"Gone where?" Worth asked. "To the Abbey with your family?"

Percy shook his head. "I have no idea. I hope so. Who were you talking about, Alston?"

"Your sister, of course. Lady Guinevere. Did you not realize? I have been squiring her all over town."

The picture was becoming clearer. He just had to find the right side for a couple of other blocks. "I thought you were escorting Lia," he said, humbly. "And you, Worth?"

"Lady Evelyn." Worth was morose. "It is hopeless. Her father is after a title."

"You are well born, and you have more money than the rest of us put together," Alston told him. "And the lady's feelings count for something, surely."

Percy agreed, but he didn't have much energy to spare for his friend's problems. "Alston, you'll need to wait until my father gets back from France. Meanwhile, my sister is at Versey Abbey, and my friends are always welcome to visit. Worth, Lady Evelyn is still in town. Tell her how you feel, and if she loves you, approach her father. Alston is correct. Your family is wealthy, and your bloodlines are excellent, even if your line of the family doesn't have a title. You won't know what he might say until you try."

He looked around the room, relieved to find that the four of them were the only people present. "Barrington, I need to know where my wife went for afternoon calls, and what upset her."

LIA WAS NOT going to worry, and she was not going to cry. Not anymore. She made the resolution several times during the trip to Thornstead Hall, and broke it just as often. She cried herself to sleep and wept again frequently during the next day, all the time lecturing herself on her own weakness.

Aunt Enid had read her a lecture on the subject. "At the very least, my nephew has been careless with your feelings, Aurelia. And his foolish friends, too. You cannot change that. If he has, in fact, taken up again with that woman, you cannot change that, either. You can only decide whether you will behave with dignity."

"Barrington says it is not like that, Aunt Enid," Lia had sobbed. "And His Grace says to trust Percy's love."

"Men are all idiots," Aunt Enid decreed. "Thornstead does love you, or so I believe. But he is a man, and men can separate their appetites from their emotions much more easily than women. Are you prepared to share him, Aurelia?"

"No," she replied, instantly, and then added, "But do I have a choice?"

Aunt Enid thought about that for a moment. "Perhaps. Let us assume that my brother and I are correct. Thornstead loves you. Which means he will not set out to intentionally hurt you. You need to make it clear that he has done so, and that he will destroy your love for him if he keeps doing so."

Lia felt a little bit better. If Aunt Enid, whose miserable marriage had given her a low opinion of the entire tribe of men, was prepared to give Percy the benefit of the doubt, perhaps Lia was not weak for wanting to do so. And being honest with Percy about how he had hurt her felt like the right thing to do.

After some thought and discussion, Lia had decided to return to Thornstead Hall. Aunt Enid and Gwen were also leaving, moving up their return to Versey Abbey by a few days so Percy could not ask them any questions.

Lia had not told her servants where she was going, and the note she had left under Percy's pillow would probably not be found until he went to bed. He had a habit of slipping a hand under his pillow as he settled to sleep, by which time it would be too late to set out for Thornstead.

Lia felt a little guilty about hiding the note instead of leaving it in plain view. Though if she had left it in the open, perhaps a maid might have opened it, and she would not have wanted it read by someone else. No. That was a prevarication. She could easily have left it with Marsh. But she chose to hide it.

*It will give him pause to find me gone. He deserves to worry a little, even if he is innocent of the worst.*

Most of the time, she believed he had not betrayed her. But now, two days later, she had realized it was her mother's voice she heard when she lapsed. Her mother's voice that told her she was not good enough for a handsome young marquess, that she was not sophisticated enough to hold his attention, not beautiful enough or fascinating enough to compete with a lovely creature like Mrs. Maxwell.

That she continued to be haunted by her mother's opinion was hardly surprising. She had been hearing her mother's complaints about her looks and her character her entire life, and Percy's compliments and encouragement for only three months. Furthermore, what he said and what he did were in conflict. It was all too easy to believe that he avoided her company because he had lost interest in her.

He was not so shallow. Had he not made sure she would be well looked after before he went away? And did he not tell her that he wished he did not have to go? She would wait and let him explain before she got upset again.

Then, inevitably, the doubts would roll over her again and she was once again in tears.

She did her best to keep up a facade in front of the servants. Not Pansy. Pansy knew her too well and was ready to tear a strip off Percy. "He deserves more than a piece of my mind, my lady. I should throw the chamber pot at him, and so I should, upsetting my lady, and you in such a delicate state."

"He does not know about the baby," Lia pointed out. She barely knew herself. She had missed her courses once, and if they did not arrive in the next couple of days, twice. But she'd detected none of the other signs Aunt Enid mentioned. No sick stomach in the mornings, or at any other time of the day. No tenderness of the breasts. No instability of temperament.

Well. Perhaps a little instability. Perhaps a tendency to cry more easily than usual. She placed a hand protectively over her belly, at present unchanged in shape or size. *You deserve parents who love one another, little one,* she told the probable child. No one knew better than her the damage that children suffered when parents held onto the past and used it as a weapon to beat one another.

It was decided, then. She would wait for Percy to follow her, and then she would fight for the type of marriage he had promised. One in which they were partners. Open and honest with one another. Faithful, of course. That was part of it. But also telling one another the truth about what they wanted and what they were feeling.

In the meantime, she was not going to sit around feeling sorry for herself. Redecorating the townhouse had given her ideas for Thornstead Hall. She sent for the housekeeper and a notebook, and set off to examine the house from attics to cellar. The nursery would need to come first, of course, but she was sure she could find plenty of work that needed to be done.

# Chapter Twenty-One

PERCY WANTED TO go after his wife, but where? West to Versey Abbey in the Cotswolds? North to Thornstead Hall? Or all the way to Northumberland, to Byrnewick? No. Not the last. She would not turn to the Harrowbys for help. Perhaps to one of her friends?

Worth volunteered the location of the ball Lady Evelyn was attending. He had an invitation and Percy knew they weren't going to refuse the son and heir of a duke, and went along. Sure enough, Lady Evelyn and Miss Prescott were present. Worth had already secured a dance with Lady Evelyn, but gave in when Percy insisted his need was greater. They approached Lady Evelyn together.

Her reaction to Percy was not reassuring. "You!" She came as close to spitting as a lady could, and her expression showed disgust and contempt. Those around her all turned to look, and a couple of them whispered to one another behind their fans.

"Lady Evelyn, may we walk for a moment?" Percy asked, offering his arm. She hesitated for a moment, and those in their vicinity stiffened like hunting dogs scenting the prey. Lady Evelyn must have noticed, for she placed her gloved fingers lightly on his elbow, and he led her away.

"If we keep walking, we can hold a private conversation," he said.

"I have nothing to say to you, Lord Thornstead," she insisted.

"I don't know what you have heard," Percy told her, "but I love my wife. I have been faithful to my wife. That is the truth, my lady."

She looked searchingly into his face, and then sighed. "If Lia believes you, I will believe you," she offered.

"That is fair. I want to tell her where I have been and why, but I need to go to her. Lady Evelyn, do you know where my wife is?"

But the answer was no, and the fourth member of their little group, Miss Prescott gave the same answer.

Percy raced around town until he found out what entertainment the Duchess of Haverford was attending that evening. It was at least possible that Lia had taken refuge with the duchess. Far more likely, in fact, than that she would go to her own mother, who was, in any case, back in Northumberland. It was near midnight when he found Her Grace, and by then he had convinced himself that she must be giving refuge to Lia, which would explain why Lia took a traveling carriage, but not one of the sturdy long-distance vehicles that could traverse the whole of England with ease.

However, the duchess denied knowing that Lia had left him and left London. Percy found himself telling her the whole story, and had his knuckles rapped figurately—and also physically, with her fan. "Don't keep secrets from her in the future, Thornstead," she warned. "If you are doing nothing wrong, don't be afraid to tell your wife. If you are afraid or embarrassed to tell her, don't do what you are afraid to speak about."

"I wasn't afraid, exactly," Percy protested. "I just didn't want to upset her."

"Very well," Her Grace acknowledged. "Your intentions were good. Is she upset now, do you think?"

Percy had to acknowledge the point. Lia had been far more hurt by the vicious rumors than she would have been if she had known the truth from the beginning. "Can you tell me where she is, Your Grace? Did she come to you?"

"No, Thornstead," she told him. "I wish she had. I would be able to relieve your worry and tell you she was safe. I would not, however, tell you where she was until she was ready to talk to you. Go home, Thornstead. Lia is a smart girl, and she has loyal servants with her. When she is ready, she will want to talk to you. Go home and wait for her to send for you."

Having run out of options, Percy had no viable choice. At home, he ignored his bed in favor of his study chair, unable to stand the scent of Lia on his pillows. He ordered the carriage for seven in the morning. He would have left that minute if there had been enough light, and if he had already carried out Lia's instructions as related by Marsh.

By half past six in the morning, he was almost ready to leave. First, though, he had to speak with Marsh and Mrs. Marsh, and go through what needed to be done to put the house to rest for the summer. They fulfilled their mentors' expectations and his own hopes by explaining the actions that had to be taken and the people who needed to be told. Thank goodness they knew what to do.

He agreed to maintain a skeleton staff of the Marshes, one footman, and two maids, one of whom was the assistant cook. "The cook has another position, my lord," Mrs. Marsh explained, "with a family that stays in London for most of the year. But the assistant cook is very good."

Percy left with a list of letters and notes that he needed to write, and promised to work on them in the carriage. He'd post the letters from Thornstead Hall and send the notes in a bundle back to Marsh to have them delivered.

"When you hear from Lady Thornstead," he instructed Marsh, at the last, praying in his heart that it was *when*, and not *if*, "tell her I have gone to Thornstead Hall, as we planned."

Marsh bowed. "I trust my lady is waiting for you when you arrive at the Hall, my lord." Percy had no such hope.

*She would not be. Why would she go home when I hurt her so much?*

He would obey the Duchess of Haverford. She knew far more about how women thought than Percy did. Percy had made what his father's shepherds would call "a reet proper mullock" of his marriage, and he would do everything and anything to fix it.

But he could not imagine it would be easy.

LIA HAD THE village carpenter and several other men pulling down fittings and taking out shelves and cupboards in all the rooms of the nursery. She stood in the center of the room, a handkerchief tied over her mouth and nose because the dust made her cough.

Elsewhere in the Hall, the housekeeper and two trusted maids were going through all the linen, returning some items to the linen closet, putting some aside to go to the seamstresses, and tearing the last pile into rags for cleaning and other purposes.

Another group of maids were taking down all the drapes and hangings in the master's bedchamber. When Percy came, if Percy came, he could sleep with her. If he still wanted to do so after he heard what she had to say. She would not be like her mother. She would not put up with her husband's peccadillos for months and then turn on him, all quicklime and gunpowder.

Nor would she ignore them completely and live her own life, as the Duchess of Haverford appeared to do. That was a better option than her mother's way, but Lia was not ready to give up on her marriage.

She was going to try being calm but honest. She just hoped she could avoid bursting into tears.

Then suddenly he was there, looking in bewilderment at all the bustle. "Lia? Are we decorating the nursery?"

Lia burst into tears.

Through the floods she realized that the servants all stopped to watch, looking awkward, as if they felt they should do something but did not know what.

Percy put his arms around her—tentatively, as if afraid she would push him away. "Come away, darling. We'll go somewhere you can sit down."

He picked her up to carry her downstairs, and she buried her face in the curve where his neck met his chest, and cried and cried.

The words he murmured as he walked just made her cry harder, so it must be mostly the baby, for what was there to cry about in what he said? "I am so sorry, my darling. Lia, I love you so much. I love you more than anyone in the world. I should not have kept secrets, but there was nothing in it, my love. I was helping an old friend, but there is no other woman in the world for me but you. I promise there never will be."

She still needed an explanation, but at least she had an apology and he had freely given her the promise she was going to demand. With that thought, she managed to stem the flood, enough to say, "I am too heavy," as he pushed open his bed chamber door.

"Damn it," he said, as another set of workers stopped to stare at their master and mistress.

"I beg your pardon for my language," he said to Lia. "Is the lady's bedchamber full of people, too?"

Lia shook her head. "I can walk," she insisted, but he clutched her tighter and strode the few paces down the hall to the appropriate door.

Inside, Pansy was putting out a fresh gown for Lia. "A cup of tea for your mistress," Percy ordered as he settled Lia in one corner of a comfortable sofa. He grabbed a footstool and placed it at her feet then looked up to see Pansy glowering at him with narrowed eyes.

"What?" he demanded, and then sighed. "I didn't do it, and I have apologized for making her think I had," he said. "Now go and get the tea, Kirsop."

"Tea for two and something for my husband to eat, Pansy," Lia ordered. "Come and sit with me, Percy. We need to talk."

"I will get you some water for your eyes," Percy said. He dampened her flannel in the jug of fresh water that Pansy must have set on the washstand and brought it over to her, perching on the edge of the sofa to tenderly wash her eyes.

"Let me start," he said. "Emily Mabberley, whom you knew as the milliner Mrs. Maxwell, used to be my mistress. Gossip had that right. I knew she wanted to open a shop, for she told me that was her dream when I ended our relationship. Apparently, she had been saving and the money I gave her was the last bit she needed."

"I wish you had told me," Lia commented. "I would never have gone to her for hats if I had known. They laughed at me, because your mistress was making my hats."

"I would have spared you all the rest if I had told you what I knew, my beloved," Percy admitted, "but I could not have told you that Emily planned to open a milliner's shop, for I did not know. I was not interested enough to ask." He shifted uneasily. "I am a bit ashamed of that, to tell the truth."

"She has closed her shop, they say, and has gone back to being a mistress. Was she unsuccessful? I do not understand, if you were not setting her up as your mistress, why you went away with her." *There. That was very calm and collected.* Lia felt all breathless and shaky, as if she had run several miles, chased by a bull.

"She has not gone back to being a mistress, and certainly not my mistress. But she has closed her shop. Let me explain how it came about."

His story made perfect sense. The mother trying to build a better life for her child. The spoilt selfish so-called gentlemen who did not think she had the right to refuse them. The importuning, the attempt to ruin her business, the threats, and the attacks on the shop.

"The others who put into the fund to help her could not leave

London, and so I went with her and her little girl to Birmingham and helped her with the paperwork to set up again. Did you know that a woman cannot open a bank account or sign a lease unless a man countersigns?" Percy shook his head in amazement.

Lia had not known, since she had never had a bank account nor a lease, but she was not in the least surprised. "It was good of you to help her," she told Percy. "It was very poorly done of you not to explain all of this to me from the first."

"I can see that now," he admitted, humbly. "I hoped you would never find out."

"Percy! That just makes it worse," Lia protested. "How am I to trust you if you think a secret between us is acceptable as long as I do not find out?"

A knock on the door was followed immediately Pansy's entrance with a tray. She examined her mistress's face as she put the tray within reach and then gave Percy a hard stare.

"That will be all, Pansy. I shall ring when I want you," Lia said.

The maid curtseyed, glared at Percy again, and left.

"All the women you know are cross with me," Percy complained. "I have had a scolding from the Duchess of Haverford and Lady Evelyn. Mrs. Marsh looked as if she wanted to add a few words, and my own aunt and sister left Town rather than talk to me."

"And?" said Lia.

Percy sighed. "And I deserve every bit of it. There is more. I didn't suspect you, Lia. You mustn't think that. But I punched Alston for trying to seduce you. And I was going to punch Worth, too."

Lia giggled. "But Percy, Alston is in love with Gwen, and Worth loves Evelyn."

"That's what they told me," he said, mournfully. "I cannot understand why, my golden girl. You are the only female I can even see. Every other female is, at best, just a pale imitation of you."

"It is fortunate, however it comes about," Lia said. "How miserable a world it would be if we all yearned after the same person."

"I yearn after you," Percy assured her. "Only you." He proved it by drawing her into an embrace and pressing a kiss to her lips, and Lia leaned into him with a sigh, her awareness of the world compressing to just the pair of them, and his mouth on hers, and the feelings that only he had ever stirred in her.

She did not realize she had begun to cry again until Percy drew back, looking at her in horror.

"Have I hurt you? Pretend I didn't say that. I know I hurt you. Tell me what I can do, my love? How can I make it better."

"I am not hurt, Percy," she assured him. "I am happy."

He frowned. "You are crying because you are happy?"

"It is the baby," she explained. "Aunt Enid says I will be less weepy in a month or two, but in the meantime, I am a watering pot. It is nothing to worry about, Aunt Enid says."

Percy was staring at her as if he had been hit on the head and knocked silly. "A baby."

Of course. She had not told him. She took his hand and put it on her stomach. "In there, Percy. A baby. He will arrive just after Christmas, Aunt Enid thinks."

Now Percy had tears in his eyes. "A baby," he repeated, and his lips spread in a broad smile. "We are having a baby." He dropped to his knees at her feet and drew her into another passionate kiss. Then, just when it was getting interesting, drew back again.

"If you are having a baby, do we have to...? Is it safe for us...?" He glanced at the bed and back at Lia.

"I asked Aunt Enid, and she said Kirkland enjoyed his rights until she was as big as a whale, so it must be safe, for she has four healthy adult children, and Pansy, who comes from a family even larger than yours, says..." Lia blushed. She was not sure she could get the words out. But they had promised each other honesty, so she whispered, "The way it takes some women, they are more eager for bed sports than at any other time."

A spark of interest lit Percy's eyes. "Are you one of those women?" he asked.

Lia looked at the bed and blushed. "Shall we try to find out?" she asked.

# Epilogue

His Grace the Duke of Dellborough had Viscount Versey, aged two, tucked in beside him, Viscount Farnham, aged eighteen months, seated on his knee, and Lady Barbara Versey, aged nine months, cradled in his arms.

The family had gathered at Versey Abbey for Isolde's wedding to the Earl of Mellingforth. His Grace was a regular visitor to the nursery, and frequently—as now, abducted Aurelia's children and Gwen's to bring them down to the family parlor.

Since Percy frequently did the same, he and Lia made no complaint. Alston was surprised, but when he mentioned it, His Grace lifted an eyebrow and declared, "It is never too young for a future earl to learn how to behave in company, Alston."

A rude noise followed by a noxious smell indicated that Alston's son, Simon Lord Farnham, was not yet a model student in the subject of polite behavior. Gareth Lord Versey, Percy's son, held his nose with two fingers and commented. "Simon 'as a stinky bo'um."

Even his grandfather joined in the laughter, and Gwen came to retrieve her boy and hand him over to the hovering nursemaids to have his clout changed. Probably, Percy reflected, his skirts, as well.

Gareth clambered onto the suddenly vacant knee, which

prompted Percy to suggest, "You will need to grow some more legs, Your Grace." Both Lia and Gwen were with child again, though it was early days and not yet known beyond the immediate family. Presumably Isolde would soon be adding her contribution to the demand for room on the ducal lap.

The duke was in conversation with an earnest two-year-old, and did not reply.

Isolde and Mellingforth came into the room from the garden. When Lia, who had been playing gooseberry, followed them, Percy felt his heart skip and his mouth go dry, even after three years of marriage. And after three years of marriage, she looked around the room until she found him, met his eyes, and smiled.

"Mama," Gareth observed, without showing any desire to leave his coveted perch.

"Hello, my treasure," Lia replied. "Did you and Barbara come down with Grandfather?"

"An' Simon," Gareth told her. "But he 'as a stinky bo'um."

"Lord Farnham has retreated from the drawing room to recover from an embarrassing personal misadventure," the duke told her solemnly, his eyes dancing.

Mellingforth edged closer to Alston and Percy. "Is this usual?" he asked, his voice hushed so that others would not hear his question. "Children in the drawing room?"

"At Versey Abbey it is," Percy assured him, not bothering to lower his own voice.

"You can't stop His Grace," Alston warned. "He simply looks at you in the way he has, and carries on doing what he chooses."

The young earl chewed that over for a moment. "I suppose if a duke does it, it must be acceptable," he concluded, just a little louder than before.

"My opinion exactly," commented the duke.

For a moment, Mellingforth looked for all the world like a startled faun, contemplating a split-second decision about whether to hide or flee. He recovered himself, and replied. "Then it must be true, Your Grace."

One of Mellingforth's eyebrows twitched slightly higher than the other, and a corner of his lip lifted. For a moment, he resembled the duke at his most sardonic, which startled Percy, who had written his sister's choice off as a naive moonling, with more breeding than brains.

*Good lord. Mellingforth might fit in with us, after all.*

Lia came to join him, slipping her hand into his. "We came inside because we saw a gig coming up the drive," she said. "We think it might be Worth and Evelyn."

A moment later, her guess was confirmed, as the butler announced their friends. "Mr. and Lady Evelyn Worthington, Your Grace."

Lia had not seen Evelyn for some time, and she and Gwen had soon separated their friend from her husband and settled in the corner for a good chat. Isolde was torn between joining the ladies and discussing her wedding, which was Worth's ostensible reason for calling.

He guessed. "Shall we take five minutes straight away to talk about the final arrangements for tomorrow, Lady Isolde? I know you must be anxious to catch up with your friends." The three of them found another corner for their discussion.

Worth, once he had made up his mind to gratify his family by seeking ordination, had proved to be an excellent pastor.

The incentive, of course, had been Evelyn. He had disclosed to her his prospects (none), his fortune (small, and largely dependent on an allowance from his family), and his love for her (all-encompassing).

Evelyn had had no hesitation in setting forth a plan for their future. As Worth had told his friends when he arrived at the club, dazed but deliriously happy, "She says she thinks I will make a good vicar and she will be an excellent vicar's wife. She says that with my allowance, the income from her dowry, and any tithes, we shall manage very well. Unless I am set against being a vicar, she says, but I realize that I am not. Not really. Not if I will have Evelyn at my side."

With Evelyn at his side, he had discarded the idle life of a wealthy city gentleman, and had embraced instead the vocation of a country vicar, on a living provided to him by Percy's father. As far as Percy could tell, neither Evelyn nor Worth had regrets about the lives they had left behind them, and they were both much loved by their parishioners.

The betrothed couple must have settled their final details with Worth, for Isolde was crossing the room, with a lingering backward glance for her betrothed.

Worth and Mellingforth rejoined Percy and Alston just as Lance sauntered into the room. He had ridden across from Oxford for the wedding, arriving a couple of hours ago. Clearly, the last couple of hours had been spent in his rooms, for he was as immaculately dressed as if he were about to step out into Mayfair to make afternoon calls.

The light-hearted but clever boy who had ridden the length of England with Percy on a quest to meet Percy's betrothed was turning himself into a Bond Street fribble, and Percy didn't know how he felt about it.

"I visited in the nursery floor," said Lance. "They'll all be down in a minute. Hasn't Tris grown!"

Shortly after his twelfth birthday, their brother Tristram had begun to shoot upwards, and Percy, too, had been struck by the difference since he, Lia, and the children had last seen the younger Verseys.

"What do you call that knot, Tulip?" asked Alston, who had been examining Lance's cravat.

"The Incomprehensible," Lance replied. "A small invention of my own." Lance's great ambition was to excel at being a gentleman of leisure.

Worth laughed when Percy expressed concern. "He will find that life less satisfying than he thinks," Worth predicted.

Any further discussion on clothing was ended by the arrival of the schoolroom crowd. Nineve carried Simon straight to his father, saying, "He is quite clean," as she handed him over.

Nineve, at fourteen already showed the promise of being lovelier, if more buxom, than her older sisters.

Unless Elaine had another growth spurt, she was going to be the shortest of the Versey girls. A merry child with a good heart, she went directly to her father and coaxed baby Barbara into her arms.

Tristram and Arthur arrived together. Though only a year apart in age, they were very different. Tris was determined on a military career, though Percy worried about how it would suit him. He was such a kind boy, with a great love of animals. He currently intended to join a cavalry regiment when he was old enough, but Percy thought it would break the boy's heart to see how horses suffered in war.

Artie was a conundrum. A bright child to talk to, he could still barely read or write. Even his name came out with the letters all jumbled more often than not. Of all of them, Percy thought, he was the one least likely to leave home. Percy wondered if they should find a job for him on the estates. Something that did not require reading and writing.

If they were blessed, His Grace would be with them for a score of years more, but he was growing older. His hair—visible now that powdering and wigs were no longer in fashion—was almost all white, and was receding from his forehead.

Sooner or later, responsibility for the estates and the family would fall on Percy. And Lia, he added, as she caught his eye from across the room and smiled. While he was hoping for blessings, he would hope for that one. That, when he was forced to step into his father's shoes, he would have his beloved golden girl at his side, helping him to pretend to be duke until the pretense stuck, just as he had, in the early days of their marriage, imitated what he had seen of his father as husband to his mother, until he and Lia had found their own pattern, their own way to be husband and wife.

As if she had heard his thoughts, she left the huddle of ladies in their corner and came to slip her hand into his. "Isolde is happy," she reported. "Looking forward to her new life as Mellingforth's countess. One less sister for you to worry about, my love."

He smiled at her, though he was unconvinced. He could not fool his beloved wife.

"I know," she said, as if he had spoken. "You will always be concerned about all of them, and all their children, too, including ours. I suppose it is part of your training to be a duke, Percy. You think you are responsible for making sure that everyone is happy and safe. Perhaps I should have said, one more brother-in-law with whom you can share the burden."

"Is Mellingforth going to keep her happy and safe?" Percy asked his wife, not doubting but looking for reassurance.

"He is not showing at his best," Lia told him. "He is an only child. An orphan raised by an elderly uncle. He has never been in a family like ours. He will adjust. He is already adjusting."

Mellingforth was showing his watch to Artie, who had a burning curiosity about mechanical devices. Yes. Perhaps Lia was right. Mellingforth caught Isolde's eye and smiled, and some of Percy's worry evaporated. That was a besotted smile if ever he had seen one, and he had. Every time he was near a mirror while thinking about Lia.

"Lia," called Elaine, "come and rescue His Grace. Barbara has had an accident."

Percy followed his wife. Perhaps they could use the baby as an excuse to go upstairs. It had been a busy few days preparing for the trip to Versey Abbey, making the trip, and catching up with the family when they arrived. A little time alone together would be a good idea.

"Given the look of satisfaction on her ladyship's face," his father was saying when they arrived at his chair, "it was not an accident but a deliberate achievement."

Lia took Barbara into her arms. "You, my child, are odiferous," she told the little girl.

The nursemaid stood ready to take Barbara away to be

changed, but Lia said she would take her to the nursery herself. "I can take Gareth, too, Your Grace, if you have had enough of him," she offered.

"Leave him with me, my dear Aurelia," His Grace commanded.

"I will walk you up to the nursery," Percy said, offering Lia his arm.

Alston rolled his eyes and Worth grinned.

Percy would have called them on their cheek, but they were quite correct. He had every intention of carrying his wife off and having his wicked way with her. Or vice versa, which was just as delightful.

First, Lady Barbara Versey needed to be washed, dressed in clean clothes, fed, and put down for a sleep, which was also delightful in its own way. Then he and Lia left the nursery.

"Are you tired, darling?" Percy asked.

"Not at all…" Lia saw her husband's wildly signally eyebrows and added, "Oh! Yes, Percy, I think I should lie down. Won't you come and lie down with me?"

"Yes, Lia," he said. "I think I should. We can just lie on the bed and see what crops up."

Lia lightly touched the fall of her husband's breeches. "I think something is cropping up already," she replied.

"With you, my golden girl," Percy told her, "always."

Most of my books are set in the Regency, broadly speaking. Technically, the Regency ran from February 1811, when the Prince of Wales was named Regent for his father the King, to January 1820, when the King died, and Prince George inherited the Crown.

In common practice, the term is used to mean a longer period, from somewhere around 1795 until the start of the reign of Queen Victoria, in June 1837.

So *The Sincerest Flattery* isn't covered by even the longer definition, being set in 1792.

1792 was three years after the storming of the Bastille, but at the time of the story, the King of France, his wife, and his children were still alive, and not yet in prison. The French National Assembly, set up in 1789, was still debating the shape of government, with those who support some form of constitutional monarchy unable to find common ground with one another, let alone those who wanted a republic. This impasse ended in August 1792, after the events in my story, with the arrest of the king for treason. In January 1793, he was tried and executed.

After the king's execution, declarations of war poured into France from various European powers and the United Kingdom (who at the time would not have thanked you for considering them European—the more things change, the more they remain the same). From then until the end of the Napoleonic era, France was at war for all but a couple of short respites.

In June 1793, the extremists took over. They ordered more aristocrats to the guillotine. The Reign of Terror had begun. It looms large in historical fiction and historical romance, but lasted only around a year.

Political instability (and executions) continued until the Directorate was formed in 1795, their power supported by the army which was now led by a young general named Napoleon Bonaparte.

In 1792, the fashionable Englishwoman was not yet wearing what we think of as Regency fashion. Nor was she wearing the huge ornate gowns and towering wigs fashionable at the time her mother made her debut. Instead, waists were still on the natural waistline—though by 1795 they had crept up to the Empire line (so-called because it was favored by Josephine Bonaparte, and therefore by the women of the French court). They wouldn't head back towards the waist again for another twenty-five years.

She was not powdering her hair, either, or wearing a wig. Hair powder had already become unpopular with the most fashionable before the British government put a tax on it.

Just a quick word about arranged marriages. Technically, the Duke of Dellborough and the Earl of Harrowby could not force their children to marry. Both the church and the law said that the free consent of the parties to the marriage was essential. Without it, any marriage could be annulled.

That said, they were both underage—Aurelia is seventeen and Percy is nineteen—and fully dependent on their families for the roof over their heads, food on the table, and clothes on their back. Add to that the social pressure on children to obey their parents, and the choice facing Aurelia and Percy was to obey their fathers and marry as they were told, or take the consequences.

Percy's allowance and his promised estate might have evaporated. Aurelia probably faced at least a beating and possibly some version of being shut in her room until she made up her mind to obey.

It was fortunate for them that they fell in love.

Have you ever wanted something so much you were afraid to even try? That was Jude ten years ago.

For as long as she can remember, she's wanted to be a novelist. She even started dozens of stories, over the years.

But life kept getting in the way. A seriously ill child who required years of therapy; a rising mortgage that led to a full-time job; six children, her own chronic illness... the writing took a back seat.

As the years passed, the fear grew. If she didn't put her stories out there in the market, she wouldn't risk making a fool of herself. She could keep the dream alive if she never put it to the test.

Then her mother died. That great lady had waited her whole life to read a novel of Jude's, and now it would never happen.

So Jude faced her fear and changed it—told everyone she knew she was writing a novel. Now she'd make a fool of herself for certain if she didn't finish.

Her first book came out to excellent reviews in December 2014, and the rest is history. Many books, lots of positive reviews, and a few awards later, she feels foolish for not starting earlier.

Jude write historical fiction with a large helping of romance, a splash of Regency, and a twist of suspense. She then tries to figure out how to slot the story into a genre category. She's mad keen on history, enjoys what happens to people in the crucible of a passionate relationship, and loves to use a good mystery and some real danger as mechanisms to torture her characters.

Dip your toe into her world with one of her lunch-time reads collections or a novella, or dive into a novel. And let her know what you think.

Website and blog:
judeknightauthor.com

Subscribe to newsletter:
judeknightauthor.com/newsletter

Bookshop:
judeknight.selz.com

Facebook:
facebook.com/JudeKnightAuthor

Twitter:
twitter.com/JudeKnightBooks

Pinterest:
nz.pinterest.com/jknight1033

Bookbub:
bookbub.com/profile/jude-knight

Books + Main Bites:
bookandmainbites.com/JudeKnightAuthor

Amazon author page:
amazon.com/Jude-Knight/e/B00RG3SG7I

Goodreads:
goodreads.com/author/show/8603586.Jude_Knight

LinkedIn:
linkedin.com/in/jude-knight-465557166

www.ingramcontent.com/pod-product-compliance
Lightning Source LLC
Chambersburg PA
CBHW060443310726

48977CB00001B/304